"IF I KISSED YOU—"

Her eyes widened. "You're going to kiss me?"

Shock made her look almost comical. "If I did, what would you do?"

Her mouth opened twice before she whispered, "I don't know."

"Would you slap me?"

That had her frowning again. "No."

He took another step toward her. "Would you push me away?"

Cheeks flushed with warm color, she shook her head. "Of course not."

"Great." Pete moved closer still. He took her coffee cup and set it on the counter. "What would you do?"

She stared up at him, her blue-green eyes shining, her lips parted. "I'd kiss you back," she said on a breathless gasp, and then she attacked him.

from "Good With His Hands"

BOOK YOUR PLACE ON OUR WEBSITE AND MAKE THE READING CONNECTION!

We've created a customized website just for our very special readers, where you can get the inside scoop on everything that's going on with Zebra, Pinnacle and Kensington books.

When you come online, you'll have the exciting opportunity to:

- View covers of upcoming books
- Read sample chapters
- Learn about our future publishing schedule (listed by publication month *and author*)
- Find out when your favorite authors will be visiting a city near you
- Search for and order backlist books from our online catalog
- Check out author bios and background information
- Send e-mail to your favorite authors
- Meet the Kensington staff online
- Join us in weekly chats with authors, readers and other guests
- Get writing guidelines
- AND MUCH MORE!

Visit our website at
http://www.kensingtonbooks.com

Bad Boys in Black Tie

Lori Foster
Erin McCarthy
Morgan Leigh

BRAVA

KENSINGTON PUBLISHING CORP.
http://www.kensingtonbooks.com

BRAVA BOOKS are published by

Kensington Publishing Corp.
119 West 40th Street
New York, NY 10018

All Kensington titles, imprints, and distributed lines are available at special quantity discounts for bulk purchases for sales
promotion, premiums, fund-raising, educational, or institu-
tional use.

Special book excerpts or customized printings can also be created to fit specific needs. For details, write or phone the office
of the Kensington Special Sales Manager: Attn. Special Sales
Department. Kensington Publishing Corp., 119 West 40th
Street, New York, NY 10018. Phone: 1-800-221-2647.

ISBN-13: 978-0-7582-0775-3
ISBN-10: 0-7582-0775-1

First Brava Books Trade Paperback Printing: May 2004
First Brava Books Mass-Market Paperback Printing: January
2012

10 9 8 7 6 5 4 3 2 1

Printed in the United States of America

CONTENTS

GOOD WITH HIS HANDS

by Lori Foster

1

MISS EXTREME CONGENIALITY

by Erin McCarthy

109

LAST CALL

by Morgan Leigh

229

GOOD WITH HIS HANDS

Lori Foster

One

Pete Watson smiled as he watched Cassidy McClannahan get out of her spotlessly clean white Ford Contour. It was a familiar thing, smiling at the sight of Cassidy. Which meant he smiled a lot these days, because he saw her every day, everywhere he went. They worked together at the Sports Therapy Center and they lived in adjoining condos, thanks to the fact that Cassidy told him when one of the units became available. They left at the same time in the morning, came home at the same time each day.

It was nice. Routine. As predictable as being married—but without the chain chafing around his neck.

And no sex.

But hey, that kept it simple and easy. Besides, he could probably have sex with Cassidy if he wanted. But he didn't. Not really.

Not bad, anyway.

The spring breeze played havoc with her super-long, too-curly brown hair, whipping it into her face until, in disgust, she dropped her grocery bag and grabbed the mass with both hands.

She was such a contradiction, so much a woman in some ways, so oblivious to her own femininity in others.

Sidling up next to her, Pete said, "You should have put it in a ponytail."

"Bite me."

He laughed. Her reaction to him fell into the oblivious category. She treated him like an asexual pal. Joking with him, putting him down sometimes. And she never, ever primped or prettied up for him. Nope, Cassidy didn't want him. Still, he could get her if he wanted to.

He just didn't want to.

Scooping up her bag, which weighed a damn ton, Pete said, "Come on, Rapunzel. I'll help you inside."

She eyed his bulging biceps as if she didn't see them every day at work. But it wasn't a look of admiration, just one of observation—the same sort of look she always gave him. Unaffected. Non-sexual.

Finally she looked away, saying, "Don't strain anything."

Yeah, right. She knew better than most that he was in great shape. "What the hell did you buy, anyway?" Part of their routine for Friday was stopping at the grocery store. Since their eating habits were like night and day, they separated in the store, but met up again in the parking lot. He'd only bought enough lunch meat and bread to last him through the week, but it felt like Cassidy had bought bricks.

While she rolled up her driver's-side window and locked her car door, she ticked off her purchases. "Baking potatoes, steak, corn on the cob, and a six-pack of pop."

"Got a big night planned?" Pete knew she didn't. Cassidy almost never dated. In fact, he couldn't remember ever seeing her date. That made him stop and think.

"Not really."

Well. That was pretty damn vague. Frowning, Pete waited to see if she'd invite him to join her. But she didn't. She never took the initiative. If he asked, she'd smile and tell him what time to show up. But why the hell did he always have to ask? Couldn't she just once extend the invitation? Another contradiction. They always enjoyed each other's company, but she never deliberately sought him out.

He loped beside her as they went up the tidy walkway to her front stoop, which was right next door to his, a mere fifteen feet away.

Assuming he'd follow, she unlocked her door, pushed it open and strolled inside, kicking her sneakers off the moment she got in. Out of the wind, she released her long hair and Pete watched as it tumbled free down to the small of her back, swishing above her plump ass.

Pete shook his head. She stayed in great shape, was always clean and well dressed, but she paid zero attention to feminine details like her hair and nails. She didn't wear makeup or perfume—not that she needed to. She always smelled great, even when sweaty. And she had a healthy, robust complexion.

Robust? Yeah, that's how normal men should think of women. Half disgusted, half embarrassed, Pete shook his head at his odd musings.

He'd asked Cassidy once about her long hair and found out she only washed and dried it. No curlers, no trims, no highlights. He'd never known a woman who didn't spend hours on her hair. When it got humid outside, her hair drew into long, bouncy ringlets that looked adorable.

Like Cassidy, her place was clean and comfortable but not overly decorated. It overflowed with plants and posters and throw pillows. By rote, Pete trailed her into the kitchen.

"You want some coffee or something?" She didn't wait for him to reply, but began filling the carafe, proving how predictable he'd become. He should politely decline and head home, maybe throw her off a bit. But he didn't.

"I can take one cup." Pete set their groceries on the counter, pulled out a kitchen chair and sat.

With the coffee preparations complete, Cassidy set out mugs and sugar before turning away. "Be right back."

"Where're you going?"

"To change. It's warm tonight."

She disappeared around the corner into the hall leading to her bedroom. Pete knew the setup of her condo because it was the mirror image of his. Where his bedroom ran to the left of the front door, hers ran to the right. He'd never been in her bedroom, though—and she'd never been in his.

Today she'd worn loose navy blue athletic pants and sneakers with the red unisex polo shirt supplied to all employees at the Sports Therapy Center.

Pete tilted his chair onto the back legs. It dawned on him that he'd known Cassidy about eleven months now. Not that he was counting or anything, but maintaining a close platonic relationship with a woman other than his sisters-in-law for almost a year had to be some sort of personal record. Usually if he knew a woman any length of time at all, he either dated her or was merely acquainted, not friendly.

The thing he'd first noticed about Cassidy—after that abundance of super-soft, crimped hair—was her focus. They'd spoken for about an hour his first day on the job, and in that time he realized that she had it together more than anyone he knew. If you asked Cassidy where she wanted to be five years from now, she could tell you. She knew where she wanted to work, where she wanted to live. She even claimed to know the type of guy she wanted to marry one day.

In comparison, Pete didn't even know where he wanted to be next week. Not that he intended to leave his job, his home, or Cassidy's friendship. But after finishing school and working three different jobs before settling at the sports center, he often felt unsettled, as if he were somehow missing the big picture.

Not Cassidy. She set new goals daily and worked

hard to reach them. Maybe that's why she didn't date—she was too busy meeting her goals. Pete frowned in thought, trying to remember if any of their male clients had ever hit on her.

No one specific came to mind, but then everyone, young and old, male and female, loved Cassidy. She laughed a lot—honest laughter, not the trumped-up, polite kind. She also had nice eyes. Sort of a wishy-washy blue-green that managed to be awesomely direct. Honest, like her laugh.

She was built well enough, of course. On the short side. A little too muscular, given all the time she spent being physical on the job, but trim and fit. She had a body guys would notice. . . .

And why the hell was he dwelling on her body, anyway?

Pete stood up and went to her patio doors. With his hands stuck in his back pockets, palms out, he contemplated the darkening sky. Looked like another spring storm on the way. Trees swayed under the wind. Heavy gray clouds raced by. He slid the glass door open so the fragrant, moist air could come in through the screen, wafting around him, stirring his senses.

Now that he'd thought of Cassidy's bod, he couldn't stop thinking of it. And that was strange, because he preferred his ladies on the prissy side. He enjoyed watching a woman fuss with her hair, fret about her nails, and reapply her lipstick. It was so intrinsically female.

Dawn, the woman he'd most recently stopped dating, had done a lot of fussing. She was a corporate exec, smart, lots of ambition, and sexy as hell in a power suit. It had teased Pete, the way she'd pair a short, snug skirt, high heels, and red lipstick with a business jacket that begged to be unbuttoned. The attire emphasized rather than diminished her femaleness. Her glasses were a bonus. The way she pulled them off whenever she meant to get intimate had really turned him on.

"Coffee's done."

Speaking of turned on . . . Pete watched as Cassidy strode back into the room. No business suits, heels, or glasses for her, but unlike Dawn, Cassidy never bored him.

Her hair was pulled up into a high, sloppy knot, haphazardly clipped into place. Long, twining hanks of hair fell loose to her shoulders, around her small ears. She'd changed into a football jersey and cutoffs. A really big jersey—and really short shorts.

Being male, and healthy, and for some reason kind of horny on this almost rainy, quiet Friday, Pete automatically gave her the once-over. Maybe there'd be a full moon tonight, or maybe the tide was high. Something, some unknown force, was making him contemplate Cassidy naked. Eyes narrowed and mouth pursed, he watched as she filled the mugs with coffee. He'd seen her in everything from sweats to bike shorts, so he knew she had lots of soft, squeezable curves to go with the muscles.

As if she felt his gaze, Cassidy looked over her shoulder, caught him staring at her butt, and looked away again. She didn't care that he was looking. She didn't care if he didn't look.

Damn abnormal woman.

Driven by some inner perversity heretofore undeveloped, Pete leaned back against the doorframe and smiled. "Your ass looks nice in those shorts."

A slight pause, then: "Thanks. You want a cookie with your coffee?"

His jaw locked. *Thanks? That's it? No more reaction than that?* Pete folded his arms over his chest. "How about I take your ass with my coffee?"

She threw a cookie at him, then dropped that delectable behind into a chair at the table with a hearty sigh. Using her toes, she snagged the chair opposite her and pulled it out enough so she could prop up her feet. "I'm so glad it's the weekend. Thanks to that tank of a guy with low back pain, I'm beat."

All week, Cassidy had worked with the man, who tipped the scales at three-fifty, on controlled, repetitive movement rehabilitation, teaching him safe movement through progression and complex exercises. That had been on top of her regulars who came in each day to work on running faster, farther. She'd been busy, no doubt about it.

Pete took his own seat. "I had an easier week. A bunch of junior high school boys working on sports conditioning. It was fun."

"You're good with kids." She sipped her coffee. "You should work with them more."

"Thanks. You know, I used to think about being a gym teacher." Before his father passed away and his brother took over the family business and everything went sideways, including all their lives. He'd gotten off track then and hadn't found his way back yet.

Cassidy nodded thoughtfully. "I can see that. You're close to having the right credits, right? It wouldn't take much to become a teacher, then you could—"

"Whoa. I didn't say I was going to do it. Just that I used to think about it."

"So what do you want to do? Work at the sports center the rest of your life?"

"I don't know." Damn it, why did she have to press him? "I'm happy there for now, so there's no rush."

Cassidy leaned her head back and closed her eyes. "I envy you the ability to keep thinking things through. It seems like I made up my mind in my teens and I've been on the same road ever since."

"You want to own a sports center someday, right?"

"A whole chain of them." With her eyes still closed, her mouth curled in a self-deprecating smile. "I've had my entire life pictured in my mind forever. First, I'd graduate with honors—"

"Which you did."

"—then learn my trade."

"Working at the sports center."

"Yeah." She shrugged. "And sometime before I got too old, I'd marry a professional man. Some guy in a suit, like Ward Cleaver." Her eyes opened. "You remember that show? *Leave It to Beaver?* Ward was always in a suit and June was always in a dress and their kids were polite, their house spotless. It seemed like the ideal setup to me. Only I don't want to wear a dress. I want to run a business in my sweats."

Used to her honesty, Pete toasted her with his coffee cup. "You look great in sweats."

"Thanks. They suit me. You know, because I'm into comfort and all that."

"I noticed." Boy, had he noticed. Especially today. She was relaxed and easy to be with, totally natural. Very appealing.

"It makes my little sister crazy. She hates to be seen in public with me."

"No way."

Wearing a sideways grin, Cassidy admitted, "She considers me a fashion disaster. But then, you'd have to meet my sis to understand. She's always perfectly groomed, manicured, and stylish." Eyes averted, she added, "Sort of like the women you date."

That had Pete frowning. It made him sound very superficial. "So you want a guy in a suit, huh?" Since he never got within ten feet of a suit, he didn't much care for that inclination, either.

Cassidy propped her chin against her hand and stared thoughtfully at the ceiling. As if picturing it in her mind, she said, "Tall, dark, and handsome, the kind of guy who looks great at black-tie events. Very serious. Dedicated to his job and his family."

Yep, she had that all planned out, too. Pete sank lower in his seat.

Her gaze met his, her eyes twinkling with suppressed laughter. "My dad is five-ten, fair, and balding, but he's got the other qualities. When I was a little girl, I'd put on his suit coat and imagine how big a man had to be to fill it out—not just physically, but intellectually and emotionally. Dad worked long hours, then got home and rolled up his shirt-sleeves to help Mom with dinner. And after dinner, he'd sit at the dining room table with my sister and me and help with our homework." She laughed at herself. "My dad is great. Mom, too."

"And your sister?"

"Holly is a charmer. Beautiful enough so things come easily to her. Especially guys."

As usual, the conversation flowed between them. Pete had never realized the significance of that before, but he was as comfortable with Cassidy as he was with his brothers and his best friends—who were all male. Huh. "Speaking of family, did I tell you Ariel is pregnant? Sam is beside himself."

Cassidy's coffee cup clicked against the tabletop as she plunked it down and leaned forward. "Sam, your oldest brother, the bad-ass cop, the scary dude who likes to put himself in the line of fire, is going to be a *daddy?*"

"Yeah, how about that?" Cassidy hadn't met Sam yet, but she had met their middle brother, Gil, when he was dropping off his daughters for Pete to babysit. Sometimes Cassidy even helped out with that. Nicki, now seven years old, adored Cassidy, as did her two-year-old sister, Rachael. "I think our nieces softened him up."

"I wouldn't be surprised. Those little angels could soften up anyone."

She looked all gentle and sweet when she said that. Someday she'd make a good mom—*whoa!* Pete snuffed that thought out with ruthless precision. No way in hell was he going to start thinking that way. It was one thing to picture Cassidy naked, especially since he couldn't seem to help himself.

He would not think of her with a kid on her hip. Therein lay trouble—as Sam had discovered.

Pete cleared his throat and concentrated on his coffee cup. "They've been married five years now and Ariel said she's ready to be a mother. She told Sam he could either be the father or not, but one way or another she was getting pregnant."

Cassidy nearly choked on her coffee. "She gave him an ultimatum?"

"I think she just hid the condoms and then got naked. Didn't take any more than that to get Sam's cooperation."

Her throaty laughter seemed to wrap around Pete, mingling with the warm, moist air, further confounding him. He pushed his chair back in a rush. "I gotta run."

Cassidy picked up another cookie. "All right. See ya later."

She didn't change her relaxed posture or even look particularly curious as to why he was rushing off. Pete snatched up his grocery bag, started out, and then heard himself say, "I'm watching a movie later if you want to come over."

"You're not going out with Dawn?"

He and Dawn had parted company three days ago when she wanted him to leave the sports center in the middle of the day to meet her for lunch. While he appreciated the enthusiasm she gave to her job, she treated his job as nothing. Shaking his head at the memories, Pete said, "That's over."

Cassidy took another sip of her coffee before shrugging and saying, "I'll let you know."

Eyes narrowed, Pete stared at her while the perils of masculine ego shoved his temper up a few notches. When he got her naked and under him, she wouldn't be so cavalier. . . .

His eyes widened and his back snapped straight. Damn it, there he went again, thinking things he shouldn't. Best to make a run for it now before he did something stupid, like jump her bones. He pivoted on his heel and stalked out. It took all his control not to slam her front door.

He would not start pining after Cassidy McClannahan. Okay, so despite her comfortable-as-an-old-shoe appearance, her femininity beamed through. It didn't matter. If he wanted a woman, he'd make a phone call and—Pete snapped his fingers—he'd have a woman.

But once in his condo, Pete put away his groceries, stripped down to his boxers, and slouched in front of the TV to watch ESPN while guzzling an icy cold Coke and munching salty chips. He didn't touch the phone. But he did zone out on the latest sport clips while his mind danced around the idea of Cassidy McClannahan stripped naked, that long hair trailing over her shoulders and breasts; Cassidy with her eyes warm and inviting instead of indifferent; Cassidy as a sexual conquest, begging for more. . . .

Before long, Pete was caught up in a full-fledged fantasy with predictable results.

He did need a woman, damn it. But he only wanted one. And she didn't seem at all interested.

Cassidy resisted the urge to head to Pete's. Little by little, their friendship drove her insane with sexual frustration. Against all common sense and her own responsible nature, she wanted the knuckle-head. Hell, she'd wanted him almost from jump.

At first, it had been his mouthwatering appearance that had grabbed and held her attention. Tall, dark, and most definitely handsome. But not a suit in sight. Not that it mattered. Her thinking had done a one-eighty the day Pete Watson got hired on at the sports center.

For most of her life, Cassidy had bought into the idea of an intellectual, suit-wearing, serious-thinking guy with advancement on his mind as the perfect male. Pete was none of those things, but oh, he was *so* perfect.

Tall and trim, long-boned with rangy muscles, inky black hair, and dark bedroom eyes that ate a woman's soul. Outside of work, you were more likely to find Pete in jeans than dress pants. A few times, she'd even caught him in his boxers. And wow, what that man did for underwear should be illegal.

He was so sexy, there was no way on earth he couldn't know it. But amazingly enough, Pete didn't play up his sex appeal. Instead, he laughed and joked and befriended everyone. He didn't seem overly keen on advancing, but then his family owned a private novelty business and Pete got regular deposits from the profits, so he wasn't exactly hurting for cash. Pete was one of those guys who had plenty of time to *find himself,* because he didn't need to settle down to survive.

So here he was, well-to-do, gorgeous, and still so darn nice. He respected people, their accomplishments and their limitations, which made him easy to be around, easier to like.

Pride and intelligence, her two most noticeable fortes, told her Pete wasn't a guy to fall for, not with his carefree, live-for-the-moment attitude. It had been pure idiocy on her part to tell him about the condo for sale next door to her. Dumb, dumb. He'd moved in a few months ago and now they had this ultrafamiliar relationship that kept them in constant but platonic contact. It was maddening.

They were such good friends that he even felt at ease teasing her about her butt. Cassidy covered her face and groaned. He'd invited her over to watch a movie. He wanted to pal around.

The big dope.

Okay, so no one saw her as a sexual being. That didn't mean she was without desire. Where Pete was concerned, sex was about all she had on her mind. Sitting on the couch with him, knowing he was that close, pretending to watch television when instead she breathed in his scent and wallowed in his warmth and gradually melted . . . it was the act of a masochist. It was desperate and pathetic. Enough already.

She'd go to the movies by herself instead. She'd glut herself on popcorn and cola and by the time she got home, she'd have herself back in control. She'd even be able to face Pete in his boxers without drooling.

Mind made up, Cassidy snatched up her car keys and headed for the front door. She shoved her feet into her sneakers, turned the knob, jerked the door open—and ran face-first into a brick wall.

At least, it felt like a brick wall. After recoiling

and almost falling, she managed another look. No wall, but close. "Duke," she said stupidly while rubbing her bruised nose, "I'm sorry. Are you okay?"

Since Duke was built like a cement slab and thus considered himself invincible, he grinned. "I'm fine." He reached out and brushed some of her tumbled hair from her face. "Sorry about that."

"My fault entirely."

Next to Duke's six-foot-six, two-hundred-and-fifty-pound frame, her younger sister, Holly, looked like a delicate, disgruntled miniature. "Cassidy, what on earth are you doing?" She eyed the keys, Cassidy's sloppy clothes, then propped her hands on her hips. "If it was any woman but you, I wouldn't ask. Most women wouldn't be seen dead wearing what you have on. But knowing you don't care how you look, and considering you have your keys in your hand, I have to ask."

Please don't, Cassidy thought.

Her sister forged on, haughty in her accusation. "You *forgot* that you invited us over to dinner, didn't you?"

Invited them? It was more like she'd had her arm twisted. "Umm . . ." Lusting after Pete had warped her brain.

"Cassidy," her sister wailed, as if the world had started to descend into hell. "You promised."

Holly was set on getting her family to worship Duke as much as she did. Because their mom and dad wanted only the best for Holly, that wasn't likely to happen. But Holly was convinced that if she got Cassidy's blessing, their parents would fall into line. Like she had that much influence? Right. Just because she was the *sensible* one.

It was enough to make a red-blooded female howl.

Cro-Magnon man—otherwise known as Duke—ushered both women inside. For a football player, he was gentle enough. But in Cassidy's opinion, her sister was too young to concentrate on anything other than her college studies. She should be thinking about her career, about gaining her independence before she got tied at the hip to a gargantuan sports aficionado.

"Holly, calm down," Duke said. "Maybe Cassidy just had to run an errand."

Cassidy snatched at that excuse like a lifeline. "Exactly. I forgot dessert." *Thank you, Duke.* "I left steaks on the counter. With it ready to rain, I figured we'd just broil them inside. Why don't you two go ahead and get everything ready while I run to the bakery?"

Holly started to protest, but Duke squeezed her into his side and smiled. "No rush, Cassidy. We'll manage till you get back."

Cassidy looked at him from under her brows. Oh, she might be sensible, but she wasn't blind. She knew that heated look as well as any woman. Duke always looked that way when he was with Holly. Well, she *would* rush, damn him. It didn't matter that her sister was old enough to make her own decisions on intimacy. Cassidy didn't intend to aid and abet.

She went out the door in a trot, and even with family drama to occupy her mind, she couldn't help thinking of Pete. Had he already called another woman to come over? His car was in his driveway, but his condo windows were dark.

She wouldn't succumb like so many other women. Sure, succumbing would be sublime, but far too temporary. And after all, Cassidy *was* the sensible one.

What a curse.

Two

Pete couldn't take it. Somehow, Cassidy, with her contrary lack of interest, had him frothing at the mouth. He never frothed. Okay, so he'd had a few semi-serious crushes in his day, the most noticeable being toward Ariel. But that was before she became his brother's wife, even before she'd met Sam. Once she'd met him . . . well, everyone except Sam had noticed that Ariel was head over heels in love with him. Seeing that had cured Pete's crush real quick, and now he loved Ariel as a sister-in-law, but certainly nothing more.

Since then he'd just dated and enjoyed life and women and the fun of being single.

But there was nothing enjoyable about how he felt right now—sort of rejected and dejected and annoyed. Why didn't Cassidy want him?

Maybe he needed to clue her in, let her know he wouldn't be adverse to the idea of some cozy time in the sack. Hell, it'd be great. They were already friends. They knew each other, trusted each other, enjoyed each other . . . so why not enjoy each other a little bit more?

Pete pulled on a T-shirt and shorts, and barefoot, went out the back to see if Cassidy was grilling yet. He'd sniff her steaks and she'd invite him to join her and he'd move from there. He'd be casual, relaxed—he'd sneak the idea of wild sex in on her. Anticipation had him semi-hard before he discovered that she wasn't in the back.

He was hot, but her grill was still cold.

Frowning in disappointment, Pete wondered if the weather had chased her inside. The sky had turned black and static filled the air. It would start storming soon, probably throughout the night. Perfect weather for making love.

Maybe they could skip dinner and go straight to the idea of sex. Feeling like a desperate voyeur, Pete peered in through her patio doors, but didn't see her. He considered his options, raised his hand to knock—and heard a noise in her bedroom. That window was open, too, and Pete stared at it, teased with the idea of Cassidy changing clothes, maybe getting in or out of the shower. . . . The sound of a soft, hungry, vibrating moan resonated out to him.

Pete's heart, thoughts, and breath all stuttered to a standstill. Was that a moan of . . . *sexual pleasure?* His reaction was swift and confusing: jealousy, possessiveness, and red-hot anger. He strained to hear more while everything masculine within him went on the alert.

Another moan reached him, then another, higher in pitch, each subsequent moan rising in excitement until they peaked—and Pete's hair damn near stood on end.

He felt betrayed!

She turned down a movie with him to have sex with someone else. Never mind that she didn't know he wanted to have sex with her.

Forcibly, Pete unglued his feet and stalked away in a temper, but even after he'd stepped into his own kitchen and slammed the door, the sound of her pleasure, sweet and deep, reverberated in his head, pounding against his skull.

Cassidy was involved sexually with someone— someone other than him. That sucked.

He'd only just decided that he wanted her, and he'd already lost his chance.

Dinner was a nightmare that had taken forever, but now it was over. The cake she'd bought was completely consumed, a pot of coffee polished off, and still Duke and Holly lingered.

Maybe she should have invited Pete over. She'd noticed his car still in the drive when she returned from fetching dessert. He could have served as a buffer, a guy for Conan the Barbarian to regale with football stories. For herself, Cassidy had heard enough about tackles, passes, and kicks to last a lifetime.

Pete was so good with people, he'd have found a way to steer the conversation, to keep it entertaining for one and all. He could have told more anecdotes about his cop brother, Sam, or his niece Nicole. He could have discussed sport-induced injuries with Duke. He could have just been there, smiling and making everyone else smile.

Cassidy didn't realize that Duke had finished his story until she caught him grinning at her. Good grief, how long had she been sitting there with that stupid look on her face while she daydreamed about Pete?

With far too much perception, Duke asked, "Thinking of a guy?" When Cassidy just gaped at him, he said, "I hope we didn't interrupt your plans. You could have invited your boyfriend to dinner, too."

Cassidy's face burned. Her *boyfriend*? Pete was not a boyfriend. He was a miserable, sexy, forever-out-of-reach pal.

Holly started laughing. "Cassidy doesn't date!" She made it sound like the most absurd thing imaginable. "She hasn't been involved with anyone since . . . gosh, when was it, Cass? Better than a year ago, I think."

Felt like ten years to Cassidy, but then, celibacy probably had that effect on many people.

Duke's smile turned sympathetic. "Now, Holly, your sister is too pretty not to date."

Pretty? Well okay, she wasn't an ogre, but . . . Duke was probably just trying to score points. Still, Cassidy found herself tucking her disheveled hair behind her ears and twittering in the age-old way of women.

"I never said she wasn't pretty," Holly protested. "But as my folks are fond of saying, Cassidy is the levelheaded one. She doesn't waste her time on guys."

Uh-oh. Now Duke was sure to be insulted. After all, what male ego would like being called a waste of time?

But to Cassidy's surprise, Duke picked a different bone entirely. "Meaning you aren't level-headed?"

Cassidy did a double take. She hadn't thought about it from that perspective. She knew her parents meant well, and she'd always taken the comments to mean Holly was the personable one, the one who got friends and compliments and dates easily. Cassidy thought they were throwing her a crumb, giving her the only credit they could. But the look on Holly's face assured her that Duke had read her sister right.

If Cassidy felt insulted for being called too responsible, how did the comments make Holly feel? Cassidy automatically reached out to her. "Holly, Mom and Dad didn't mean—"

Holly gave her brightest smile. "I bet you were wishing us gone so you could get to bed, huh?" And then to Duke, "Cassidy's an early bird. You'd think she was eighty-seven instead of twenty-seven, with the way she conks out so early."

Cassidy started to deny that accusation, but Holly's eyes were pleading, so instead she fashioned a wide yawn. "Sorry. I did have a really busy week."

Duke pushed to his feet and gently hauled Holly up and into his side. He was a demonstrative man and he couldn't seem to keep his hands off her sister.

He was so attentive, no one could miss how he felt about Holly.

Teasing, Duke said, "I still think it was a guy. I've seen that look before."

Holly playfully swatted at him. "Not lately, you haven't."

"Not from anyone but you." He kissed Holly's nose. "It was really nice of you to have me over, Cassidy. Next time is my treat."

"Great idea, Duke." Holly hugged his arm while giving Cassidy a beseeching look. "Maybe you can talk Mom and Dad into joining us."

They acted like lovesick teenagers, Cassidy thought, and really, Duke was so very nice to Holly, would it be that bad if they were in love? "Sure, I'll see what I can do."

With a grateful squeal, Holly embraced her. "Thanks, Cass. I know this whole relationship thing is out of your league, but—"

Duke laughed, cutting Holly off. "She hasn't been living in a cave, Holly. Come on. Let's make a break for the car while the rain has slowed down."

Cassidy watched them go. The rain had been furious earlier, with lots of thunder and lightning, but now it seemed to have settled into a steady but gentle downpour. Duke made a point of holding his jacket over Holly's head. He opened her door for her, touched her cheek, and smiled at her with love and affection. Cassidy sighed. No one ever looked at her like that. She could see why Holly was smitten.

With food for thought and a final wave to her sister, Cassidy locked up. She turned out all the lights in her condo, took a quick shower, pulled on a tank top and panties, and climbed into bed. Her window was still open and the cooler breeze drifted over her face, her body. She'd probably end up chilled in the night, but for now she needed the fresh air.

She couldn't sleep. Thoughts of her sister in love tangled with thoughts of Pete. Why couldn't he dote on her the way Duke doted on Holly? She rolled to her back and answered her own question: because Holly was everything she wasn't—fun, beautiful, sexy.

Pete's last girlfriend had been the young executive type. She'd stopped in the center to pick him up, usually too early, which Cassidy could tell annoyed Pete. Not that he showed it, she just knew him really well. Maybe that's why things hadn't lasted with Ms. Corporate Exec.

Cassidy propped her arms behind her head and watched the shadows on her ceiling. Because she lived next door to Pete, she'd watched the women come and go. Usually a woman lasted about two weeks before Pete got bored. Any woman who set her sights on tying him down was bound for disappointment.

She certainly wouldn't expect anything lasting from him. Well, other than their friendship, which seemed pretty strong. But Pete liked women like her sister, polished to a soft glow, ultrafeminine, and very ladylike.

She didn't fall into any of those categories, so

she didn't stand much of a chance at gaining his attention even on the short term. Not that she'd go out of her way anyhow. She had her pride.

But pride ran a cold second to kissing, touching, and being held. Maybe if she just gave Pete a nudge to let him know she was interested, he'd pick up from there. She couldn't be too obvious. For her entire life, she'd been au naturel—what you saw was what you got. She wouldn't change who she was—not for Pete, not for anyone. But maybe she could just try a few small refinements.

Cassidy chewed her lip and considered her course of action.

A trim for her long hair was way past due; she'd just been too busy, and too unconcerned, to deal with it. But thinking of the too-curly mess it had become, she decided to set an appointment in the morning. And she could dab on a really subtle fragrance, something naturally earthy, like musk. While she was at the mall to get her hair trimmed, she'd also pick out a scent.

Pete had noticed her shorts, so she'd wear them again, maybe with a low-cut top. Her cleavage wasn't anything to crow about, but she wasn't flat-chested, either.

What did she have to lose?

Rolling to her side, Cassidy wondered if Pete would even notice the small changes. She would never be the type of woman he gravitated to, but they were friends, so maybe he wouldn't mind getting more intimate with her.

She'd put her plans into action tomorrow—and hope he didn't already have a date.

* * *

Pete was up with the sun. After hearing that disturbing moan—disturbing on too many levels—he'd tried turning in early. But sleep had been impossible and he'd spent hours tossing and turning, thinking of Cassidy over there with someone else while his muscles cramped and protested. He'd tried to block the awful images from his mind, but they remained, prodding at him like a sore tooth: Cassidy with some suit-wearing jerk; Cassidy getting excited; Cassidy twisting and moaning.

Cassidy climaxing.

He couldn't stand it.

By seven, he was showered, standing at his closet and staring at the lack of professional clothes. Oh, he had a suit, the one he'd worn for his brothers' marriages. Gil had fussed, trying to insist that he buy a new, more expensive one, but Pete refused. He hated the idea of shopping for the thing, trying them on, getting fitted. Then he'd have to pick out a shirt, and a tie, maybe cuff links. . . . He *hated* suits.

But Cassidy loved them.

Stiff and fuming, Pete jerked on khaki shorts and a navy pullover, then paced until it got late enough to go to her place. She generally slept in on Saturday mornings. He knew her schedule as well as he knew his own. Right now she'd be curled in bed, all warm and soft and . . . He couldn't wait a minute more.

He went out his back door and stomped across the rain-wet grass to her patio. He pressed his nose against the glass doors, but it was dark inside, silent. Daunted, Pete looked around, and discovered that her bedroom window was still open.

Shit. What if the guy was still in there? What if he'd spent the night? What if, right this very moment, he was spooned up against her soft backside?

A feral growl rose from Pete's throat, startling him with the viciousness of it. No woman had ever made him growl. He left that type of behavior to his brother Sam, who was more animal than man.

Now Gil, he was the type of man Cassidy professed to want. A suit, serious, a mover and shaker. A great guy, his brother Gil. So what would Gil do?

He'd be noble for sure, Pete decided. Gil would wait and see if she did have company, and if so, he'd give them privacy.

That thought was so repugnant, Pete started shaking.

To hell with it. His fist rapped sharply on Cassidy's glass door.

A second later, her bedroom curtain moved and Cassidy peered out. "Pete?" she groused in a sleep-froggy voice. "What are you doing?"

"Open up." Pete tried to emulate Gil, to present himself in a calm, civilized manner. "You alone in there?" he snarled.

Her eyes were huge and round in the early morning light. "No, I have the Dallas Cowboys all tucked into my bed. It's a squeeze, but we're managing."

Pete sucked in a breath. *"Cassidy . . ."*

"Of course I'm alone, you idiot." Her frowning

gaze darted around the yard in confusion. "What time is it?"

She was alone. The tension eased out of Pete, making his knees weak. "I dunno, seven or so." The chill morning air frosted his breath and prickled his skin into goose bumps. "Time to get up and keep your neighbor company."

"Seven!"

He took five steps and looked at her through the screen. She had a bad case of bedhead and her eyes were puffy, still vague with sleep. She looked tumbled and tired and his heart softened with a strange, deep thump. "Open up, Cassidy."

Still confused, not that he blamed her, she rubbed her eyes, pushed her hair out of her face. "Yeah, all right. Keep your pants on." She started to turn away.

"What fun will that be?"

Her head snapped back around. Seconds ticked by before she said, "Get away from my window, you perv. I have to get dressed."

The thump turned into a hard, steady pulse. "Don't bother on my account."

But she'd already walked away, so she missed his sentiments on the matter. Pete thought about peeking, knew he wouldn't and went back to the door to wait. Impatience hummed in his veins. He was a man on a mission, a man driven by testosterone and the ancient, savage need to stake a claim.

The fluorescent kitchen light flickered on and seconds later, her door slid open.

Assuming he'd come in without a greeting, Cassidy slunk away to the sink to start the coffee. Around an enormous yawn, she asked, "What's wrong? Why are you up so early?"

Pete soaked in the sight of her. Now seeing her with new eyes—new lusty eyes—he realized just how appealing she appeared with her long hair hanging in ropes around her shoulders and her skin flushed and warm. Plaid flannel pants hugged her behind and her black tank top molded to her breasts. Her feet were bare, her toes curled against the tile floor.

With the morning air so cool, her nipples had puckered.

Puckered nipples had never taken out his knees before, but now Pete groped for a chair so he wouldn't collapse into a horny heap in the middle of her kitchen. Like Pavlov's dogs', his mouth started watering. He could just imagine pulling that skimpy top up and over her head, baring her breasts, taking a plump nipple into his mouth. . . .

In between measuring out fragrant coffee grounds, Cassidy glanced up at him. "Pete?"

"I couldn't sleep," he mumbled, staring in awe at those breasts, mesmerized by the possibilities. He'd never really thought about her breasts before. But boy, she had them. Nice ones, too. Sort of small but perky, like the rest of her.

Someone had touched that lush little firm body just last night. Someone other than him. Pete hated that thought.

"So I don't get to sleep either?" The coffee-maker started to hiss and spit. Cassidy pulled out a chair and slumped boneless in her seat, putting her head on her folded arms. Thick, curly hair went everywhere.

Pete didn't think about it—he just reached across the table and drew his fingers across a long tendril, feeling the texture, the weight and warmth. He was close enough, so he leaned forward and brought it to his nose, breathing in the fragrance of her shampoo.

Cassidy froze. By small degrees, she tipped her face up until her eyes were visible above her forearm and she could lock gazes with him. He still had hold of her hair, still had it pressed to his nose.

She rose up a bit more. "Uh . . . Pete?"

Neither of them blinked. "Yeah?" He sounded hoarse, but damn, her hair was soft and sweet—as erogenous as her silky skin or a peek at that luscious behind. He imagined how her hair would feel slipping over his chest, his stomach, his thighs. . . . He dropped his hand and sat back.

Cassidy continued to stare at him. As if moving away from a dangerous animal, she slowly pressed her spine into the back of her seat. Her breasts were soft and round under the clinging shirt, trembling with her fast breaths. Her tight little nipples jutted forward.

Pete tried, without much effort, to keep his attention on her face. It was futile.

Cassidy shoved back her chair. "I'll, ah, I'll be right back."

Pete stared up at her with a sense of déjà vu. "Where're you going?"

"I have to . . . brush my teeth and stuff." She ran off before he could stop her.

Pete got up and paced. He felt insane, a little lost, and a whole lot aroused. Once the coffee finished dripping, he poured two cups, doctoring Cassidy's the same way she always took it, with lots of sugar and cream. He even rummaged through her cabinet and found some prepackaged brownies, knowing she'd want one.

He was leaning against the sink, sipping his coffee and thinking of the deliciously depraved things he wanted to do to her, when she shyly came back into the kitchen. Pete stalled with the cup to his mouth.

She hadn't changed clothes, but she'd brushed out her hair and neatly braided it, leaving flirty little curls to tease her temples, her nape. Her face was pink, her lips shiny with clear gloss.

She'd fixed up for him?

Very slowly, Pete set his coffee aside. "I was thinking, Cassidy . . ."

She swallowed hard and charged into the room, grabbing her coffee with near desperation. After downing half of it, she wiped her mouth and in the process removed most of the gloss she'd just applied. Pete grinned. She was . . . adorable.

How come he'd never noticed that before? He remembered how, as soon as he knew Ariel wanted Sam, he'd stopped thinking of her sexually. She became family to him. Had he done that with Cassidy, relegating her to the category of friend and not allowing himself to think of her in any other way? He hadn't wanted to screw up with Ariel, to alienate her or his brother. And God knew he valued Cassidy's friendship too much to risk it.

Visibly bracing herself, Cassidy prompted him, saying, "Yeah? You were thinking?"

Usually they were comfortable with each other, but now she seemed edgy. Pete didn't like that, so he decided to ease into things.

"Are you dating anyone?" When she said yes, then Pete could suggest she date *him*, and they could move on from there.

But Cassidy shook her head. "You know I'm not."

Pete drew back, narrowing his eyes in thought. "You can tell me anything, you know. We're . . . friends."

"Sure." When Pete just waited, she said, "I don't have time to date."

Pete blinked. If she wasn't dating, then it had been what—a one-night stand? No. He shook his head. Cassidy wasn't into those any more than he was.

He decided to approach the idea of sex from a different angle. "You didn't come over to watch the movie with me last night."

She blushed. *Blushed*. What was that about?

"I know." She shifted her feet. "I had . . . other stuff to do."

Yeah, he knew what other stuff—like moaning out an orgasm. He locked his jaw and clenched his teeth. "Another guy to see?"

The blush gave way to frowning annoyance. "I just said no, didn't I?"

"But . . ." Why was she fudging the truth? "You're saying you didn't have a date last night?"

Exasperation sharpened her tone. "How many ways can I say it, Pete? I'm not dating anyone. I haven't had a date in a year. You see me every damned day, so I'd think you'd know it."

No date. Pete stood there for fifteen seconds before other ideas started squeezing past his confusion. Ho boy.

If she hadn't been with a guy, that meant she'd been *alone* when he heard that soft, excited, and sexual moan. And if she'd been alone and moaning like that, then she'd been . . .

His abdomen clenched with sexual images so vivid he thought he might collapse. Tenderness rolled over him, too. *She'd been alone.* All by herself. He stared at her, feeling both soft in the heart and hard in the crotch.

Bless her heart. He wanted to smile and hold her. He wanted to strip her naked and pull her down to the floor.

It was still up in the air exactly what he'd do, but he knew where to start. Throbbing with need, Pete took a small step toward her. "If I kissed you—"

Her eyes widened. "You're going to kiss me?"

Shock made her look almost comical. "If I did, what would you do?"

Her mouth opened twice before she whispered, "I don't know."

"Would you slap me?"

That had her frowning again. "No."

He took another step toward her. "Would you push me away?"

Cheeks flushed with warm color, she shook her head. "Of course not."

"Great." Pete moved closer still. He took her coffee cup and set it on the counter. "What would you do?"

She stared up at him, her blue-green eyes shining, her lips parted. "I'd kiss you back," she said on a breathless gasp, and then she attacked him.

Pete staggered back from her assault. And it was an assault. She had a death grip on his neck, her mouth plastered to his so hard his lips were smashed against his teeth. The small of his back landed with jarring impact against the sharp edge of the counter.

"Mmmrrrmm." Pete tried to speak, to tell her to slow down, but she wasn't exactly a weak woman and he didn't want to hurt her. When he tried to pull back, her fingers locked into his hair. Now that hurt.

Pete turned so she was the one nailed against the counter. He covered a breast with his hand.

That got her attention.

Got his, too. Boy, she felt good.

Cassidy freed his mouth and groaned, "*Pete.*"

Her eyes were closed, her heartbeat hammering madly against his palm. He smiled and said, "Cassidy."

She tried to kiss him again, but Pete dodged her mouth. "Take it easy, okay? How about you just stand there looking like you look, and let me do the kissing?"

"Was . . . was I bad?"

"Maybe just a little out of practice."

Her lashes lowered to hide her eyes. "Sorry. It's been over a year."

Shocked and appalled, Pete paused in his ascent toward her mouth. "A year since you've been kissed?"

"Yeah." And then, defensively, "I've been busy."

But not too busy to pleasure herself last night. Oh man, that was fodder for many fantasies to come. Had she been thinking of him? Now his toes were curling.

"Jesus, I'm glad I woke you up." He pried her fingers out of his hair.

"Me, too." She tried a grin. "So, uh, now what?"

A loaded question for sure. Pete caught her waist and hefted her up to the countertop. "That's up to you, but I'd say you have a year's worth of kissing to make up for."

Cassidy smiled. "Then let's get started."

Three

Cassidy had to fight against swooning. All it took was a braid in her hair, and Pete wanted her? Who knew?

Her hair was so long that braiding it was an awkward pain in the butt, a lesson in flexibility, but hey, if it turned Pete into a ravening animal, she'd braid it every single day.

With her fanny on the countertop, she was able to look down at him. But he didn't meet her gaze. No, he was staring at her chest. More specifically, her nipples, which even now were stiff against the thin material of her tank top.

It was a little embarrassing, definitely not something she was used to. She'd sort of figured on Pete being more of a challenge.

Clearing her throat, Cassidy asked, "So did you come over here just for this?"

Distracted, he said, "Yeah." And then his hands

covered her breasts and his eyes closed as he murmured, "Damn, you feel good."

She would have slid right off the counter except that Pete was there, standing between her knees, keeping her in place.

His thumbs brushed over her nipples and it felt so good, so electric, Cassidy slumped back and banged her head on the wall. Now half reclining, she used her elbows to support herself and absorbed the wonderful sensation of being touched by Pete Watson.

He leaned forward, murmured something low, and then his mouth was at her breast, his lips plucking at her nipple through the material of the shirt. Cassidy groaned and said, "I was thinking about this last night."

"I know," he whispered in between taunting little nips with his teeth.

That momentarily stumped her. "What do you mean, you know?"

He paused, his hands stilling on the hem of her shirt. His dark brown eyes looked velvety and warm when they met hers; then he shrugged and tugged the shirt above her breasts, baring her to his gaze. He swallowed and color slashed his cheekbones. "I was thinking it, too," he admitted in husky tones. "Something happened between us yesterday, that's all I meant."

"Oh."

His mouth, scalding hot and damp, closed around her stiffened nipple.

"*Oh.*" Cassidy arched her back, offering herself to him, amazed at the intensity of the feelings he gave her.

Pete sucked languidly. His tongue swirled around her, his teeth occasionally nipping before sucking softly again. "You taste good, Cassidy."

She was in the most awkward position, cramped against the wall beside her sink, her legs half dangling off the counter at either side of his lean hips. She couldn't move much, couldn't really lie down or sit up. "Pete?"

He switched to the other nipple, latching on hungrily before slowing down, teasing with his tongue and teeth. "Hmmm?"

"Let's go to my bedroom."

His head lifted. His eyes were almost black now, heavy-lidded. He was breathing hard, his lips wet. "Yeah."

Before Cassidy could push off the counter, he put his arms around her hips and lifted, holding her tight to his chest, her legs around his waist as he made his way down the hall.

With one big hand splayed wide over her behind, Pete growled, "You know where this is headed, right?"

Hands braced on his shoulders, Cassidy gave him a blank look. The friction of his hard abdomen against the soft apex of her thighs was enough to leave her brainless. She nodded. "We're going to have sex. At least I hope we are."

Pete gave a rough laugh, surged into her room, and dumped her on her bed. He immediately followed her down, sprawling out over her, catching her hands and pinning them beside her head. "Damn right we are." His smile faded. "But I have to know you won't have regrets, Cassidy."

"Why would I?" she asked, when what she really wanted to say was, *Get on with it*.

"We're good friends." Slowly, Pete leaned down and touched his mouth to hers. A tender, almost loving kiss. Not sexual so much as emotional. It confused and elated her.

Between soft, small kisses to her lips, her chin, her throat, he whispered, "Very good friends. I value that. You're important to me. I don't want things to get . . . weird between us."

Meaning he didn't want her to start getting clingy. She understood that. To a freewheeler like Pete, she must seem like a complete stick-in-the-mud. The sensible part of her brain nagged at her, saying it wasn't too late to back out before she got hurt. But she'd been sensible all her life and damn it, she was lonely.

Eventually they'd part ways. In a year, two at the most, she'd have enough money saved, and enough experience, to open her own sports center. She couldn't see Pete working for her, so their friendship would likely wane. She hated that reality, even as she accepted it.

He was interested now. She was more than interested. For once she snuffed her sensible thoughts and went for broke.

Cupping his face, she held him back. Her fingers sank into the cool, silky thickness of his dark hair while her thumbs stroked his cheeks, luxuriating in the rasp of beard stubble, the lean hardness of his jaw. Cassidy smiled at him. It wasn't easy and her lips felt stiff, but she managed it. "I have long-term goals, Pete. You know that, just as you know how determined I am. I'm not going to throw all my plans into the wind just because we sleep together."

He looked far too serious and solemn. "Cassidy . . ."

"Shhh." She leaned up and took his mouth, loving his taste, even loving him a little. "I want you. I think you want me."

"You know I do."

She let out a breath. "We're both adults, both available, and as you said, we're friends. I trust you, more than any other guy I know. That's enough, isn't it?"

He ducked his head, and for one agonizing moment, Cassidy thought he was going to pull away. Then he moved to her side and put his hand on her belly. "I guess it'll have to be."

She had no idea what he meant by that, but his fingers were on her bare skin, teasing her abdomen before dipping under the waistband of her flannel pants. His baby finger tickled her navel, making her muscles pull tight in reaction.

Pete leaned over her and took her mouth, somehow making a mere kiss so much more—deeper, hotter, more intimate. She was still assimilating the wonder of that when his fingers pressed lower, into her panties, then tangled with her pubic hair.

Against her mouth, he said, "No, don't stiffen up." His fingers felt hot, calloused. "I'm sorry if I'm rushing things, but I'm dying to touch you."

Dying to touch her. Cassidy sighed and parted her legs a bit. She wanted him to touch her. Everything about this felt magical: his delicious scent surrounding her, the heat of his muscled body pressed all along her side. The gentle, careful way his hands moved over her.

With his hand still cupping her mound, Pete rose on one elbow. "Look at me, Cass."

It was a struggle to get her heavy eyes open and focused on his face. Their labored breaths seemed to find a matching rhythm. Pete stared at her, his eyes smoldering, intense, and his fingers parted her, gently stroking, easing—he sank one finger deep inside her.

She didn't mean to, but Cassidy pressed her head back into the mattress, closing her eyes to hold in the sensations.

Pete went still. "Open your eyes, honey. Come on, look at me."

She panted, struggled to get control of herself, and finally, her bottom lip caught in her teeth, met his gaze.

"You're already wet." He looked at her mouth, smiled. "Don't bite your lip. Ease up. That's it. Now how does that feel?" He pressed in, pulled back.

There were no words, so Cassidy just nodded.

"Good?"

"Yes." She lifted her hips against him and groaned. "Very good. But not enough."

"Does this help?" He pushed a second finger into her. "Damn, you're tight."

"Oh God."

"Come on, Cassidy," he tempted softly. "Keep your eyes open. Let me watch you, let me see what you feel." He pulled his fingers out, slowly pressed them back in, out, back in. "You can move your hips with me."

Because she couldn't *not* move, she did.

Groaning, Pete said, "Yeah, like that." He ducked his head and captured her nipple, suckling, tonguing. Sucking hard.

Whenever Cassidy had thought about sex with Pete—and she'd thought of it a lot—it hadn't been like this, with them both dressed, him more so than her, and lying on her bed with him doing things to her. She'd imagined it being a reciprocal event, her touching him and kissing him and ogling him in the buff.

"Pete, please."

As if her words snapped him out of a daze, he sat up in a rush. "Let's get rid of this, okay?" He peeled her shirt completely off her, then his own.

Oh wow. Cassidy stared at his bare chest, lightly furred in dark hair, taut with muscle, wide and hard. If the sports center would change its policy about wearing polo shirts, they'd get more customers. Women would flock in to see Pete in nothing more than shorts, she was sure of it. When she got her own place, she'd talk him into letting her use him for a poster.

"Now these."

He reached for the waistband of her flannel pants and Cassidy was overcome with shyness. What would he think of her naked? Would he enjoy the sight of her body as much as she enjoyed his?

"Lift your hips."

She gulped down her nervousness and did as he asked and, just like that, she was naked. Pete sat back beside her, looking at her body in minute detail, taking his damn time.

She started to tremble. Despite his requests, she closed her eyes and even turned her head to the side, waiting in an agony of suspense to see what he'd say. But he didn't say anything at all.

She felt his breath on her belly and jerked. "Pete?"

His lips moved over her skin; he nuzzled with his nose.

"Pete!"

"You smell so damn good." He ended that statement with something of a growl and then his hands were on her upper thighs, pulling her legs open.

Shock kept Cassidy immobile. Surely he didn't think to—oh yeah, he did. Her head fell back again. *"Pete."*

After one hot kiss to her vulva, he slid off the side of the bed. "Keep talking to me, Cass. I like it."

Her eyes widened. Such an inane thing to say to her! Cassidy almost smiled, but she was too hot, too turned on, to find any real humor in the situation. And now that he'd requested it, she couldn't think of a single thing to say.

Pete kept kissing her inner thighs, easing them farther and farther apart with his forearms holding them there. When she was inelegantly sprawled, he stared down at her, his eyes half closed, his lips parted, his face flushed. His expression very intent, he moved closer, closer. Moaning, he sank his strong fingers into her tender thighs, and stroked his tongue into her.

For Cassidy, it was as much the idea of what he did, as the physical feel of it, that had her ready to explode. No one had ever kissed her there. The few dates she'd had that resulted in sex had been perfunctory and unsatisfactory. The men had rushed to get her naked, rushed to get inside, then rushed to leave.

Pete didn't seem to be in a rush at all. In fact, in that moment, he rumbled, "I could do this all night."

She didn't think she could take it all day.

"Talk to me, honey. Do you like this?" His tongue moved over her swollen lips, pressed deep inside.

"Yes."

"And this?" He stabbed with his tongue, short, quick strokes.

A quaking had started deep inside her, radiating out to her legs, making her lungs constrict, her heart thunder. She choked, "Yes."

"And how about . . . this." Very gently, he closed his mouth over her clitoris and flicked with his tongue and Cassidy knew she was lost.

"Yes, yes, *yes*." The climax took her completely by surprise. She hadn't expected it. Not so easily. Her whole body went taut and hot, shaking uncontrollably, her hips lifting and twisting against his mouth, her hands gripping the sheets tight, trying to anchor herself.

"Oh God." It felt like she'd die, like she'd never be the same again. Even after the crushing pleasure faded, her body continued to pulse and shiver and she still couldn't get enough air into her lungs or any strength into her limp limbs.

Reality swam around her, not quite within reach. She felt good, alive and sated and weak. She knew that Pete had moved, that he'd stood up, but she couldn't seem to gather her wits. Incredible aftershocks of sensation shimmered through her.

Then Pete was over her, his chest crushing her breasts, his hairy thighs wedging between hers. He held her face while speaking softly. "I should wait, I know it, but I can't." Something hard pressed against her sex. She was sensitive, still swollen, and she flinched. "Forgive me, Cassidy."

He thrust into her—heavy, thick, hot, and hard—and Cassidy melted in renewed pleasure. There was nothing tentative about the way Pete began moving, stroking steadily, already groaning, heat pouring off him.

"Ah . . . Christ," he said, and grabbed her face to hold her still for his voracious kiss. He was wild, his tongue in her mouth, his body smothering hers. The hair on his chest abraded her nipples, his abdomen rubbed against her belly, her thighs ached from the unfamiliar position, and Cassidy felt the swelling eruptions start again, building, overflowing.

She locked her ankles at the small of Pete's back, inadvertently sending him deeper, to a spot that was almost pain, the pleasure was so fierce. Sobbing, she tried to pull her mouth away enough to breathe, but he held her too tight, too close. He drove into her faster, harder, and when he stiffened, his hips jerking, Cassidy came with him, swallowing his groan and giving him her own.

Happiness, euphoria, cocooned her. Pete was still atop her body, their warmth sealing their damp flesh together. His breath had finally calmed in her ear and she felt him withdrawing as he lost his erection.

"Mmm." Lazily, she trailed her fingertips down his spine. His skin was sleek and hot, a little sweaty. "That tickles."

He didn't move. "What?"

"Your leaving me."

"Oh. Yeah, that happens when I get wrung out." Sluggishly, Pete forced himself up on stiffened arms. Their gazes met, hers a little timid, his triumphant. He smiled. "You're incredible."

Warmth flooded Cassidy's face. "Thank you. You, too."

His attention drifted from her eyes to her mouth. "Wanna do it again?"

Cassidy felt him growing hard once more. Her eyes widened. "But . . ."

Laughing, Pete rolled to the side of her. "In a little bit, I mean. Hell, I have to regain my strength." He reached over and absently patted her thigh. "I know the manly thing to do would be to hightail it into the bathroom to get rid of the rubber, but I'm not sure I'd make it. You got any tissues in here or anything?"

Cassidy stared at her ceiling, astounded by the turn of events. She, Cassidy McClannahan, the *sensible* one, was being queried by a gorgeous man on how to deal with a spent condom. She chuckled and forced herself upright with renewed energy. Pete was sprawled beside her, one hand on his chest, the other near her hip. His eyes were still heavy, a crooked smile still on his mouth.

"I guess I'm stronger than you." She swung her legs off the side of the bed and stood—then staggered.

Pete chuckled. "Yeah, right."

"Be right back."

As she headed into the hall, he said, "You're always saying that to me."

It didn't occur to Cassidy that she was naked until she stepped into the bright light of the bathroom and saw herself in the mirror. Gads. Her once-tidy braid now looked like a frayed rope. Little hairs stuck out everywhere. Cassidy jerked out the rubber band, brushed her hair, and decided against braiding it again. It'd take too long, especially considering she had a naked man in her bed.

She wet a washcloth, wrung it out, and headed back to Pete with the small bathroom trash can in hand. She could feel her hair feathering against the bare skin of her back, reminding her of her nakedness. Now that she'd thought about being naked, she felt more self-conscious. She peeked into the bedroom, saw Pete had pushed himself up against the headboard, and knew there was no help for it. At least he was naked, too. A nice distraction, that. Trying not to look embarrassed, Cassidy waltzed in.

Pete leered at her. "I like your hair like that. Last night, I was thinking about all that hair sliding over me while we made out."

Cassidy drew to a stunned halt. "You were?"

"Yeah. What did you think about me?"

"Ummm . . ." To give herself time to formulate a

safe answer, because after all, she couldn't tell him she'd been mooning over him forever, she came in and handed him the trash can and cloth. It was an amazing thing, watching Pete peel away a condom and use the washcloth as if having an audience of one very interested woman didn't affect him at all.

"Cassidy?" He dropped the cloth over the side of the bed and caught her hand, tumbling her onto his chest. "Snap out of it, woman."

She *had* been watching the process rather fix edly, she realized.

With no real assistance from her, Pete arranged her next to him, pulling one of her legs over his lap, her arm over his chest and tucking her face against his shoulder.

The position was so comforting, but so alien, Cassidy felt stiff. "This is new to me."

"Yeah?" His hand smoothed her hair, her shoulder. "Do tell."

Not in this lifetime. "I thought it was crass to talk about stuff like that."

"I don't want details." He shuddered at the thought. "But how come this is new to you? You're twenty-seven, right? Same as me?"

"Yeah." Disgruntled, she tangled her fingers in his chest hair and frowned up at him. "I didn't say I was a virgin. I just haven't done this much. And usually the guy didn't stick around asking stupid questions afterward."

Pete seemed to be chewing that over before coming to his own conclusions. "So you've been with the wham-bam-thank-you-ma'am kind? That's pathetic."

She sighed and nestled closer. She could stay like this forever. "I know."

"Hey, I didn't mean you." He tugged on her hair to get her face tipped up to his. "I meant the jerk who walked. What an idiot."

"Idiots. Plural."

"So how many idiots have you been with?"

This time she gave his chest hair a tug. "That is none of your business and you know it. I haven't asked how many women you've been with."

"You can if you want to. Like I said, we're friends. I realized yesterday that we talk a lot. About everything."

Did he seriously think she wanted to tally up his conquests and converse about them? "No."

"I'm as comfortable with you as I am with the guys."

And that was supposed to reassure her? Cassidy thought about slugging him. She pulled her fist back, ready to poke him in the ribs.

"No guys ever kissed you between the legs before, huh?"

Oh God. Her arm fell to her side and she ducked her face against him. Maybe she could just sink into the bedding. Maybe she'd get lucky and disappear. No, Pete was still there. Still waiting.

"Cassidy?"

Beyond annoyed, she sat up and glared at him. "I may be new at this but I still don't think this is normal after-sex conversation, even between very good friends."

"I liked it." He grinned shamefully. "You taste good."

Cassidy thought her eyes might cross. He had

no shame, no modesty, no understanding of the restrictions on polite conversation.

Giving up, she fell backward on the bed and pulled a pillow over her face. Her words muffled by goose down, she said, "You're outrageous. Will you please stop?"

"No." The bed dipped and shook as Pete moved. "In fact," he said, from somewhere near her knees, "I wouldn't mind doing it again. Right now."

Hot, moist breath touched her, obliterating all her objections—and someone knocked on her front door.

Four

Pete groaned at the intrusion. Where his palm rested on the inside of Cassidy's thigh, she was warm and firm and silky. "You expecting company?"

"No." Cassidy removed the pillow, twisted, and looked upside down at her alarm clock. "It's nine-thirty already." She flopped flat again and said to Pete with evident surprise, "I thought we'd only been in here a little while."

Grinning, Pete squeezed her leg. His fingertips were *that* close to her pubic hair. "Time flies when you're having fun." The knock sounded again and he sighed in disappointment. "Want me to get that?"

"Good God, no!"

She scrambled out of the bed, gloriously bereft of clothing. Her ass was round and soft, her waist trim, her legs sleek. That long hair swung around her, caressing her back, sides, shoulders. Pete lounged back and crossed his arms behind his head, enjoying the show.

"It could be my parents."

Right. June and Ward Cleaver. Pete made a face that she didn't see. "What do you want me to do?"

She jerked on a shirt and wrangled into her flannel pants. On her way out, she said, "Just be quiet." She closed the door behind her.

Pete was on his feet in a flash. He pulled the sheet off the bed and wrapped it around his hips. Carefully, not making a sound, he eased out of the room and followed Cassidy down the hall. He had just peeked around the corner when Cassidy unlocked her front door and pulled it open.

Gil stood there on her stoop with Sam beside him. "Morning, Cassidy. Did we wake you?"

Cassidy, poor girl, pressed a hand to her chest and stared. From Pete's vantage point, she seemed to be in shock. "Uh . . ."

Next to Gil, Sam stuck out his hand. "I'm Pete's brother, Sam. Gil thought you might know where he is."

Cassidy gave a very limp handshake and said again, "Uh . . ."

Both his brothers were here, looking for him? Pete stepped around the corner. "What is it? What's wrong?"

Her eyes so wide they looked ready to fall out of her head, Cassidy turned to face him. Gil gave him the once-over, making particular note of the sheet, and started fighting a grin. He cleared his throat, looked up at the ceiling, shifted his position.

Sam, who apparently saw nothing amiss, didn't

so much as blink. "Everything's fine. We were just going to head out on Gil's boat and thought you might like to tag along. Sorry if we interrupted. Gil said you hang out here a lot."

It struck Pete then, exactly what he'd just given away. He looked at Cassidy, but she was beet-red and mute with incredulity. Damn it, he'd embarrassed her.

Gil cleared his throat again. "We can see you're otherwise engaged. Later."

He and Sam started to turn away, but Cassidy said, "No, wait." Using both hands, she shoved her hair out of her face. "We, ah, I had to go out now anyway."

Pete reached out and took her upper arms. "Cassidy . . ."

She wouldn't quite meet his gaze. "I need to go to the mall. And then I have to visit my parents and . . . you should go. Go with your brothers. Go on."

She actually shooed him.

Pete crossed his arms over his chest. "Can I get my shorts first?"

Poleaxed, she laughed too loud. "Yeah. Your shorts. I'll get them for you." And she practically ran out of the room.

Sam said, "Am I missing something?"

Gil grinned. "I believe the world just shifted."

"Ha ha." Pete walked to the front door and held it open. "If you two hooligans want to wait at my place, I'll be right there."

"What, and stand around outside? Your place is locked up." Gil started for the couch. "We'll just wait here."

"No."

"Yeah." Sam joined Gil, saying thoughtfully, "Do you remember a certain baby brother making our romantic lives hell?"

"I have a vague memory of that, yes."

Pete had tussled with his brothers many times. But not in a sheet. Odds were if he tried it now, he'd end up bare-assed and that just wouldn't do. He didn't wrestle with certain things flopping about unprotected. "Fine. But you're only embarrassing her, not me."

Sam, the only blue-eyed one of the brothers, stretched out his long legs in ragged jeans. "You mean like Ariel was embarrassed when you caught her in my boxers?"

"*That* was funny," Pete declared.

"Or when you tried to find out which Web sites featured Annabel on them?" Gil asked.

"I was curious." Then with disgust: "Come on, Gil. I was just teasing you then and you know it."

Sam settled in with a grin. "We'll be waiting."

With nothing else to do, Pete stormed into Cassidy's bedroom. She was perched on the edge of the bed, still pink but now dressed in jeans and a knit shirt. As if they could hear her, she whispered hopefully, "Are they gone?"

Pete threw the sheet aside. "Hell, no. They stuck their asses to your couch and they're not leaving until I leave with them." He grabbed up his boxers and yanked them on.

"I see." She licked her lips with her gaze glued south of his navel. "Maybe I'll just wait in here until then."

"Coward." Pete eyed her as he zipped up his shorts and grabbed for his shirt. "You don't have any reason to be embarrassed, you know."

"But I'm the sensible one. How sensible is this?"

Oh, now that stung. Eyes narrowed, he stalked to her and, as she hastily leaned back, caged her in with his fists on the mattress at either side of her hips. "What exactly does that mean, Cassidy?"

She swallowed hard. Braced on her elbows, her breath fast and shallow, she hissed, "You know what I mean."

Her hot breath brushed his mouth, and damn it, he wanted her again. "Explain it to me."

"You're a . . . a carouser." Once she said it, she warmed to the topic. "A hound dog, a hedonist. You're never going to settle down."

Pete went very still. He was . . . well, hell, he was hurt. And a little confused. Cautiously, he asked, "Did you want to settle down?"

"Yes! You know I do—someday." Her gaze was defiant. "I have my plans for the future, remember?"

"That's right." Plans that didn't include him. Pete straightened away. If he didn't put some distance between them, he'd be kissing her again and they both knew where that would lead. "You want a guy in a black tie, a corporate dude who's just like Daddy."

"Don't you dare be snide!" Temper shot her off the bed so she could glare up at him. "At least I have plans beyond getting laid!"

A tap sounded on her bedroom door and Cassidy nearly fell over.

Whipping around, Pete barked, *"What?"*

"We can hear you, and since it appears this argument won't be over any time soon, we're going to go ahead and mosey over to your place. Don't keep us waiting."

Eyes huge, her hand clutching his wrist, Cassidy whispered, "That was Sam?"

"Yeah." Pete ran his free hand over his face, far too frustrated for a guy who'd just had over-the-moon sex.

"He *heard* me." She freed her death grip on him to cover her mouth. "Ohmigod."

"Now don't faint." Amusement at her reaction took away some of the sting of her disapproval. "Sam's heard worse, believe me. And if I had to make a guess, they were cheering you on."

"But you're their brother."

"Exactly. It's no fun to pick on a girl, anyway."

"Woman," she clarified distractedly.

"What?"

"I'm a woman, not a girl." Then: "This is so embarrassing. I'll never be able to face them again."

Pete put his arm around her. "Sure you will. You're my helper when I babysit, remember? And someday I'd like you to meet my sisters-in-law. They're terrific." He led her out of the room and to the couch that Sam and Gil had vacated. He felt safer getting away from the bed, where he could think clearer. Not much clearer, considering she looked well-loved, but at least this room wasn't scented by their lovemaking, too.

And it had been lovemaking, he realized. Not

just sex. He'd had sex. Hell, he loved sex. But what he'd done with Cassidy was something . . . richer. Only she didn't seem to know it.

He frowned, trying to figure out what to say to her.

"You should go."

That pissed him off more. She did her best to rush him out the door. Talk about a wham-bam-thank-you . . . sir. "Look, Cassidy, we should probably get a few things straight."

"All right, but make it quick. I don't want your brothers to come back here."

His annoyance rose. Why had he never realized what a bossy, irritating woman Cassidy could be? "You want me to cut to the chase? Fine." He stood over her, forcing her to tilt her head back to see him. "I'm. Not. Done."

She scooted back on the couch. "Not done with what?"

"Not what, who. One time having you isn't near enough." Color flooded into her face until she looked sunburned. "Now don't start getting wide-eyed on me again. I don't intend to get in the way of your grand plans. I'm sure your suited Romeo will still be out there after we've finished exploring this . . . connection."

Her long hair hid her face from him. Her fingers twined together in her lap. Then she nodded. "Okay."

"Okay?"

She looked up, and she was smiling. "I want to explore it, too."

Well. That hadn't been as hard as he'd expected. "Great. So from now on, don't go shoving me out the door."

"Tell your brothers not to interrupt and I won't."

That made Pete smile. "If I told them that, they'd probably hang around as much as possible. It'll be better if I just don't say much about you at all."

Her wry expression told him just what she was thinking.

"Don't judge me by your own standards. I'm not embarrassed to be sleeping with you. I'm just trying to protect you from them."

"Why would they bother me?"

"Because I bothered them when they were—" Pete gulped. He'd almost said, *falling in love.* That'd really have her tossing him out the door. She didn't want anyone like him, not permanently anyway. She wanted a suit, a stuffed shirt.

Maybe he should meet her dad. Hmmm . . .

"What?" Cassidy gave him a funny look. "What are you thinking?"

"Oh, nothing." Shaking his head, Pete said, "We just like to rib each other, that's all."

"Okay then." She stood and started ushering him to the door. "Go and let them rib you so they won't embarrass me."

"Yes, ma'am." Pete pulled her into a hug first. "Cassidy? You were phenomenal."

Her grin was cheeky and fun. "Thanks. You, too."

Pete stepped outside and was just about to close the door behind him when Cassidy said, "Pete?"

Such a cautious voice. Turning back, he raised a brow.

Very softly, she said, "I'm not at all embarrassed to sleep with you."

"No?" That made him feel better—although he wasn't sure he believed her.

"No." She pushed the door almost closed. "In fact," she said through the narrow opening, "I'm looking forward to sleeping with you again."

The door snapped shut and the lock clicked into place. Pete stood there, grinning like an idiot, oblivious to his brothers watching from the stoop next door—until Sam said, "Yeah, it's love. I recognize the signs."

"Most definitely," Gil agreed.

Pete jerked out of his daze. There wasn't anything he could do about his brothers ribbing him, not after the way he'd goaded them back during their courtships, but he could at least move it to someplace private to protect Cassidy. She was embarrassed enough already. Eventually she'd have to get used to his brothers . . . or would she?

"Eavesdropping?" Pete grouched. "Don't you two have anything better to do?" Fishing his keys out of his pocket, he strode to them and unlocked his front door.

Sam eyed him in the intimidating way only an older brother could. Given the older brother was a certified bad-ass, intimidation came easily. "You don't look too worried about being in love."

Gil bent to see Pete's face. "He's not blanching even a little."

Pete laughed. Yeah, he thought he just might be

in love. What to do about it—that was the big question. He pushed his front door open with a flourish. "You might as well come on in."

Sam snorted. "As if you had a choice in that."

By rote, all three brothers headed for the kitchen. Didn't matter where they were, the kitchen was the official meeting place for anything important. Pete assumed this meant they considered his situation with Cassidy important, not just fodder for harassment.

He opened his fridge and tossed Sam a frosty can of Coke, then handed one to his quieter brother. Pete popped the tab on his own and started to drink, but Gil snatched it out of his hands.

"You two are such hillbillies." He turned to Sam, but Sam had that touch-my-drink-and-you're-in-trouble look. Sighing, Gil rinsed Pete's can under the tap and dried it. "Here. If you don't have enough breeding to use a glass, at least clean the thing."

So saying, Gil got down a glass and filled it with ice.

Sam had already guzzled half his Coke from the "dirty" can, and now he tipped it at Pete. "I'm more concerned as to whether or not you're using protection than if you get a few dust germs off your drink."

Pete took a long swallow before saying, "You know, Sam, when I was a teen—hell, even when I was in my early twenties—it was amusing the way you constantly reminded me about that. But in case you missed it, I'm grown now. And I'm as responsible as you or Gil."

Both brothers cracked up.

When Gil saw Pete's fuming face, he choked down his laughter. "Sorry. Okay, so maybe where birth control is concerned you're cautious enough."

"Thank you."

Sam was still snickering, which only drove home Cassidy's point that Pete wasn't a sensible choice for any wise woman to get involved with. Even his own brothers thought him reckless. That burned his butt big-time.

Gil took a seat at the table. Sam hopped up on the counter. Pete lounged against the wall—and waited.

"So," Gil said. "Are you in love with her?"

"Maybe."

Sam eyed him. "You really don't seem too worried about it."

Shrugging, Pete admitted, "I'm more worried about what she thinks." It took the rest of his Coke and three deep breaths before he screwed up the nerve to spill his guts. "She thinks I'm irresponsible, too."

"Too?"

With a wry look, Pete pointed out, "Wasn't that you two just laughing your asses off at me?"

"Oh, now hey, we're you're brothers." Sam straightened with annoyance. "We're allowed to give you shit. You need it."

"Exactly," Gil agreed. "But if Cassidy really thinks that about you, then she just doesn't know you well enough."

"Don't get any ideas about clueing her in," Pete warned. "Our relationship is . . ."

"Delicate?"

"I guess."

Sam leveled him with a look. "Sex was good?"

"None of your damn business!"

Sam held up both hands, but he was grinning. "Such a reaction," he said to Pete, "means one of two things—either it was great and it has you floundering, or it was awful and you just wish it hadn't happened."

Thoughtfully, Gil shook his head. "No, I've gotten to know Cassidy. She's not awful at anything."

"An overachiever?" Sam asked.

"Something like that. She's one of those really organized women who knows what she wants and goes after it. She's got like a five-year plan and a ten-year plan. Hell, probably a twenty-year plan."

"Looked to me like she wanted Pete."

Gil shrugged and took another drink. "All things considered."

Pete really wished it was that easy. Sure, Cassidy had slept with him—then more or less told him he couldn't get in the way of her goals for a committed relationship. He rubbed the heels of his palms into his eye sockets, wishing he could figure her out. One thing was plain, though. "She's into guys in suits."

Gil rolled his eyes. "Yeah, so wear a suit."

Everything always seemed so cut-and-dried to Gil. He was one hell of a businessman, making plans and decisions with absolute certainty. Nothing ever threw him off course. He was more suited to Cassidy than Pete would ever be. Thank God Gil was already married. "I can't exactly wear suits to work out in the sports center, now can I?"

Slapping his hands onto his thighs, Gil said, "I have a solution."

Sam groaned. "Here we go."

"Shut up, Sam." Then to Pete: "Take a job with me. People love you. You'd be great at sales pitches, talking to the board, dealing with consumers. . . ."

"But you'd have to wear a suit." Sam shuddered.

"That's the whole point, Sam. He said Cassidy likes suits."

"So why the hell isn't she wearing them? Did he ask her that?" Sam hopped off the counter. "The answer is not to do something you'd be miserable doing."

Gil stood, too. "Why would he be miserable working with me?"

His brothers were both nuts, Pete realized. And he loved them. "I wouldn't be miserable, but damn, Gil, you're so good at it I'd be trailing behind. And Sam's right, I can't change my life for her."

Sam slung a heavily muscled arm over Pete's shoulders. "I say stick with the great sex. It'll win her over for sure."

"Yeah," Gil conceded, "that just might do the trick."

All three brothers laughed. It didn't solve Pete's problem, but being with his brothers today was just the distraction he needed. "Are we going out on the boat or what?"

"We're going." Gil led the way out the front door. "It's too nice a day to stay inside. But

Annabel and Ariel are planning a baby shower or something, so they couldn't go along."

"So I'm second choice, huh?"

Gil winked. "Over my wife? Always."

"I'm driving," Sam told them as he slipped on his mirrored sunglasses.

Gil snatched the keys out of his hand. "No, you're still shaking over the idea of Ariel being pregnant. I'd just as soon reach the boat alive, thank you very much."

Driving down the road with the setting sun in her face, Cassidy thought about all the time she'd spent at the mall. She'd done some shopping, and in the process, she'd ventured into a salon where she lost a good two inches of hair. The beautician had wanted to take off more than that, but Cassidy was too cowardly to do too much at once. She promised the woman she'd look at her hair when she got home, think about it, and maybe come back soon.

Now at least the ends were smooth instead of poofing out like dandelion fluff. She liked the softer look. To her, it made a huge difference, making her wonder if taking off a little more might be a good thing.

In the passenger seat of her car, a pretty pink bag rustled in the current from the open window. Inside that bag were her purchases of new underwear. Skimpy, sexy panties and two matching wisplike bras that she couldn't believe she'd bought, and doubted even more that she'd wear. They didn't look all that comfortable, but then, for the first time in her adult life, comfort wasn't the point.

On top of the bag rested a small box of positively sinful perfume. She'd loved the earthy, seductive scent the moment she dabbed it on her wrist. When she got home, she'd dab it in other places.

Having sex with Pete had turned her into a carnal-minded monster. All she could think about was seeing him again.

But for now, duty called.

Cassidy pulled into her parents' driveway, noting both cars. Good. She'd get this over with in one visit. Taking the walkway around to the side door, she entered the kitchen and caught her folks smooching. Some things, it seemed, never changed. In all the years they'd been married, her father continued to dote on her mother. As refined as he often seemed, he wasn't above cuddling.

Grinning, Cassidy said, "Knock-knock."

Dressed in a lightweight summer dress and matching sandals, her mother looked chic and flustered. Her father just laughed and came to Cassidy for a hug. "Cass. What are you doing here?"

He always smelled of the same familiar aftershave, even on the weekends. Unlike most men in movies, books, and the ones she knew in real life, her dad was predictable in everything he did. Every single day, without fail, he got up at six. He exercised, drank coffee, and read the paper. He was dressed, shaved, and had eaten his breakfast by eight. He didn't fret over losing his hair, but he did fret over his family.

Today he wore a natty, short-sleeved oxford shirt tucked into dark trousers. She had never seen her dad in shorts. Even when he golfed.

With typical fatherly affection, he hugged Cassidy right off her feet.

Avoiding his question for just a moment more, Cassidy went to her mom and embraced her as well. "Hey," she said to her blushing mom, "if a man and wife can't make out in their kitchen, then I don't want to ever be married."

Her mother laughed. "Oh, stop."

"We just finished dinner, honey. Want me to warm something back up?"

"No, thanks, Dad, but I'll take some tea." While her father poured three glasses of sweet tea, her mother sat with her at the table. Cassidy waited for the comments on her hair, for them to notice and ask her why she'd done it. She had her reply all planned out, and Pete wasn't a part of it. But neither one even mentioned her hair. A little disappointed by their lack of reaction, Cassidy said, "Holly came to see me last night."

Her father set the tea in front of her and took his own chair. "That's nice. You girls don't get to visit enough anymore with you working so much and Holly in school."

"She, ah, had Duke with her."

Her mother let out a breath. "She really is hung up on that boy."

Cassidy nodded. "They're in love, Mom."

With a sound of annoyance, her father said,

"She's twenty-two, Cass. She doesn't know what love is yet."

"Actually, I think she does." Because that wasn't what her parents wanted to hear, Cassidy chose her words carefully. "You'd have to see the way she looks at him to know what I mean. She's never looked at any of her other boyfriends like that. And Duke is wonderful to her. I know he's not who you would have wanted for her. . . ."

"He hopes to be a professional athlete. That's the equivalent of a young man who dreams of becoming a cowboy. *Most* outgrow that fantasy."

Cassidy shrugged. "From what Duke told me, he has a good shot at it. I bet if you see them together you'll realize that Duke is a really nice guy"—Albeit a bore—"and that he loves Holly, too. Isn't that the most important thing?"

The doubting expressions on her parents' faces didn't look promising.

In for a penny, in for a pound. "Why don't we all get together?" Cassidy made the suggestion with a bright smile, trying to sound chipper about the idea. "You can get better acquainted with him."

"I want her to finish school."

Cassidy knew that stern tone only too well. "I know, Dad. And I think she will. But if you keep disparaging Duke, she might, *just might* do something stupid like marry him now."

Being a logical, levelheaded guy, her father reluctantly conceded. He turned to his wife. "Gina, what do you think?"

Her mother frowned in consideration. "We do have that benefit at the country club tomorrow."

"Perfect," her father exclaimed with a smile.

"No," Cassidy said at the same time. "I mean, that's a formal thing. I thought we could just get together at my place to grill out or something."

"But this would be the perfect opportunity to see Duke in a different setting. I've met the young man twice, not at length, but enough to know he might not have any great social skills off the field. Let's see if he'll do this for Holly," said her father.

Cassidy groaned. "But then that'll mean I have to dress up, too."

Her mother took her hand with a smile. "A painful prospect, for sure. I don't know why you shy away from dresses."

Because she looked and felt like a dolt in them.

Her mother wasn't above maternal bribery. "We need you there, Cassidy. Isn't that right, Frank?"

"Absolutely."

"You've always had such a good, sensible influence on Holly," her mother added.

Sensible. Right. What would they think if they knew she'd started a torrid affair with Pete? It might be worth telling them just to lose that hideous "sensible" label.

Cassidy pushed to her feet. "All right. I'll talk with Holly and set something up, then let you know." She kissed her mother's cheek, hugged her father again, and started out the door. But at the last second, she paused. "Mom, you know Holly is pretty smart. Just because she's beautiful doesn't mean she's lacking in brains."

Her dad laughed. "Honey, we know one asset doesn't rule out the other. Look at you." He winked. "Beautiful *and* smart."

Cassidy blinked at him.

"Holly's just young," her mother said. "We can't help but worry. About *both* of you."

Cassidy would have replied, but hearing herself referred to as "beautiful" put her in a stupor. She'd never thought of herself that way, and she wasn't sure she'd ever heard her father say it, either. Usually they harped on her brains, her common sense, and her determination.

She was still dazed when she stopped by the dorm to see Holly. Amazingly enough, her sister was in. Unusual for a Saturday night, but then Holly said they would be hooking up later.

Cassidy thought Holly would surely notice her hair, and again, she rehearsed how she'd explain the sudden attention to her appearance. But Holly just inquired as to why she was there, then started dancing in excitement at the idea of dressing up for a formal charity event. Holly, at least, loved the idea. But then Holly was a typical woman who adored spiffing up in her best duds.

Holly raced to the phone to call Duke, who agreed with no apparent hesitation at all, making Cassidy wonder if she was the only person on earth who detested formality.

Then she smiled. No, Pete hated it, too. And he suited her so much better than a businessman ever would.

Five

Cassidy assumed Pete was still out with his brothers when she got home. His car was in the drive, but his condo was dark and quiet. She hesitated, unwilling to look too desperate, then went next door and knocked.

No answer.

She was amazingly bummed by that, so much so that she gave herself a stern talking-to and marched her sorry butt into her own place. She had plenty to do before the evening anyway.

Oh God, what if he didn't come over that evening either? She'd only had sex with him once but was already suffering withdrawal. Her hands were shaking, for crying out loud. No, she wouldn't angst over it.

She threw her new undies into the wash on a delicate cycle. She always washed new clothes before wearing them, but especially underwear.

These had to be line-dried instead of going into the dryer. What a pain. Pete was already affecting her life, making her too conscious of her sloppy appearance when it had never mattered to her before.

After the wash finished and she had the new items hung up to dry, she jumped in the shower. Lingering under the spray, Cassidy forced herself not to rush, not to listen for the phone or door. But the second she got out, she checked her answering machine, which showed a great big, fat "0" calls. She stuck her head out the front door, trying to see if Pete was home yet. He wasn't, and she wanted to smack herself.

Wearing only an enormous navy nightshirt, Cassidy paced around her condo. Later, when the panties were dry, she'd put on a pair just in case Pete did show up. In the meantime, she was making herself nuts.

Two hours later, she was propped in front of the television with a snack, oblivious to the movie she'd turned on. A tap sounded on her kitchen door.

She jumped—actually jumped—from her seat. Forcing herself to slow, Cassidy smoothed her hair, wiped the bread crumbs from her cheese sandwich off her shirt, and walked into the kitchen.

Pete stood there at her patio door, his hair damp from a recent shower and with a little too much sun on his face. He had one long, muscled arm above his head on the doorframe, the other stretched out to the side of the frame. He grinned when he saw her and just like that, Cassidy went weak in the knees and hot in secret places. Boy, she had it bad.

Unlocking the door, she slid it open and said, "Why do you always come to this door—umpff."

Pete had his mouth all over her, as if he'd missed her just as much. One of his hands held the back of her head, his long fingers wrapped around her skull, while his tongue stroked into her mouth, tasting her deeply. His other hand was at the small of her back, going lower and lower until he cupped her bottom and squeezed her in close.

"Damn, I've thought about your mouth all day. That was the most boring boat trip I've ever taken."

Cassidy licked her tingling lips and struggled to get her eyes open. "Yeah?"

"My brothers had endless comments to make. The lake was choppy. And chicks in bikinis kept flirting with us."

Cassidy shoved back with a frown. "Oh, and I just know you hated that."

Pete's grin widened. "You sound so snide." He caught her and pulled her close again. "With Gil and Sam both hitched, it was up to me to send the girls off with smiles."

"But you sent them all off?"

He chuckled outright. "Snide and suspicious. Of course I did. Now if you were in a bikini . . ."

"Right. I wouldn't be caught dead . . ."

"Did you do something to your hair?" He frowned, lifted a lock and ran his fingers down to the end. "It looks different. Shorter."

Ohhhh. He noticed. Cassidy felt her heart turn

over in her chest at the same time she started blushing. No one had noticed—but Pete had. "I just got it trimmed," she mumbled.

"You lopped a lot off."

"Just a couple of inches."

Pete didn't comment, just kept examining it. Then the hand on her bottom shifted and he growled, "Are you wearing panties?"

Oops. She'd forgotten. Before Cassidy could stop herself, she glanced into the laundry room off her kitchen where the new underwear hung across a line. "I—"

Pete followed her gaze and his eyes darkened. "Well, what have we here?"

"Pete." She grabbed the waistband of his shorts when he started that way, and ended up dragged across the linoleum floor. "You leave my laundry alone."

Of course, he ignored that order. Cassidy went from embarrassed to mortified when Pete fingered the panties, examining the lace and silk. Then his gaze swung around to her lower body.

"You naked under that shirt, Cass?"

She backed up. The big-bad-wolf look on his face had her giggling nervously. "Maybe."

"I think you are." He released her underwear to stalk her. "Much as I'd like to see your sweet ass in those little bits of nothing, I think I'd just as soon see it bare."

She clutched the material of her nightshirt tight around her thighs. "Is that right?"

"Come here, Cass."

"No." She shook her head and giggled some more.

"You want me to chase you?" His gaze brightened. "I'm up to a few games if you are."

"No! I didn't mean—"

"Better run," he suggested. *Now.*

His expression was so hot and intent, Cassidy didn't question him further. She just whipped around and fled. She felt Pete behind her, heard his big feet pounding on her floor, and her heart shot into her throat. She ran as fast as she could, and all the while she kept giggling hysterically like a ninny of a schoolgirl.

She darted behind the couch, squealed when Pete went over it, and dashed down the hall. He was toying with her, she realized, when his fingers brushed her bottom again and again but he didn't bother snagging her. Her open bedroom door offered the only escape, so she flew inside and tried to slam it shut, but Pete didn't give her a chance. She screamed in surprise when he surged in right behind her.

Backing up, breathing hard, Cassidy watched him.

Pete's wicked grin was full of promise. "Nowhere else to go, Cass. Now be a good girl and lift the shirt and let me see if you've got on underwear."

It was impossible to wipe the smile off her face. But at the same time, her heart beat so fast she thought she might faint. "You know I don't."

"Let me see."

The back of her knees hit the mattress, bringing her to a jarring halt. Slowly, feeling like a tease, she caught the hem of her shirt—then flashed it up and back down again.

Pete laughed. "That was too fast."

"It's all you get."

"Not even close." He advanced and Cassidy caught her breath. Slowly, he took the bottom of her shirt and pulled it up, up, until it rested above her naked breasts. Somehow she felt more bared than she would have without the shirt. "Hold it there."

Feeling light-headed again, Cassidy did as she was told.

Until Pete went down on one knee.

She whimpered. *Whimpered*. She wasn't even the whimpering type, but she'd heard the ridiculous sound come out of her throat. . . . His fingers parted her, stifling all coherent thought.

A gasp, another whimper, then a soft groan. "*Pete.*"

"I kept wondering," he said huskily, "if you really tasted as good as I remembered." With his fingertips still holding her open, he looked up at her. "You do."

And he must have meant it, given how much tasting he did for the next ten minutes. Cassidy's knees were shaking, her legs like noodles, when she finally called a halt. "I have to sit down."

"How about lying down instead?" Pete stood, tugged her shirt the rest of the way off, and began stripping his own clothes away. "I should see to you first," he said, while staring at her breasts, "because the way I'm feeling, this won't last long."

"I don't care." Cassidy couldn't wait a second more and went to work on his fly. She had his shorts off in a heartbeat. He was fully erect. Breath held, she cupped him in her hands and stroked the length of him, reveling in the velvet texture over tensile steel. She glanced at Pete's face, saw his eyes were closed, his jaw locked, and felt more powerful than she ever had in her life. "I want to taste you, too."

He ground his teeth a moment, then swallowed. Locking his dark gaze with hers, he murmured, "Be my guest."

It was Cassidy's turn to kneel, and she took her time, feeling him, playing with him. His thighs were rock hard, his big feet braced apart, his hands fisted at his sides.

She'd never done this, but she'd certainly read about it. Curling her fingers tight around the base of his erection, she brought him to her mouth and licked—slow, soft, wet.

Pete dropped his head back and groaned.

He was a little salty, very warm, and she liked it. A lot. Opening her mouth, Cassidy drew him in, moving her tongue, teasing, then sucking just a bit.

In a rough, hoarse voice, Pete said, "You're something of a tease, aren't you?"

"Mmmm." If it meant doing more of this, she thought she could be.

"Oh, hell," Pete complained around a broken laugh. "That's it. That's enough." He caught her shoulders and pulled her up. "It's been too long and my control is obliterated."

Cassidy felt herself hauled upright and said with some surprise, "But it was only this morning—"

"In the bed you go."

He was moving at Mach speed, not giving her time to think. "What about you?"

"I need to fetch the raincoat first. Trust me, I'll be right with you." Pete snatched up his shorts and dug through the pocket for his wallet. Waving one condom at her, he said, "After this, I'll head next door for reinforcements." He tore the package open and rolled the rubber on with ease, proving just how much experience he had at this sort of thing.

Cassidy didn't care. He was wonderful, a fabulous lover, and he'd noticed her haircut. She opened her arms to him.

There were few preliminaries this time. Pete settled between her legs and kissed her hungrily while cupping her breasts, teasing her nipples. Unlike the first time, he didn't drag out the foreplay. Within minutes he used his fingertips to open her. Cassidy felt the broad head of his penis pressing inside.

"Hold on to me, Cass," he told her. "This is going to be a rough ride."

Just hearing him say it thrilled her, and she wrapped her arms tight around him seconds before he lifted her hips and drove forward. They both gasped.

Around a groan, Pete said, "You feel so fucking good. Too good."

The power of his thrusts rocked the bed and had the springs squeaking rhythmically. Cassidy put her legs around him, gripped his shoulders, and gave herself over to the incredible sensations of physical pleasure and emotional fulfillment. God, she knew she loved Pete. Nothing else could explain why she wanted to both weep and laugh with joy. She did neither. As her climax approached, she tightened, moaned, cried out—and felt Pete join her with a resounding, husky groan.

Yep, she loved him.

Now what?

Pete didn't exactly mean to fall asleep with her. Staying over with a woman wasn't something he ever took for granted. It wasn't something he normally did, because it signified advancement in the relationship and there'd been only a few times he'd felt comfortable with that level of commitment. But after running back to his place to grab a box of rubbers, he'd returned to Cassidy and cajoled her into modeling her new underwear.

She was such a turn-on, blushing while wearing something so sexy, laughing at him while her eyes glowed with the same powerful lust he felt. He loved watching her come. He loved holding her. He just plain loved being with her.

All through the night, while she slept soundly in his arms, he was aware of her. He'd slept little, but then, he had a soft, naked woman beside him, and everything about her fascinated him.

He hated it that she'd cut her hair. What if it had been his teasing comment that prompted her to do it? Her hair was a big turn-on for Pete. Not styled, totally natural, totally female. Like Cassidy.

Sometime during her third screaming orgasm, Pete realized he loved her because of her naturalness. Strange, when usually the really polished women appealed to him. But his relationships with them had always been polished, too. Tidy, shiny, and very surface. He'd never harassed any of them or had them laugh at him. He'd never just been himself with them.

Cassidy murmured in her sleep and her fingers tightened in his chest hair. She'd kept a death grip on him all night. Pete liked that. It gave him hope that she felt just a modicum of the desperate need he experienced.

Carefully prying her hold loose, he lifted her hand and kissed her fingers. She stirred, but didn't quite awaken. He examined her small hand with the short and clean, unpainted nails. She wore no jewelry. Because she was asleep and wouldn't know, he rubbed her fingertips over his lips, his chin. They were a little calloused, yet he thought Cassidy McClannahan was about the most feminine woman he'd ever known.

He brought her palm up and pressed it to his mouth.

"Pete?"

Her slumberous eyes were sexy as hell. Enticing. "I love touching you," he said before he could censor that L-word out. Then he decided, what the hell. "I love the way you feel and how you smell. And how you taste." He drew her finger into his mouth and curled his tongue around her, sucking lazily.

Eyes smoldering, Cassidy stared at his mouth while hers opened to accommodate her accelerated breaths. She pressed closer, her breasts flattening against his side, her thigh sliding across his boner with tantalizing effect.

Pete closed his eyes and licked his tongue down

to the seam of her fingers, probing gently. Cassidy said, *"Pete,"* with unmistakable yearning—and her phone rang.

At first, they both ignored it. Then a young woman's voice sang into the answering machine, "Hey, Cass. I wanted you to know that Duke and I are coming by your place tonight before the benefit. We figured we'd ride together so you won't be able to forget us. Again." She giggled, said something muffled to someone. "Duke said you should invite your mysterious boyfriend. It'll round out the night and give Mom and Dad someone to focus on besides him."

Jolted into frenzied motion, Cassidy shoved herself away from Pete and dove out of the bed. She stood there looking at him, the fingers he'd licked curled protectively against her naked chest. In a horrified whisper, she said, "That's my sister."

Thinking of strangling her, Pete narrowed his eyes. "She can't see us, Cass, and she can't hear you."

"I don't care." She turned her back on him, affording Pete a fine rear view. "I'm still embarrassed."

"Why?" Pete heard the phone disconnect and pushed himself up against the headboard, settling in for a confrontation. "Because you lied to me about your boyfriend?"

She whipped around so fast, her tangled hair flew out and her breasts jiggled. "I do not lie, damn you, and you owe me an apology."

Confusion swamped Pete. "Then what was your sister talking about?"

Cassidy scrubbed both hands over her face.

"Duke and Holly came over the other day. Duke's an athlete and boring beyond belief, especially when he starts gabbing on about football, but Holly worships the ground he walks on. At one point I zoned out and Duke is hell-bent on believing I was mooning over a guy."

"Were you?"

She frowned and blushed at the same time. "Yeah, but he's not a . . . a boyfriend."

"Who is it?" Knowing she'd mooned over some guy put Pete in a killing mood.

The way she crossed her arms under her breasts plumped them up like an offering. She thrust her chin up, adding to Pete's suspicions. Then, taking the wind right out of him, she said, "You."

"Me?"

"I told you he wasn't a boyfriend." She paced away, came back. "Remember you said we were both thinking about sex? Well, I was. I suppose Duke knows the look and he wanted to tease me."

A queer little feeling settled into Pete's stomach. *She'd been thinking about me.* He really did need to get this all sorted out. "So Friday night, when you didn't ask me to dinner even though you had enough beef for four, and you didn't come over to watch the movie with me, it was because your sister and Duke were visiting?"

"The steaks were for them, yeah." She rolled one shoulder. "But I wouldn't have watched the movie with you anyway."

"Why not?"

Her look told him that should have been obvious. "Because I was already . . . well, lusting after you. I didn't want to put myself through that."

His damn heart ached. "I'm sorry."

She waited two seconds, then shrugged and scampered back into bed. "Trust me. You've made up for all my suffering."

Pete pulled her up to sit on his lap, arranging her so she faced him, her legs folded at either side of his hips. Holding her thighs, he asked, "Your sister insinuated that you'd forgotten about them?"

Wiggling her bottom, Cassidy grinned. "You sure you want to keep talking about this? I can think of better things—"

"Cass."

Rolling her eyes, she sighed. "After all your teasing, I totally forgot about them coming over. I was on my way out the door when they showed up. I was going to go to the theater and see a cheesy movie and eat popcorn until I was sick, but I lied and told them I was going for dessert."

"Aha." Pete smiled widely. "I thought you didn't lie."

"I don't." She smoothed both hands over his chest, leaned down and kissed his nose. "Not to you."

She started to sit up again, but Pete pulled her back for a longer, more satisfying kiss, then allowed her to settle against him. The position was nice, with her knees drawn up by his hips, her belly flush against his. He smoothed his hands over her bottom, offered up so nicely. "So they were here alone in your place?"

"Yeah, why?"

Should he admit it? He grunted at himself. He wanted her to always be truthful with him, so he had to be truthful, too. "I think I heard them making whoopee."

Cassidy started in surprise, but Pete held her secure. "That's insane. Not in my home!"

"Afraid so. I heard a lot of sexy moaning."

"Oh, God." She covered her face.

"I assumed it was you."

Her head jerked up. "That's why you kept asking me who I was seeing?"

"Yep." Pete grinned, tightened his hold, and said, "But when you insisted you weren't seeing anyone, I assumed you were playing solitaire."

"Who moans over solitaire?"

His grin widened. "You misunderstand. I heard those moans, Cass. I thought you were . . . alone."

She still looked confused.

Sighing, Pete said, "I thought you were flying solo. Taking care of business. All alone."

In slow progression, confusion gave way to understanding and her eyes flared. "You thought—!"

"Yeah."

It was probably the toothy grin that got to her. She punched him. Hard. Groaning, Pete grabbed his ribs, then had to grab her to keep from getting another shot.

"Jerk!"

When he laughed, she tried to scamper away. Pete wrestled her down, making a point to let her come close to slipping away, again and again. He liked wrestling with Cassidy. The match finally ended when he got her flat on her back, used his knee to open her legs, and thrust inside her.

They both went still, breathing hard. Cassidy

struggled to get her hands free, only to wrap them around his neck. "You win," she told him huskily.

Pete pressed his face into her shoulder. He wasn't wearing a rubber and no way in hell would he do that to her. "Promise me you won't move."

"But I want to move. I want you to move."

"I'm not wearing anything."

"Oh." She nudged his shoulder. "Well, go get something."

"In a second." Pete smoothed her beautiful hair away from her face. "So?"

"So what?"

Watching her expression, Pete pressed in a little tighter, making Cassidy inhale sharply. He knew he was playing with fire but he was willing to use whatever coercion he could.

"Can your mysterious boyfriend accompany you to the benefit?" Though the question sounded light, Pete's apprehension was so great, his lungs hurt. He couldn't recall anything mattering quite so much to him.

Cassidy froze. "It'll be boring."

"Maybe I'll liven it up a little." Shit. She probably didn't want that. He frowned and started to retract that statement when she smiled.

"That's what I was thinking the other night when Duke accused me of daydreaming about a guy. I kept thinking if you were there, it wouldn't be so bad."

Ah damn, now she had him feeling all mushy inside. Softly, he urged, "Then let me be there."

"It won't just be Duke and Holly tonight." She

stared at his chin while chewing her bottom lip. "Mom and Dad are going to the benefit, too."

Every muscle in Pete's body drew so tight, he felt brittle. He wasn't good enough for June and Ward? "You're afraid I'll embarrass you."

"No!" She rushed to reassure him, then scowled. "How could you even think such a stupid thing?" Just as quickly, she softened. "Mom and Dad are great and I'm sure they'll like you."

"Then?"

She let out a long, grievous sigh. "It's a dressy thing. A formal event at the country club. Dad will probably break out his tux."

"I promise not to wear shorts." How he'd find something appropriate on such short notice, he didn't know. Gil would probably have a variety of tuxes in his wardrobe, though, and they were about the same size. . . .

Cassidy was laughing. "I wish we could both wear shorts. I'd sure be more comfortable in them." She sighed, then said, "If I invite you along tonight, will you please *get a damn condom?*"

At least she wanted him sexually. As Sam and Gil had assured him, he could work from there. And he'd start right now. He'd take her five ways to Sunday, make her scream, beg. He'd devastate her with pleasure. "Yes, ma'am. Be right back."

But as Pete finished rolling on the condom, Cassidy said, "I have, you know."

He turned to face her. She was sprawled in the bed, sleekly muscled, strong in ways that only a woman could be. Damn, he adored her. "Have what?"

"Thought of you."

"Yeah?" He stretched out next to her.

"While flying solo, I mean."

Pete's heart all but stopped. Well, hell. He looked at her, knew he was lost, and fell on her like a starving man. Later. He'd devastate her later. For now, he just had to have her.

Six

She still couldn't believe Pete wanted a date with her and her family. Didn't that signify . . . something?

Since he left early that afternoon, she used the remainder of the day to buy new pantyhose—a chore that made her grimace—and while she was out, she decided to have her hair trimmed a little more. Not just because Pete noticed, she assured herself, but because she'd like it.

By the time the beautician finished, her once witchy, waist-length hair now hung to just below her shoulder blades. Still long, but much tidier and more manageable.

Cassidy located her one and only black dress at the back of her closet. She removed the dry cleaning bag and tugged the dress on over her head. It was a simple dress with sleeves, a high, round neckline, and a straight fit that fell to just below her knees.

It was . . . *comfortable.*

Seeing herself in the mirror was almost depressing. Give her a scythe and a hood and she'd pass for Death. Cassidy groaned and dug out her black-heeled pumps. They didn't help. Now she looked like a cross-dressing Death.

To make matters worse, Pete knocked on her door before she had time to consider any alternatives. Not that she had any, owning only that one black dress. It'd have to do. She hoped Pete wouldn't turn tail and run when he saw what a formal misfit she was.

For once, he came to her front door, and when Cassidy opened it, she almost fell over.

Pete wore a tux.

Her gaze traveled all over him and still she couldn't take it in. All spiffed up, he didn't even look like Pete. He looked good, no two ways around that. Just . . . different, not *her* Pete anymore.

And she'd once thought she wanted a guy who wore suits? How stupid.

He was busy fiddling with a black tie. "I'm lousy at this crap. Never done it enough, I guess. Can you help?" He looked up then and got caught. A frown pulled down his brows and Cassidy waited for him to question her choice of dress.

"You cut your hair again?"

Whoa. No mention of her black tent? She cleared her throat. "Technically, the beautician did."

He forgot all about his tie. Releasing the tie so it fell to his chest, he propped his hands on his hips and glared. "Why the hell do you keep cutting it?"

Beyond Pete, Cassidy saw her mother and father pull up to the curb, and behind them, Duke and Holly. Oh boy. Let the fun begin.

Oblivious to their audience, Pete caught her shoulders to regain her attention, then moved her back so he could step in. "I like it long, Cassidy."

"It's still long." Nervously, Cassidy watched as her family plus Duke approached, all of them very attentive. Her parents had expected to deal with one nonconforming boyfriend. Now they were faced with two.

"Not as long as it used to be." Pete looked bedeviled, then blurted, "Was it something I said? Because if it was, forget it. I love your hair."

"No." Cassidy tried to quickly explain that her parents were right behind him. "Uh, Pete . . ."

He wrapped his hands in her hair, crushing fists full as if savoring it. "I don't want you changing on me, Cass. I adore you just as you are."

Her mouth fell open.

Pete stepped closer. "I adore you enough to get into this damn monkey suit to impress Ward and June—though God knows I have no idea about this stupid tie, so you're going to have to help me with it."

From behind Pete, Duke said, "I can do that if you like."

Pete turned, saw the crowd, and gave a sheepish grin. Both Duke and her father wore tuxes, and to Cassidy's surprise, Duke looked very comfortable in his.

"Let me see," Pete said. "You must be Duke, because you're definitely not Ward."

"Right in one." The two men shared a hardy handshake.

"And this has to be Cassidy's pretty little sister, Holly."

Holly twittered a laugh. "That's me," she said, then realized she'd just complimented herself and blushed.

Pete cleared his throat and faced her father. "And you must be—"

Fighting a grin, her father stuck out his hand. "Not Ward."

Pete winced. "Sorry. I was just, uh . . ."

"Going by Cassidy's description? She's told me that before, too. Where she sees a resemblance, I'll never know."

Relaxing at the easy banter, Pete accepted his hand. "It's nice to meet you, Mr. McClannahan."

"Anyone who adores my daughter has to call me Frank. And this is my wife, Gina."

The obligatory greetings were performed without Cassidy's help. She sank back against the wall and closed her eyes. Pete said he adored her and everyone had heard. He'd noticed her hair again when no one else did. And he didn't notice her hideous dress, even though both her mother and Holly were there, providing awesome comparisons.

Her mother said, "Cassidy, he's right. You've done something to your hair."

"Twice," Pete pointed out.

"It looks lovely," Gina said, earning a frown from Pete, and when Holly agreed, he looked ready to fume.

Duke stretched out his massive arms to include everyone and herded them inside. "Why don't we move this indoors? We have a little time before the benefit starts."

Cassidy remembered the purpose of this blighted soiree and launched into compliments aimed at Duke. He kept Holly at his side while reciprocating. "I usually only dress up for weddings and funerals. But considering how much time I spend in sweaty jerseys, I like to trade up every now and then."

Near Cassidy's ear, Pete murmured, "This feels like the latter."

She shushed him. "Mom, Duke has the record for touchdowns at his college. Isn't that impressive?"

"Very," Gina said.

Duke pulled Pete around and began knotting his tie. "Thanks. I was pretty pleased about it."

Holly beamed at everyone. "He also made the dean's list."

Frank gave his attention. "Excellent. What's your major?"

With the tie finished, Duke threw his arm around Pete's shoulder, nearly knocking him off balance. "Business. If I don't make it in football, I'd like to open my own sporting goods store. Maybe build up to a chain."

"Good plan," Pete said, then scowled when he noticed Cassidy was staring at Duke.

The differences in the two men hit Cassidy. Both were big and strong, but next to Duke, Pete looked leaner, more refined. Definitely more handsome—but then, that was just Cassidy's opinion. Holly, apparently, felt just the opposite.

Because Pete kept giving her odd looks, Cassidy

said, "I'll put on a pot of coffee." She ducked out of the room, anxious for a moment to herself. Pete had said he adored her. It wasn't love, but it was better than a quick fling. Maybe she could build on that.

She had her back to the kitchen entrance, waiting for the coffee to finish, when warm male hands slid around her waist. Pete's scent enveloped her, so warm and familiar. Curse the stupid benefit—she'd rather lose their clothes and cuddle in bed.

Next to her ear, Pete rasped, "Why the hell do you keep staring at Duke?"

Did he sound jealous? No, that was absurd. Because she wasn't about to tell Pete that she'd been comparing them, she shrugged. "He looks different in a suit. Nice." She twisted around to face him. "My parents will be pleased."

"He doesn't normally wear a suit."

"What an understatement. Duke is a jock through and through. But that business degree surprised my parents." She smiled. "I think old Duke is full of surprises."

"You like him?"

She realized she did. How could she not like Duke when he was so good to her sister? "You know, I really do. He's not flighty like I thought. He's got a plan, and a backup plan. And he's going after what he wants."

Pete groaned, then tucked his face against her neck. "You know, Cassidy," he murmured, and she could feel his lips on her skin, "I was thinking there were a few things—just small things—that you could possibly change about yourself. What do you think?"

Heat rushed into her face. "The dress is awful, I know."

Pete straightened. "What?"

Holding out the sides of the hideous tent, she repeated, "This dress. But it's the only black thing I own."

Confused, Pete shook his head. "I like you better in shorts, sure, but you look great no matter what you wear." He smoothed his hands up and down her sides. "You're such a goal-oriented person."

What that had to do with her dress, Cassidy didn't know. "Sensible Cassidy, that's me."

"Sleeping with me wasn't all that sensible. You told me so yourself."

"I've changed my mind on that. Sleeping with you is one of the best decisions I've ever made."

"Yeah?" He started to grin.

From behind them, her father said, "Well, I think we can segue right into good-byes."

Cassidy gasped, Pete turned, and they both saw that it wasn't just her father standing there. Her mother, Holly, and Duke were all within earshot. Well, hell. Couldn't they have made a little noise? Cleared a throat? Whistled?

Without missing a beat, Pete asked, "Is it time to go already?"

Frank stepped into the kitchen. "For us, yes. But my daughter looks tortured at the moment, so perhaps she'd like to skip it."

All eyes turned to Cassidy. She wanted to shrink in on herself. "Uh, no. I'm all right. Really. I can—"

Duke smiled. "We're getting along fine, Cassidy. You don't need to run interference, though Holly and I both appreciate the effort."

Gina hooked her arm through Frank's. "It's not that we don't want your company, but I think Pete has a few more things to say." Gina turned to Pete. "Cassidy has always been an overachieving tomboy. Put her in a dress and she's miserable. She'll be happier staying here and, ah, working things out with you."

Cassidy groaned. Her mother's attempts at matchmaking weren't all that subtle.

Her father sent her a fond look. "My sensible Cassidy. She'll have things squared away in no time."

Just what was she supposed to square away? Pete?

Pete left the ball in her court. "Whatever you want to do is okay by me, Cass."

No way did she want to go, but she'd feel guilty if she didn't. "You've already rented the tux. . . ."

"Naw. I borrowed it from Gil." Pete flashed her a grin.

"Then it's all settled," her mother said before Cassidy could reply. Behind Pete's back, Gina gave Cassidy the thumbs-up. "We can see ourselves out. Have a nice night, kids."

Her family managed a mass exodus in record time, leaving a heavy silence behind.

Pete zeroed in on Cassidy. "About that dress."

He looked so intent, she started to fidget. "Horrible, huh?"

"Let's get it off you."

So he wanted to head straight to bed? Did he intend to just skip past everything else that had been said? Would he now ignore his statement about adoring her? "In a hurry, are you?"

Pete nodded. "If you strip, I can, too."

Relief sent a grin across her face. Slowly, she pulled the knot from his tie and opened the top button of his dress shirt. "Poor baby. You're really uncomfortable in this suit." Almost as uncomfortable as she was in the dress. Of course, Pete looked delicious, while she didn't.

"Yeah, but for the right incentive I can suffer through anything." The way he said that left no confusion: he considered her the right incentive.

Using the tie like a leash, Cassidy led him down the hall to her bedroom. Her heart beat fast in anticipation. "Then by all means, let's get you out of it."

He followed along willingly enough, but as Cassidy closed her bedroom door, he said, "About those changes I mentioned . . ."

Did he have to keep harping on that? To distract him she pushed the coat off his shoulders and finished unbuttoning his shirt. "Let's get this off you."

"But I wanted to talk."

"We'll talk in bed." She reached for his belt, and Pete gave up with a groan. The dress pants came off easier than his stiff jeans, and in no time, Cassidy had him buck naked. He looked so gorgeous, and for the moment, he was hers.

Remembering how he'd teased her earlier, chasing her and wrestling with her, Cassidy decided to get back a little of her own. She picked up the length of black tie and beckoned Pete into bed.

His dark eyes glittered. "What are you going to do?"

"Just have a little fun." She patted the mattress. "Put your sexy self right here while I lose my dress."

"Now, there's an idea." With no sign of modesty, Pete stretched out on her bed, his arms folded behind his head, one leg bent. "Go ahead. I'm ready."

Man, he looked good on her sheets. Sighing, Cassidy said, "No you aren't. Not yet." She went to the bed and looped the tie once, twice around his erection. "Leave that right there for a moment."

Eyes wide, Pete stared down at his decorated penis. "Uh, Cass . . ."

After kicking off her pumps, she reached beneath her dress and stripped off the strangling pantyhose. Forgetting the tie, Pete gave her his undivided attention.

Cassidy smiled, pulled her dress up, over her head, and tossed it aside. Now that it was gone, she felt better. She'd burn that thing before she wore it again. Now she stood in front of Pete in her new underwear, and judging by his expression, he liked what he saw.

Striking a pose, Cassidy asked, "Is this the kind of change you mean?"

Pete's gaze was glued to her belly. "What?"

"You want me to change. Does the sexier underwear help?"

As if someone had doused him in ice water, Pete shot upright on the bed. Furious, he growled, "I do *not* want you to change!" Then almost as an afterthought, he said with less heat, "I like the panties, though."

Cassidy propped her hands on her hips. "You said I could change a few things."

He groused and grumbled his way out of the bed to tower over her. The tie remained looped around his penis, the long ends dangling down. Cassidy pursed her mouth to keep from snickering.

Pete didn't even seem to notice. "Not your hair or your clothes." His vehemence made the tie shiver. "Not anything that's *you*."

Cassidy stepped closer and smiled up at him. "That doesn't make any sense, Pete."

He ran a hand over his head, drew a huge breath, and blurted, "I love you, Cassidy McClannahan."

That statement, sort of falling out of nowhere, rendered them both mute. Pete scrutinized her, waiting. All Cassidy could do was stare. She tried to reply, but nothing would come out of her throat. He loved her. Tears threatened.

Seeing that, Pete groaned. "Ah, damn it, Cass, please don't cry."

No, she wouldn't. She sniffed, took several necessary breaths, and licked her very dry lips. "So . . . you love me?"

"I do."

He sounded almost wrecked about it. Here he was, the most gorgeous, wonderful, impossible man she knew, in *her* bedroom, wearing a most unconventional black tie, declaring himself and looking morose about it. Cassidy covered her mouth but she couldn't stifle her euphoric giggle.

Pete's eyes narrowed. "You aren't going to cry now?"

She shook her head. "No." And she smiled.

Clearing his throat, Pete said, "Good." He propped his hands on his hips and took an arrogant stance as if he didn't have a black tie embracing his manhood. "So do you think you could change your mind about wanting a guy in a suit?"

She wanted him. "Maybe. What do you have in mind?"

Pete rubbed the back of his neck. "I did some thinking today. I'm going to get my teaching degree. I only need a few credits—"

Excitement shot through her and Cassidy threw herself into his arms. "Pete! That's wonderful. I've always known you'd make a great teacher."

Pete held her away. "A gym teacher, Cass. No suits."

"Yeah, so?"

Exasperated, Pete shook her. "You want a black tie kinda guy. You told me so, remember?"

Feeling very impish, Cassidy pointed out, "You're wearing a black tie right now."

His expression was comical. He looked down and said, "Damn. I forgot." He reached for the tie but Cassidy caught his hands.

"I love you, too, Pete. Just the way you are. I can be myself with you. If you were a guy like my dad, then I'd need to be a woman like my mom, and I'm not."

"You're beautiful."

Oh, see, how could she not love him? Ready to swoon, she said, "I'm glad you think so."

Pete bent his head and kissed her, long, deep, and the next thing Cassidy knew, they were on the bed. With a little maneuvering, Pete got between her thighs and then she felt the head of his erection pressing in. "I need you, Cass."

"Yes."

He pushed her hair away from her face. "I don't have anything with me."

"Will you marry me?"

He grinned. "That was my next question to you."

"Yes."

"Good." He pressed in, the friction incredible, the pleasure complete. They both groaned. "Do you want a big wedding?"

"My mother will insist."

Pete quickened his strokes. "All right." His arms tightened, holding her closer. "I guess I can borrow Gil's tux again."

"Whatever."

"You want kids?"

"Sure." She barely knew what she was saying, but she knew she loved him and didn't want him to pull away. Not now. Not ever.

"Me, too."

"Pete?"

"Yeah?"

She wrapped her legs around him and arched her back. On a gasp, she said, "Shut up."

"Yeah." Pete slid his hands down her back to her hips and lifted. The position pressed his chest closer to her breasts, abrading her already stiffened nipples. Cassidy cried out at the onset of release.

"I love you," Pete told her again, and that did it. She came, squeezing him tight, moaning and shivering. And just as the wild contractions ended, Pete went taut over her, grinding out his own orgasm. Cassidy knew she could end up pregnant, but it didn't worry her. She was twenty-seven, on track with her career, and now ahead of the game with love.

Pete slumped against her, boneless and breathing fast and hard, giving her all his weight. But she didn't mind. Not at all. In fact . . . "Pete?"

He grunted.

Hugging him, Cassidy said, "I love you in your jeans. And you're pretty loveable naked."

He puckered up enough to press a kiss to her shoulder, then went limp again.

Cassidy caressed the long length of his strong back. "But Pete," she whispered, still a little in awe and more than willing to tease, "the way you wear a black tie is phenomenal."

Two seconds passed before Pete stiffened and shoved himself off her. "Oh, hell." He stared down at his lap, where the mangled black tie was crushed. "I think it's ruined."

Cassidy started laughing and couldn't stop. "You *think*?"

He tugged it loose and dropped it over the side of the bed. "I'm going to have to buy Gil a new one."

"Maybe we'll buy ten."

"Ten? Why?"

So happy she was ready to burst with it, Cassidy said, "I've decided I like the effect black ties have on you."

Slowly, Pete grinned. "Fine by me. As long as I don't have to wear the suit with it."

MISS EXTREME
CONGENIALITY

Erin McCarthy

One

CJ White hated Wyatt Maddock. She hated the way
he walked, always leading with his dick, and hated
the way he talked, like he was determined to coax
a giggle from every woman he approached.

She hated the way he grinned, all white teeth
and wolfish charm. She hated the way he propped
his feet up on her desk at work, and she hated the
way he was leaning over Special Agent Dempsey
right now, whispering in her ear as he held her
close enough to inhale her, breasts first.

Yep, she hated him and every single minute of
the last lousy three months that she'd been stuck
working this insider-trading case with him for the
Bureau. It hadn't been as bad before, when they'd
been working a price-fixing investigation, because
she'd had Agent Knight to buffer her from Wyatt's
stupidity. On this case it had been just the two of
them until tonight.

Yet despite that stupidity, somehow Wyatt had managed to snag the exciting side to this investigation. Their boss Nordstrom had claimed Wyatt fit the corporate image, and she had to admit he was right. The man dressed like a CEO instead of an FBI agent, and could charm the bite off a snake. So Wyatt got to head off to the Chicago stock exchange every day and play stockbroker undercover, while she got stuck transcribing tapes, filling out forms, and dealing with Nordstrom and his temper tantrums. Then, at the end of each long day spent playing secretary, she had to deal with Wyatt and his amusing stories of his adventures as a fake financial whiz.

Which didn't amuse her at all.

"Hey." Fingers snapped in her face. "Get that table cleared, we're running behind."

CJ looked at the man frowning in front of her and promised herself she would be a good FBI agent and not fling him over her shoulder like she really wanted to. His name was Fisher Carter, and he was just one more reason to hate Wyatt. Somehow it just had to be Wyatt's fault that she was stuck being a catering assistant to Fisher at Sharecron's annual Christmas party/offensive display of wealth and ego. Sharecron was the target of their current investigation, and the company was knee-deep in insider trading.

"Sorry, Fisher, I'll get right on it." CJ started slapping dishes onto the metal cart she had pushed over to the table.

The plan was that Wyatt was supposed to use his image as corporate playboy to feign drunkenness and whisk his date off down the hall to his office for a little Christmas cheer in private. Really, he was going to search the computer database for evidence. CJ was supposed to be the lookout, making sure no one followed him, since he needed a good agent covering his back.

At least, that had been the official reason given to her by Nordstrom. Somehow she thought it wasn't coincidence that Brandy Dempsey, a blond and buff agent just helping on the case for tonight as Wyatt's date, looked a hell of a lot better in a dress and heels than she would. CJ didn't even own a pair of heels and she suspected her hair was stuck into the permanent shape of a ponytail.

Not that she cared that she was here wearing a waitress white shirt and Wyatt was in an expensive tux, looking like he'd been born in it. She had too many concerns in life to worry about being anything but comfortable in her clothes. Let Brandy deal with Wyatt Maddock and his roving hands, which were now sitting right above the curve of Brandy's ass. Like that was necessary.

She snorted as she finished loading her tray, hearing Wyatt's deep laugh as he bent over Brandy's neck. She should be absolutely grateful that she'd been spared the hell that Brandy was enduring in the name of the Justice Department.

Hell. Hah.

Because that was the real reason CJ hated Wyatt.

She hated him because every time she looked at him, she wanted him. In her bed, over her, under her, sliding into her hard and deep, pleasing her the way he had pleased so many other women, reminding her that somewhere locked inside her frozen body, she was still a woman.

Like that was going to happen.

He didn't think of her that way, and even if he did, she'd never let him. He was all wrong for her, the exact opposite of what she needed in her life right now, when she needed to concentrate on her son.

So if Wyatt ever did decide he was up for a challenge and put the moves on her, he'd be wearing his balls like earmuffs.

Let's see how Pretty Boy liked that with his tux.

Wyatt was having trouble breathing. Brandy's chest was too large to allow for adequate air circulation as he pretended to stumble and plant a kiss on her cleavage.

Brandy gave a laugh and shoved at him. "Oh, stop it, Wyatt."

He shot her a grin as he straightened up and sucked in some air. Brandy was good at this bimbo bit. Maybe he should ask her out for real.

In a low voice, he said, "Is White watching? We should probably head out now. If anyone gives a shit, I think we've proved I'm drunk and horny."

Not that he thought anyone would notice. This party was unlike anything he'd ever seen actually sponsored and paid for by a corporation. It was like a prom for adults, but the alcohol was legal, and there was slightly less hairspray. Half the room was dancing to the Cher impersonator, while the other half was engaged in various forms of drunken debauchery with spouses, not always their own. Weirdest of all was a woman hired to sit in a bathtub of pink balloons, encouraging men to pop her bubbles.

It almost made him regret he'd never joined the private sector.

Truthfully, he found the whole thing borderline disgusting. He liked to have as much fun as the next guy, but this was over the top for a business function.

"Yeah, White's watching, looking a little put out, in fact," Brandy murmured.

Wyatt glanced over at CJ and winced. He should have felt that cool breeze of disdain blowing over him, even muffled by Brandy's breasts. White was ripping linen off a table, her ponytail bouncing, her mouth set into a scowl. He knew that scowl well, was subjected to it on a daily basis.

CJ'd had it out for him since the minute they were assigned to a case together nine months ago and her attitude had never wavered.

Which had to be the only reason he felt this bizarre attraction to her. It was annoyance that she was immune to him. That she was the first woman that he could ever remember who blatantly didn't like him, and made no pretense of the fact that she thought he was an unpaid gigolo. It was obviously all just a blow to the ego, which fueled his interest. There couldn't be anything else to it.

The desire for CJ certainly didn't spring from her looks. He'd seen five-year-olds with a better sense of style. Her clothes were all about two sizes too big, and she walked around in shoes that could be worn in military combat. As for breasts, it was anybody's guess if she actually had them.

"CJ always looks put out," he told Brandy, flashing her a grin. "She's uptight. Unlike me."

Brandy caught his change of tone. She raised an eyebrow and he once again appreciated the picture she made in a red-hot evening dress, blond hair piled up high, legs long and toned, painted toenails. The kind of woman he enjoyed.

He went for it, giving her hand a caress. "So, how about we do this date for real tomorrow night?"

Brandy gave a laugh. "I don't think CJ would appreciate me trespassing on her property."

That stunned him into stopping all pretense of dancing. He gaped at Brandy. "I'm not White's property. I'm White's *nothing*." Less than nothing. He was the sludge in the sink pipes, according to White.

"Well, you could be if you wanted to." Brandy tugged his hand, forcing him to start swaying back and forth again. "Trust me, I know when a woman is jealous, and if looks could kill, you'd be digging me a hole right now."

Jealous? CJ was jealous of Brandy? The idea took hold for a split second, maybe because it appealed to him, and then he dismissed it. Hell, the idea was ridiculous. White was probably just pissed that she got stuck slinging plates of half-eaten cheesecake while he was playing the partygoer.

He'd spent nine months trying to figure CJ White out. He certainly wasn't going to get any closer to the truth about her tonight.

"Let's head for the hall, Brandy."

"Got it."

Wyatt turned and caught CJ's eye. He gave a slight nod and waited until she nodded back.

Then he made a big show of stumbling, grabbing Brandy perilously close to her breast and saying loudly, "Let me show you my office, baby. I've got a really big . . . desk."

Time to go to work and forget all about CJ White and his desire to peel off those baggy-ass clothes and discover what she was hiding under there. And then show her his big desk.

Half an hour later, he was done, having poked around in some computer files in his office, Brandy standing just inside the door, ready to cover for him if anyone walked in. It had gone smoothly, but he hadn't found anything of value. Nordstrom was going to be pissed, and that vein in his head would throb in a way that always freaked Wyatt out.

Couldn't be helped. There was nothing he could detect in the computer files to help their case when he did a quick visual search, though he had managed to bug his phone in hopes of taping a revealing phone conversation. A minor success, nothing more.

The minute they stepped into the hall, he sensed a problem. Several women were huddled together, laughing in a drunken giggle, hanging on to the wall like they were on the people mover at O'Hare and needed the wall for balance.

He pulled Brandy to his side, hoping they wouldn't attract any attention, but the women glanced up. And the redhead with cleavage he could drive a truck through shouted, "Brandy? Brandy Dempsey? Ohmigod!"

Brandy cursed under her breath and murmured, "Sorority sister." Then to the redhead, "Hi, Patti!"

"What are you doing here?" Patti wobbled over, her voice carrying the length of a football field, making Wyatt wince and look around nervously.

The alcohol had clearly dulled her sense of hearing as she continued to blurt out with volume that rivaled a rock concert, "Aren't you an FBI agent? I heard that, and I thought—no shit! Brandy's a fucking fed—unbelievable!"

Hell. Wyatt thought fast, well aware of how dangerous it could be to the case for anyone to know who he or Brandy was. A little desperate, he reached out and touched Patti's arm.

He said, "Brandy, aren't you going to introduce me to your gorgeous friend?"

Patti swiveled her head, and her delight turned to calculating interest. "Oh, well, hello."

"I'm Wyatt." He lifted her hand and kissed it softly. "It's a pleasure to meet you."

"The pleasure is all mine." Patti flipped her hair over her shoulder with her free hand. As drunk as she was, the movement challenged her balance. She pitched forward and Wyatt caught her by the arms.

"Oh!" In a flash, she was pressed up against him, her thigh pursuing his with predatory accuracy. "Thanks."

Damn. How he got himself into predicaments

like this was anybody's guess. Wyatt smiled at Patti, the sorority lush, and nudged Brandy with his foot.

She got the hint. "You know, Patti, God, it's good to see you, but I really have to go to the restroom. Can I leave you with Wyatt for a minute?"

"Absolutely," Patti purred, her voice dropping an entire octave.

It was for the good of the case, he reminded himself, trying not to inhale Patti's forty-proof breath, worried he might get drunk from secondhand fumes. With Brandy gone, and Patti distracted, they wouldn't have to be concerned about her screeching out words like "FBI" and "fed" and blowing their cover. Being mauled by a drunk tart was a small price to pay, and hey, he was a team player. If she weren't plastered he might actually enjoy it.

What he didn't count on was the hecklers.

"Whoo-hoo, Patti—you go, girl."

"Now you've got him, what are you going to do with him?"

"Next drink is on me if you kiss him."

The women had gone wild, whistling, hooting, and egging Patti on. His back was against the wall, literally, and he was trying to formulate a plan to get out with his dignity and body parts intact when she grabbed him by the cheeks and smothered him with her mouth in a wet, grinding kiss.

He'd never again have to doubt the meaning of the phrase "suck face."

*   *   *

CJ was hovering in the hallway by the elevators, trying to be discreet. Maddock had been gone a long time and she was starting to get concerned. That concern magnified when she saw Brandy emerge from the office pool where the receptionists and other entry-level employees worked.

Brandy didn't see her, but went back into the reception area, where the party was still raging.

CJ hesitated a minute, then started through the maze of cubicles toward the hallway that led to the larger offices in the back of the building. Brandy wasn't supposed to leave Wyatt, and that she did was alarming. CJ felt under her loose black pants for the handgun. Reassured, she moved steadily, cautiously.

Heavy breathing came to her attention and she automatically went for her gun again before she realized a couple of partygoers were sweating in a swivel chair together. They glanced at her but didn't break stride, major organs thankfully covered by the woman's black dress.

"Sorry." CJ walked faster. Geez, this company was full of perverts. She'd seen more sexual acts tonight than in six months of watching HBO.

She rounded the corner, and caught sight of another. Only this pervert she knew. And the woman wrapped in his arms wasn't Brandy, but a flaming redhead in an electrifying dress, who was ramming her tongue down Wyatt's throat.

CJ ground to a halt and stared in horror. It was like roadkill—you didn't want to look, but you had to. She would have preferred checking out squirrel guts. Fury swept over her, intense personal disgust that she could ever find this man attractive, followed by anger that after all these months of working this case, he could jeopardize it by acting like a vagina-seeking missile.

Assessing the situation, which included planting herself in the center of the hall so no one could leave, she observed the redhead's skirt inching its way up as she really worked Wyatt over. Poor guy. His jacket was getting wrinkled from all those desperate fingers gripping it.

She imagined the dry cleaner saw a lot of Wyatt.

When the woman's fingers rose into his light brown hair, artfully tousled, CJ lost her patience.

"Excuse me." Time to extract him before he caused actual damage to this case. And just for being a hormone-driven hound dog, CJ was going to make sure Agent Maddock went to bed alone tonight as punishment.

The redhead didn't break stride as her tongue swam laps across Wyatt's mouth. CJ grimaced. If she could see the woman's tongue from where she was standing, something was really wrong with her technique. Then she realized that Wyatt's arms were waving behind the woman's back and that his lips appeared to have clamped shut, denying access.

"Mr. Maddock?" CJ said, loud and clear. "I hate to interrupt . . ."

That was a big-ass lie.

"But you just got a phone call. I guess your cell phone is off? Anyway . . ." She tried to sound nonchalant, instead of malicious and furious like she felt. "Your boyfriend is just desperate to talk to you, so I think you should call him back."

The red whore—oops, she meant red*head*—

stumbled backward, nearly falling onto the floor on her behind. "Boyfriend? What?"

"Oh, damn, that's a shame." One of the women lingering with a martini glass on the opposite side of the hall shook her head.

The other two nodded in agreement.

Redhead looked stunned, her hand coming up to wipe at her lips.

Wyatt stood stock-still, every ounce of blood in his face draining away, leaving him with tight lips, narrowed eyes, and taut muscles that clenched in fury. She'd never seen quite that expression on his face before.

It was a good look.

Getting him that mad almost might have been worth the hellish night except that she still wasn't convinced he hadn't compromised the case. Besides, she wouldn't be so immature as to actually enjoy riling him. Much.

She expected him to refute her boyfriend claim, so he could pick up his tonsil tango with the redhead where they'd left off. But he just straightened his jacket and said, "Thank you."

He strode off, without even a good-bye to the woman in red, leaving CJ to trail behind him in his wake, with a distracting view of his butt in those tuxedo pants.

It was wrong to feel the way she did. It was repulsive, spineless, and unnatural to lust after someone she didn't even like. Yet she couldn't drag her eyes off him, slowly raking from head to toe, taking in the rigid pull of his broad shoulders beneath the tux jacket, the confident stride of firm, long legs, and his shiny black shoes.

He was tall, muscular, in shape but not brawny or stocky in any way. His hair was a little on the long side of respectable for the Bureau, but she had never seen him in anything but well-made, perfectly fitting suits.

He was testosterone in a tux and she was boring in baggy.

Which only served to infuriate her more.

When they reached the elevators and Wyatt turned to speak, she held up her hand. "Save it for the car. I want to rip your head off in private."

Along with a couple of other parts.

Two

When they reached the lobby, Wyatt strode for the parking garage, feeling really damn insulted.

Gay. CJ had said he was gay, of all things. Jesus.

It shouldn't matter, didn't matter, but it did, and no matter how many times he told himself she'd said it on purpose to piss him off, it still filled him with the need to show her exactly how straight he was.

Fuck privacy. Her little performance back at the office hadn't been private. And he needed to tell her how he felt about it before he popped a blood vessel. She had said she wanted to rip his head off. Well, the feeling was definitely mutual. Or maybe he wanted to do something more along the lines of screw her brains out.

Gay. Hah.

Wyatt stopped next to the front security desk and whirled around. CJ drew up short, just avoiding hitting him.

He said, "I cannot believe you said I was gay! That's the third joke like that you've made about me in the last couple of months. I don't make cracks about your personal life, so stay out of mine."

Her brown eyes widened. "Then you really are gay? Damn, Maddock, I'm sorry, I was just joking. If I had known . . ."

"No, I'm not gay!" Far from it. Not when he was lusting after CJ's mystery breasts and strategizing how he could get in her shapeless pants in five steps or less.

Then she shocked him by reaching out and nailing him on the arm. It wasn't a girl swat. It was a punch. His muscle was tight when she'd impacted, and now he reared back in pain, his arm stinging.

"Then you are such a complete jackass, Maddock! Why are you screwing around with drunken bimbos when it could jeopardize the case? Screw the bimbos on your night off."

"I'm not screwing any bimbos." Lately. His appetite for bimbos had decreased since he'd become preoccupied with pissy FBI agents in half-ass ponytails.

"Then explain what I just saw back there. And why did Dempsey leave?"

CJ was breathing hard, her cheeks tinged with pink, her brown eyes snapping at him. She blew a few strands of hair that had escaped her ponytail out of her eyes.

Wyatt wanted her warm breath on him. Everywhere. Which really did make him a jackass.

"Lower your voice, for God's sake." He glanced

around the empty lobby. "For your information, I saved the case tonight. That woman was about to blow our cover."

That was greeted with a snort of disbelief. "That's not all she was going to blow."

Irrational desire flared with anger that she thought so little of him. "You know, what the hell is your problem? I'm a damn good agent, White. I do my job. When have I ever let you or the team down on anything? I don't need this shit from you."

"Yeah, well, I don't need to work with somebody who can't go five minutes without coming on to a woman." She paced a little before stopping in front of him again. "I'm going to ask Nordstrom for a transfer to a different case."

"What? Don't be an ass." She was going to risk Nordstrom's wrath and derail her career because she didn't like him?

The flat of her hand landed on his chest, between the lapels of his jacket. Her hand was warm, her eyes were hot with fury. Wyatt inexplicably, and without warning, went hard.

"Don't talk to me like that."

And she shoved him backward.

Preoccupied with lust, he lost his balance and hit the reception desk with the back of his thighs. "Knock it off, White."

"I can't work with you anymore, Maddock. I'm serious. But maybe *you* should ask for the transfer, since you're the problem." Then her finger came up and waved in his face.

Wyatt watched that delicate finger, marveled that CJ was so feminine beneath her scowl and her attitude. What would she look like in bed? His bed. Would she rein in, hold on tight the way she did at work, or would she let go, screaming out her pleasure, or whimper in demure delight?

He snatched her finger out of the air and shoved it down by his side. "Why should I transfer? You're the one who has the problem, not me."

Her finger twitched in his grip trying to break free, and he held her tighter. They went through a thirty-second tug-of-war before she gave up. Her chest was rising and falling under the waitress getup and she held herself tense, like she wanted to pull back but was afraid to move.

"I can't. . . ." And her normally tough, no-nonsense voice cracked just a little. Her eyes dropped, hiding.

That flash of vulnerability did him in. For the first time, he could see what Dempsey had seen. CJ wanted him just as much as he wanted her.

He wrapped his arm around her, pulling her unresisting body up against his. He couldn't feel much through the clothes, just her basic outline, confirming his suspicions that she was carrying quite a package under those baggy suits. He'd give just about anything to see her dressed like Brandy had been tonight. And then, immediately following, dressed in nothing.

"Hey, CJ, did you ever notice something?" He couldn't resist this opportunity. She might pull her gun on him, but having her in his arms was just too good to pass up.

"What?" She sounded grumpy, like his niece did when she missed her nap.

It was cute and sexy, and he had clearly lost all sense of reality if a cranky woman who hated his guts turned him on.

"Did you ever notice that I want you, CJ? I don't understand you and you really kind of scare the crap out of me, but I want you just the same." Wyatt allowed his fingers to stroke her back as he bent over her just a little so he could press a kiss alongside her ear. She was so soft and warm, he just wanted to sigh.

CJ squirmed a little in his arms, but she didn't pull away. "You'd want anything with two legs and breasts."

He grinned. "Oh, do you have breasts? I couldn't even tell."

Her hand came out to shove him again, her mouth turned down in a fierce scowl. Wyatt reached out and cupped her breast through the layers of clothes, blocking her push. "Oh, hey, you do. Feel pretty good, too."

She froze, then tried to step back. He held her firmly in place with his other arm, and brushed across her nipple.

That only seemed to tick her off more. "Cut the crap, Wyatt. You're just doing this to prove a point, aren't you?"

He thought the only point he was making was that she was driving him fucking nuts and that he would just about pay money to see her naked. Apparently he hadn't been clear enough.

"The only point I'm trying to prove is that I want you." He dipped his nose into her hair, noting how CJ smelled very much like a woman. He had never detected her scent standing next to her at work, but holding her against him now, leaning over, running his mouth and nose over her smooth hair and skin, he could smell a soft, sinful, clean smell.

Outdoor sex. That's what popped into his head. "And you want me, too, CJ. Don't you?"

At some point, her hands had dug into his shirt, gripping him as she studied his shoulder. Lips just a hairbreadth from his, she whispered, "You're a disgusting human being."

It lacked any conviction, spoken in the softest voice he'd ever heard from her.

He still cupped her breast and he squeezed, dragging a low gasp from her, which she quickly masked by clearing her throat.

He said, "You're not any prize either, you know."

She gave a little laugh, and damn if she didn't lean forward a bit, causing his thumb to make contact with her nipple again, buried behind her bulky shirt and bra.

"You're such a Pretty Boy," she insulted him, even as her breath hitched and her thigh shifted between his.

Her neck was begging for a kiss. Wyatt gave it one, then sucked softly, drawing her warm flesh into his mouth. CJ's nails dug into his chest.

"Hard-ass," he murmured into her ear.

Her hands went around his back under his jacket, inviting interesting chest-on-chest contact.

CJ had been hiding a C-cup, by his best educated guess.

"Bonehead . . ."

Wyatt cut her off, locking his mouth over hers and giving her a kiss he'd been tasting for months.

CJ clung to Wyatt like a barnacle and counted herself among the many women conquered by his tongue. Oy, he knew how to use it.

Here, as he ran it along her bottom lip. There, as he teased her mouth open with it. Everywhere, as he raced inside, the hot, possessive, dominating kiss ripping the air out of her lungs and sending heat pooling in her practical, waist-high panties.

It didn't surprise her that he was good at this.

What shocked the hell out of her was her own reaction. Her own wet, sliding, grinding, eager, and desperate reaction, her nails on his back, her hips bumping forward, her tongue reaching out to plunder his mouth in return. Her moans of encouragement, her leg locking around his, the telltale dampness between her thighs.

She was out of control. The orgasm-free years since her son had been born had caught up with her, and she was overwhelmed by the need to toss Wyatt down on the security desk and have her way with him.

That would teach him.

When he reached for the top button on her shirt, she found the courage to break off the kiss with minimal whimpering.

Wyatt let her pull back, but he still held her and

he still worked her buttons. The first was free and he was on to number two. "Come home with me."

Hello. CJ swallowed hard as the second button gave way. He pressed a warm, moist kiss into the opening of her shirt.

"Are you crazy or just stupid? We have to work together."

"Mmm, your sweet talking gets me hot. Call me stupid again." His tongue dipped down low, sliding a wet path between her breasts.

Instead of yelping in delight like she wanted to, she yanked his head back and said, "I'm serious."

His eyes locked with hers. His grip on her ass— *hell, when had he done that?*—loosened and she took the opportunity to scramble back away from him.

His breathing was ragged, like her own, and his hair was sticking up, which made him look even sexier, which gave her yet another reason to hate him. He looked amazing and she probably looked like a startled rabbit.

In a waitress shirt.

"I have a deal for you, White. One where we both get what we want."

"I don't want to hear this." He couldn't possibly know what she wanted, that for just once, she wanted to shed her responsibilities and act as selfish and unrestrained as Wyatt did.

Not for one minute did she regret her son, Sam, despite his autism, but she was just so tired. Sam got the majority of her energy, then her job sucked up the rest, and she'd forgotten what it was like to be free from worry, to live in the moment. How could he understand that?

Wyatt's main worry was probably that his brand of hair gel had been discontinued.

"I'll take the transfer, CJ. You don't have to."

That got her attention. But she shook her head. "You can't. Nordstrom won't let you, you know that. I know he won't let me transfer either, since we're in the middle of a case. I was just blowing smoke before."

His hands clenched. "You know, you need to stop using words like 'blow.' Just erase them from your memory, or you're going to find yourself flat on your back on this desk."

Tempted to say "blow" in a clear, loud tone, she clamped her lips shut and stuck her hands behind her back.

Though he looked suspicious, he continued. "I don't mean a transfer to another case. I meant after the investigation, I'll transfer to another field office."

Her pursed lips fell open. "You'll leave Chicago?"

He shrugged. "Sure, why not? I don't have any family here, no wife, no girlfriend, no attachments. Maybe I'll go somewhere south."

It was too good to be true. He was volunteering to take himself and his sexy smile far away from her. "What's the catch?"

"No catch. You just have to agree to spend the night with me tomorrow. All night. And there will be no sleeping involved." He closed the gap between them, running his thumb along her bottom lip. "What do you think?"

She thought it was time to hurt him. "Are you

bribing me? That you'll move only if I have sex with you?"

It was disgusting, outrageous, and gave a whole new meaning to the term "indecent."

She was going to do it.

He may be a pig, but he was a gorgeous pig and the man could work a nipple.

Like he was doing to her, right that moment. Brushing, rubbing, rolling . . . good God.

Just imagine what he could do with the rest of her.

"Don't think of it as a bribe," he said in a low voice, his feet edging between hers so that her legs spread automatically. "Think of it as two people getting exactly what they want. We both want to have sex with each other, but we both know a relationship between us would never work."

CJ tilted her head as his lips moved across her neck. "That's true. Because I hate you."

Maybe hate was too strong a word. But she seriously disliked him. She really did.

"I know." The idea didn't seem to bother him as he navigated his way down to her cleavage.

It really was the perfect solution. She got to quench her thirst for Wyatt's body, then never had to set eyes on him again after this case ended. "I accept your deal."

She allowed her fingers to snake around his back and tug his shirt out of his pants. Gliding across his hard, muscular back, she let her eyes drift closed. It may be a huge mistake to sleep with Wyatt, but it was going to feel really good doing it.

"Just one more thing."

Stiffening, she glared at him. She should have known. Her mother always said if it was too good to be true, it usually was. "Oh, here it comes. Sixty seconds after I agree, and you're already adding contingencies."

The corners of his mouth lifted. "Just one. I promise." He tugged on her ponytail. "While you're at my house, you have to wear whatever I want."

Not.

"I don't think so!" He'd have her wearing half of Frederick's of Hollywood. The small half. No way she was covering her backside in something the size of a slingshot.

"Then the whole thing is off."

Damn, she should have known he'd pull that. Digging her nails into his back, she enjoyed it when he winced. "So what does that mean, like anything?"

Nothing could induce her to put tassels on her breasts or stuff herself into a leather bra. Or worse. "You're not going to want me to wear edible underwear, are you?"

His eyebrow rose. "Only if you want to."

Hah.

Of course she didn't . . . well, maybe if . . . no, absolutely not. There was wild, and then there was just unnecessary. If he was hungry, he could have a fruit roll-up. It'd be about the same thing.

"Fine." If she was going to do this, she might as well do it right. He could slut her up within reason. He'd probably have it off her in five minutes anyway. She let him press a hard kiss on her.

Then she added in warning, "But I'm not wearing anything that hurts."

"Damn," came his strangled reply.

CJ kicked her shoes off by the front door of her apartment and sighed. It wasn't even eleven, but she was exhausted. Yet she knew sleep wouldn't come easy tonight. Not when she had just made out with her coworker, who just happened to be exactly the type of man she swore she would never be involved with again.

Not only had she kissed him in a lobby, she had agreed to spend the night with him and wear whatever he wanted. She should be appalled, not looking forward to it. But somehow she couldn't muster up the necessary outrage, not when she wanted so desperately to just let go for once. To do something wild and selfish and irrational.

Padding softly up the stairs in her socks, she saw a light on in her mother's room. She knocked, then opened the door. "Mom? I'm home."

Her mother, nestled in her easy chair and tucked under a quilt, looked up from her book and smiled. "How was work, Christine?"

"Fine." She felt the urge to laugh and squelched it. Leaning against the doorframe, she said, "How was Sam for you tonight?"

Worry ate around the corners of her heart, as it always did when she thought about her five-year-old son, but her mother just smiled.

"Oh, we had a good time. We read his favorite book and watched a Christmas special on TV."

CJ honestly didn't know how she would handle raising a child so difficult to understand and communicate with as Sam was if it weren't for the constant support of her mother. She sometimes wished that she could find the inner peace about Sam's autism that her mother had. CJ just loved him and worried about him and hoped for the best.

"That's good." She hesitated, looking down at the carpet, hoping like hell she wasn't blushing. Almost thirty years old, and she was embarrassed to confess that she had plans to spend the night with a man. "Are you busy tomorrow night, Mom? Because I may have to stay out overnight."

Her mother looked surprised, with good reason. CJ had been quite firm with Nordstrom that she couldn't take cases that kept her away longer than twelve hours or required travel.

"That's unusual," her mother said, putting her bookmark in her novel. "But I can be here, sure."

"Thanks." CJ made the mistake of meeting her mother's gaze and she felt heat blaze across her face, giving her away in Technicolor scarlet. "Lying Slut" might as well be stamped on her forehead.

But her mother just studied her, a slight smile on her face. "Christine, do you have a date tomorrow?"

Reduced to fifteen years old and caught with John Wilson's hand on her breast, she squirmed. "Sort of."

"That's wonderful. I'm so pleased you're getting out of the house. It's not normal to be your age and never go out with men." Her mother tucked her graying brown hair behind her ear. "It's been three years since Scott left and as far as I know, you've never been on a date in all that time."

This wasn't a date either. It was sweaty sex with Wyatt, probably involving sheer black lingerie and multiple orgasms. That was her hope anyway. The orgasms, not the Band-Aid-sized bra.

When she didn't say anything, her mother continued, her tone casual but curious. "It must be beyond a date if you're thinking about spending the night. Anyone I know?"

There were certain places CJ didn't want to go with her mother, and the bedroom was one of them. Yet her mother looked calm and unperturbed, as if they talked sex every day, giving each other advice on the best positions and how to please your man during oral sex.

CJ was mortified. She said reluctantly, "I'm going out with Wyatt Maddock."

And now her mother knew precisely what she was planning on doing with Wyatt. All night.

"Wyatt?" Her mother finally looked ruffled. "Oh, my. Make sure you take condoms, Christine."

His reputation preceded him.

With no idea what to say, CJ just nodded. "Of course."

She hadn't even given any thought to protection. Just the idea of going to buy condoms made her want to call this whole thing off. She couldn't just assume Wyatt would have condoms, though she thought it was highly likely he owned stock in Trojan. She hadn't bought condoms since she had been training at Quantico.

Immediately after that she had met Scott and they had gotten married, and he had provided the protection until he had walked out two months after Sam had been diagnosed.

Thinking out loud, she said, "I guess I'll go buy some tomorrow."

Her mother said, "Oh, I have some you can use." And she stood up and riffled through her dresser drawer.

"*What?*" Oh, Lord, her mother had condoms. "Why do you have those?"

Okay, so that was an asinine, idiotic, obvious question, but her mother *baked*—she wasn't supposed to have condoms.

Holding the half-empty—*good God, half-empty*—box out to her, her mother said in amusement, "It's been over ten years since your father died. I'm only fifty-five."

Taking the offering, CJ backed up. "I'm going to bed." To stare at the ceiling and ponder how between Wyatt and her mother, her psyche had suffered irreparable damage tonight.

"Good night, dear."

"Good night." CJ bolted down the hall, stopping at Sam's bedroom door and peeking in on him.

His bedroom was tiny, but CJ had been grateful to find a three-bedroom town house to rent after her mom had moved in with her six months after Scott had left. She relied on her mother in a way she hadn't been able to rely on her carefree, life-of-the-party husband, even before they had found out Sam was autistic.

Though sometimes she just ached with wanting

to make life easier for Sam, as she watched him sleep, his chest rising and falling beneath the dinosaur sheet, she knew she wouldn't trade him for anything. Every moment with him was a pure gift, an appreciation for every accomplishment and a joy that he was her child. Unfortunately, his father hadn't felt the same way.

CJ didn't touch Sam, knowing all too well from experience that if he was awakened, it could take hours to get him back to sleep. But the sight of him snuggled up to his stuffed puppy, peaceful in sleep, made her smile. Awake, sometimes Sam looked downright tortured, but asleep his mind was at rest.

Every minute of every day for the last five years she had done everything with Sam in mind, first and foremost. But tomorrow night, she was going to do something just for her. Wyatt was a better man than her ex—she knew that just from working with him every day. He was a hard worker, responsible, honest. But he was still a playboy, and while that was all wrong for her on a daily basis, she had an idea it would be all right for one night.

She needed to let go, to live, to burst out of the confines of her life and give her body some much-needed attention. The oil in her car got changed every three thousand miles, the blades in the lawn mower sharpened every spring, and this was no different. Just a little tune-up, to make sure all her parts were still in working order.

Closing Sam's door, she headed toward the bathroom, the condoms still in her hand, excitement surpassing fear and nerves. This was going to be quite a night.

Maybe she should have let Wyatt get edible underwear after all.

He was acting like a girl. After switching the tablecloth in his dining room twice, Wyatt commanded himself to get a goddamn grip.

This was CJ. She would probably be happy with beer nuts on the couch.

That was actually something he liked about her. Unlike so many acrylic women he dated, CJ was not high-maintenance.

Yet he didn't want her to look around his apartment and draw any negative conclusions about him. For some weird-ass reason, he wanted CJ to like him. Or at least not to hate him. And to not be disgusted with herself for wanting to jump his bones.

He figured that's where a lot of CJ's animosity came from. She was pissed at herself for being attracted to him. Which he could relate to. He was having a hard time accepting his own body's response to her.

Why that had him tied up in knots and wasting the better part of a day dragging out his fake Christmas tree and sad-looking ornaments so his apartment would look more . . . something he had no idea. Most years he didn't even put the tree up if he wasn't dating anyone seriously, which he hadn't been for a good three years now, and if he did, he sure didn't do it the first week in December. But there it was, a little on the scraggly side with a crooked star on top.

After the tree, he had come close to electrocuting himself stringing white lights around his enclosed patio, and as he quickly set the dishes on the red tablecloth he had found in the back of one very dusty cabinet, he wondered if he shouldn't have gone out with Brandy Dempsey tonight instead. At least he knew what he was doing, where he stood with a woman like that. With CJ, he felt like he was swimming in pudding.

Maybe it wasn't too late to cancel the whole damn thing.

The doorbell rang.

His cock leapt forward in greeting. His gut cramped painfully. His mouth went drier than the wine.

Or maybe he should cut the crap and just rip her clothes off the minute she walked in the door.

When he opened the door and ran his eyes over her, she crossed her arms defiantly.

"Hi," he said.

"Hi," she mumbled to the hall carpet.

"Come on in." He stepped back to let her in, amused out of his nervousness. CJ looked like she'd turn and run home with the slightest provocation.

It leveled the playing field.

She hadn't let him down with her choice of clothing. He had been expecting her to arrive in something about as feminine as a Glock gun, and the oversized brown corduroys and beige cable-knit sweater certainly fit that description. She either shopped in the men's department, or she had borrowed the outfit from Bill Cosby.

As usual, her hair was pulled back, and he thought to wonder exactly why CJ wanted to make herself as unattractive as possible. Maybe once he had her wearing what he wanted, she would tell him. Wearing what he'd spent the other half of the day shopping for when he wasn't wrestling with Christmas decorations.

Knowing CJ, though, she was just as likely to pull her gun on him, or give him a shove, than to spill her secrets. And hell, maybe she just liked to be comfortable.

Reaching out, he took her hand and tugged her to him. She dug her heels in, making a sound of annoyance and rolling her eyes.

"First things first," he said, bending over her to fill his nostrils with her scent.

Her lips parted, giving her away despite her stubborn expression. She expected a kiss, wanted one. Wyatt brought his mouth close to hers, his shoulders tense as he watched the way her chest rose and fell, her lips shiny and damp, dewy with anticipation.

"First, this has got to go," he murmured without touching her, then straightened up, enjoying her little rush of impatient breath.

Digging into her hair, he found the rubber band holding the ponytail in place and with both hands, he pulled until it snapped.

"Oww, Wyatt, that hurts." She reached up to grip her hair at the temples and he realized too late he was pulling her hair.

"Dammit," she complained, pulling away from him.

"Sorry, but babe, you need a new look. Bad." Extracting the broken band, he waited for her hair to fall around her shoulders, to soften into exotic waves and enlarge the way her brown eyes looked.

It didn't happen. Her hair just fanned out slightly, the back still tucked into ponytail position, the sides drooping a little. "Christ, CJ, you look like a lion."

She stuck her hands into her hair and rubbed and shook. It didn't help.

"My hair was wet when I put it up—it probably dried that way. Which is why you should have left it alone."

She didn't add *dumb-ass,* but it was definitely implied.

And he was having trouble not laughing. She looked like she'd waged a war with static and lost.

"Do you have a brush or a comb or something?" She tucked some strands behind her ears, but they immediately bounced back out. Holding her hair flat against her head, she glared at him.

"In the bathroom." Why in the hell he still had a hard-on was anybody's guess, but not only did he, his cock throbbed as he was reminded of the outfit he had waiting for her. "And you might as well change while you're in there. Everything you need is on the bathroom counter."

Anticipation hummed through his veins.

"Change into what?" She eyed him with suspicion.

Like he'd tell her. He didn't exactly trust her reaction. In fact, he might just have to key-lock the front door to ensure she stayed.

"You'll see. Go on in there like a good girl and get changed. It's all part of our agreement, remember? I can be gone by March at the latest. . . ."

Wyatt planned to take a hell of a memory with him when he transferred.

Three

Somebody in the apartment was on crack, and it wasn't her. CJ stood in the bathroom and gaped in horror at what Wyatt wanted her to wear.

It was a dress.

With *flowers* on it.

Pink and peach flowers on a black background, and little sleeves that landed just below the shoulder in a ruffle. Who wore a sleeveless dress in December?

Not her.

Of course, she didn't wear dresses. Ever.

"Maddock!" Grabbing the offending garment, she stormed out of the bathroom.

"What?" Wyatt called from behind the closed door of his bedroom. "I'll be out in a minute, I'm changing."

Why, CJ couldn't imagine. He had answered the door in jeans and a T-shirt and it had gotten her pretty hot.

"I'm not wearing this . . . thing!"

He laughed. "It's just a dress, CJ. If you remember, you agreed to wear anything I wanted."

Crinkling the dress into a soft, silken bunch of crumpled flowers, CJ stared at his bedroom door. "I thought you meant slutty underwear, not a dress!"

Okay, that didn't come out right. She bit her lip and turned toward Wyatt's Christmas tree. The tree surprised her. The dress surprised her. The table set with real dishes and candles, ready for a romantic meal for two, stunned her. It seemed she had made some snap judgments about Wyatt, not all of which were correct.

His head poked out of his door, and he was smirking. "I know how much you want to wear the slutty underwear, since you've brought it up twice now. Don't worry, I got that, too. It just goes on under the dress."

The door closed again, which was a good thing or she would have hit him in the face with the floral foo-foo dress from hell.

CJ stood there in indecision. She liked her own clothes. Granted, she had really gone the slob route lately, wearing a size too big and occasionally veering into the men's department, but they were always clean, and matched. She didn't like clothes that drew attention to her, and in her early days with the Bureau she had fostered an image of tough girl in tough clothes so no one would be tempted to delegate her to undercover prostitute roles.

She wasn't a girly-girl and dresses made her feel vulnerable.

He could forget the dress. She wasn't wearing it. "Wyatt!"

His door opened all the way and he strode out, adjusting his jacket. Her protest died in her mouth. Oh, hell, he was wearing his tux. Shit, shit, shit.

How could she stay strong, true to herself, when he was standing in front of her looking like every woman's fantasy? Or at least her fantasy. No, every woman's fantasy.

His short, light brown hair was carelessly tousled, green eyes were dark with desire. He filled that tux from one end to the other with hard muscle, broad shoulders, and long legs, and when he stopped and stuck his hand in his pocket, it felt like lightning had struck her right smack between the thighs. She felt fried like bacon.

She wanted him. Every classy, sexy, hard, masculine inch of him and the only way to do that was to put on a dress. Her life was full of cruel ironies.

There was only one option available. She flung the dress at him, ticked off beyond belief. "Eat the damn dress, Maddock. I'm not dressing up like a . . . like a . . ."

He caught the dress one-handed. "Like what? A woman? It's not that big of a deal."

His eyes rolled over her and she tried not to shuffle. She pushed the sleeves up on her bulky sweater, suddenly aware that it really was an ugly sweater. And then there was her hair. She hadn't taken the time to look for the brush, sideswiped by the dress the minute she'd entered the bathroom, and it occurred to her that she wasn't exactly a sexual prize.

It was a wonder the man didn't look at her and laugh hysterically.

"I have this crazy idea that you've got an incredible body under those sacks you wear, and I wanted to see it. I also want to have dinner with you, and if you sat down at the table in a black lace bra, neither one of us would even touch the food, so I thought it might be nice if you wore a dress over the slutty underwear. Nothing sinister about that."

No, there wasn't and CJ felt like a big, baggy idiot.

"Fine. Give it to me," she snapped, holding out her hand.

Wyatt narrowed his eyes. "You're not going to pump bullets into it, are you?"

"No!" Fire would destroy it more thoroughly, and that would have to wait until tomorrow. "I didn't even bring my gun."

He started to hold the dress out, then pulled back. "Are you going to put it on?"

"Yes. I, CJ White, do solemnly swear to wear the ugly-ass, shower curtain–looking dress for a period of at least one hour. After that, I'm not responsible for my actions. Happy?"

"Thrilled," he said, looking anything but.

She ripped the dress out of his hands and headed for the bathroom. This was why she never dated. It was a pain in the ass.

Someone had stolen her breasts and replaced them with the bottom half of two watermelons.

Yikes. CJ stared into Wyatt's bathroom mirror at her flesh spilling up and out of the top of the black lace bra he had provided. What had looked so tasteful and simple lying in the lingerie-store box on the counter looked outrageous actually on her body.

Yet the thing appeared to fit. Everything was where it should be, it's just she was used to bras acting as support, worn for function. This thing was designed solely to produce eye-popping cleavage, and that it had. CJ wondered if she should worry that Wyatt had managed to guess her bra size correctly. What that said about a man she couldn't even imagine.

The panties fit, too, even if they were about as comfortable as a Pap smear. She kept reaching down to pull them up, only to realize they were up as far as they were going to go. But if she had to assess herself, she didn't look half bad. As far as sexy went, it had her white, waist-high panties and industrial-strength athletic bra beat.

Next the dress. CJ slipped it on over her head, struggling to get it to shimmy down over her body. After several false starts, she had the thing in place and was reaching behind her back to zip it. The dress fit as well, which made Wyatt really scary, in her opinion. The contortionist position only allowed her to zip it up to her shoulder blades, but that would have to be good enough. There was no way she was waltzing out there unzipped and asking Wyatt for help.

Digging around in Wyatt's drawers, she found a hairbrush, but nothing else of interest. No sign of a woman, or women, hanging out in his bathroom on a regular basis. Though he did have a bottle of kids' Flintstones vitamins.

Wetting the brush, she managed to tame her hair. Sort of.

Then there was nothing left to do but put on the strappy little shoe-sandal things and head out there.

If she didn't trip and fall on her behind first.

Wyatt was getting impatient. How long did it take to put on a dress? Not this long.

She wasn't going to do it. He should have known not to push quite so hard. He should have kept it to the bra and panties, and let her put her own clothes over top. That would have been a big enough thrill, sitting through dinner, knowing she was wearing sheer lace under her guy clothes.

But he had wanted to see the whole package, selfish SOB that he was. He just hoped this didn't make her bolt.

Convinced that she wasn't wearing the dress, he almost swallowed his tongue when she opened the door and stood there, looking sexy as sin and all woman, the black dress nipping in at the waist, hugging her thighs, and trailing down to mid-calf. Her bare legs looked smooth and toned, and even though she wobbled a little as she ground to a halt in the sandals, she still made him go hard.

And that was just the bottom half. The top half had him clamping down on his lips so he wouldn't groan out loud, and hoping like hell he wouldn't come in his pants. *Damn.* CJ had been hiding a killer rack under those baggy sweaters.

The dress did a little crisscross thing, cupping each breast, and her whole upper chest was exposed to him, creamy flesh descending down into cleavage so healthy he could rest a coffee mug on it. Yet despite her concerns that he would go for slutty, it was a very tasteful and feminine dress. It wasn't anything other women didn't run around in all the time, but the combination of never having seen CJ wearing anything even remotely close to that, and those curvaceous mounds of pale skin popping out and waving hello at him, had him wanting to sit down and take a deep breath.

"You look . . ."

"Stupid," she said and crossed her arms over her breasts, ruining the view.

"Don't put words in my mouth." *Put your breast in my mouth instead.*

"You look amazing."

"The amazing CJ White, that's me."

He didn't care how sarcastic she was being, she *was* amazing. He was absolutely floored at how gorgeous she was, but that she still managed to look natural. She wasn't wearing any makeup, didn't need to with those wide brown eyes and high cheekbones. Her lips were shiny without benefit of lip gloss, and now that she'd pulled a brush through her hair, it fell right to her shoulders where he had anticipated, framing her face softly.

"Thank you for wearing the dress." He appreciated it more than she could imagine.

She looked ready to be flippant, but then a mere, "You're welcome," came out of her mouth. Turning to the table, she added, "What are we having for dinner?"

"Beef tenderloin. Is that okay?"

Squeezing her lips together, she nodded. "Is it ready?"

"Yes. Have a seat." As he headed toward his small kitchen, he hit the PLAY button on the remote for his stereo. Frank Sinatra filled the room, crooning softly.

CJ snorted. When he looked at her in question, she said, "You're really good at this, aren't you?"

He frowned, not liking her implication. "What do you mean?"

But she just shook her head. "Nothing."

That was a lie, and he knew it. CJ thought he was some kind of male slut, which wasn't even close to the truth. Just because he dated different women, and hadn't had a serious relationship in a while, didn't make him some kind of serial dater.

Pissed off, he said, "If you don't like the music, I can turn it off."

As he plunked a bowl of dinner rolls down on the table, she sat with her hands folded in her lap.

"Touchy, Wyatt. Geez. I take it I'm the first woman who didn't appreciate Ol' Blue Eyes playing while you seduce me."

So that was it. She was feeling like a bedpost notch. Little did she know that she was unlike any woman he'd ever dated, and that he had gone to more trouble in twenty-four hours than some women saw from him in two months. "Actually, you're the first woman I've ever invited to my apartment for dinner."

He was surprised to realize it was true. He usually took a woman out, then went to her place if either of them was inclined to take it to the next step. It was better that way, less personal, and easier to disentangle himself in the morning.

CJ looked like she thought he was full of shit, but she stood up and said, "Let me help you."

This was more awkward than he had ever imagined. But awkward pretty much summed up his relationship with CJ to date. That and aggravating. Except for the night before, when they had kissed in the lobby. Nothing awkward or aggravating about that.

So when they sat down at the table, ready to eat, the wine uncorked, Wyatt thought it might be easier to talk about work.

"I heard the Delco case will be going to trial in February." Delco was the previous case they had been assigned to, a major pharmaceutical corporation involved in price-fixing.

"That's fast. Where did you hear that?" CJ smoothed her napkin out in her lap, studying her fingernails.

"Knight told me. I talked to him today."

"What's he up to?"

"Wedding crap. Reese is planning a bigger wedding than Knight expected."

CJ looked up at him with a cynical smile. "Tell her to save her money. You spend twenty grand on a wedding and then half the happy couples get divorced."

"Why so cynical? You been divorced?" Wyatt had never even come close to getting married, though he had nothing against it. If he were ever dumb enough to fall in love, he imagined he'd want to get married, too.

"Yes."

That startled him. He'd been kidding, not really thinking that CJ was speaking from personal experience. "Oh, hey, foot in mouth. Sorry." Then because he was a nosy guy and he wanted to know CJ, understand her, he asked, "What happened?"

She shrugged. "It didn't work out. He moved out. We got a divorce."

Not that he had expected her to break down and confess her deepest, darkest secrets, but getting CJ to open up was like pulling teeth. He had worked with her for almost a year, and he knew what he had observed about her. She was hardworking, reliable, quick with her wit, and damn smart, but he knew nothing about her life, how she lived, what mattered to her.

Ignoring his dinner, he sipped the wine and said, "Talk to me. Tell me something personal about you. I want to get to know you, CJ."

CJ didn't want Wyatt to know her. She was already sorry she'd blurted out that revealing remark about divorce statistics. It was important to her to stay private, because if she started opening up, telling Wyatt about herself, then she was going to wind up involved with him emotionally.

Which would make her vulnerable. Out of control. Able to be hurt.

Sex was one thing. She'd give him that gladly. But if he thought they were going to be friends, well, she'd rather talk orgasms with her mother.

"It's a boring story. What about you, Wyatt? Tell me about you." Then she stuffed half a roll in her mouth so he couldn't expect her to say anything for at least a minute and a half.

Leaning back in his chair, he held his arms out,

which stretched his jacket and showed off his chest, though she didn't think he was aware of it. Her fingers itched to get beneath his tie and rip it off, thigh wrapped around him, FBI femme fatale on the loose.

"I'm an open book, babe. What you see is what you get. I work, I hit the gym, I hang out with some old friends from college from time to time, and I watch TV."

He made it all sound so innocent. "And you date, don't forget that."

With a laugh, he bent forward again, reaching for his fork. "Yeah, I date. Jealous?"

Please. She was not missing a single thing. Which didn't explain why she hotly blurted out, "I date, too." Once a decade or so.

Given that look on his face, she didn't exactly have him fooled. But he only said, "No, I meant are you jealous of my dates?"

A snort left her before she could contain it. "I'm not usually jealous of big hair and even bigger boobs."

Wyatt's eyes dropped to her chest and lingered. "With good reason."

Heat flooded her face. Shoot, she had walked right into that one. Unable to think of a snappy comeback, she took the other half of the roll and threw it at him. He caught it midair as she said, "Stop staring at my chest."

Like that was a smart thing to say. It made it even worse, since he looked both amused and smug. God, he reduced her to a bratty twelve-year-old starting a food fight. Or maybe that wasn't him. Maybe it was the embarrassing awareness that she might have been missing something for the last three years. She was so out of touch, she didn't even know how to have a simple dinner conversation or respond to light flirtation without acting childish.

But Wyatt only said, "I haven't even started looking yet." Then he lifted the roll she'd thrown at him and bit it.

Not liking the idea of her spit mingling with his, CJ leaned forward and held out her hand. "My roll, please."

Of course, his tongue had been in her mouth the night before, but that was different. How, she didn't know, but she'd figure it out later when her nipples weren't hardening and her already-too-low panties weren't sliding down.

He shook his head. "Come and get it."

The roll waved slowly back and forth in front of her.

"There's a whole bowl full right here," she said, pointing out the obvious, not wanting to play his little games. Or maybe her little games, since she had thrown the roll in the first place.

"But it drives you nuts, doesn't it, that I have *your* roll?" And he took another bite.

He knew how to bait her too easily. But then he'd had nine months' practice doing just that. For five seconds, she watched him chew, making "mmm-mmm good" sounds, before she gave it up. She had kicked off the dumb little shoes and now she stood up barefoot, padded around the table on the soft carpet, and reached over him for her roll.

Just as she was about to grab it, Wyatt jerked his hand back, so that she wound up leaning dangerously far over him before pulling back, empty-handed. "Very funny."

He just laughed, then taunted her with the bread again.

Knowing she should be mature and just let him have the stupid half-eaten lump of dough, she still did the exact opposite. After all, wasn't this whole night supposed to be about giving in to impulse? Having fun? Playing games with Wyatt was fun.

She made another quick grab for the roll, only this time when he pulled back, she lost her balance and fell hard against his shoulder. Before she could say Slick Rick, he had her in his lap, hand on her thigh, settling her bottom nice and close against his waist.

Under normal circumstances, he wouldn't have gotten her down, but the dress had her off balance. It was hard to move wrapped like a floral mummy.

"You did that on purpose." CJ mustered a glare, even though she really just wanted to lean back against him and purr. Or laugh.

It had been a really long time since she had indulged in this kind of silly bantering. For all she professed to be annoyed by Wyatt, secretly she enjoyed their verbal byplay. There were days she looked forward to going to work, just because she was anticipating sparring with him. Not that she'd ever admit to that, not even under the torture of wearing stilettos every day.

"I'm sure you don't believe this, but I don't sit around devising plans to piss you off."

His hand was on her knee, stroking, making her itch and ache and want to squirm. "So you just spontaneously piss me off?"

"I guess you could say that. But maybe if I ask you ahead of time, we can avoid the whole problem."

There was a trick here, she just knew it. An April Fool's or Halloween kind of trick, where she was going to be left empty-handed, feeling slightly ashamed.

She turned to him. Big mistake. Big, fat, eight-hundred-pound-gorilla mistake. He was right there, watching her. Two inches or less from her mouth. She could smell the wine on his breath, feel the heat of him surrounding her, see the light stubble on his chin.

"Would it piss you off if I kissed you right now?"

That was the trick and as far as tricks went, it wasn't a bad one. CJ was on the verge of tugging him by the tie over to her anyway. She shook her head. "No, that would be okay."

More than okay. Orgasm okay.

"Just okay?" He made an impatient sound.

"Well . . ."

Her words died as he took her mouth, slow and deep, covering her, hand gripping her knee as he tasted her. There was nothing tentative about Wyatt as he sucked the tip of her tongue, sliding, owning, dominating the kiss, leaving CJ breathless and clinging to his shirt. Geez, he had the trick *and* the treat.

He was melting her innards, heating her up from the inside out, like microwave brownies, smushy and gooey, hot liquid. And they hadn't even gotten past the opening round. Yet.

Wyatt seemed inclined to change that. His hand was inching up past her knee, sliding under the dress, teasing and light along her thigh, while his mouth dropped down to kiss her neck and her shoulder. When his tongue darted across the top of her breast, she only managed to hold back a groan by biting down hard, but nothing could stop her head from lolling back.

Wyatt pulled away immediately, leaving her skin flushed and damp from his tongue and her nipples tight with frustration.

"I don't want to rush you," he said.

He had to be joking. "No, no," she murmured, sounding as desperate as she felt. "You're not rushing me."

If anything, he was going too slow. She had no problem with heading straight for the hard stuff. Like his erection pressing into her, right between her cheeks. If she weren't wearing Dumb Dress, she would swivel around and spread her legs on either side of him. But given the confines of rayon, she'd probably wind up pitching herself to the floor and ripping the dress.

And if she tore it, she'd never get to wear it again. Not that that was a bad thing.

But before she could plan a course of action, Wyatt said, "Is this rushing?"

He cupped her breast, and before she had a breath to moan, he kissed her hard, the rhythm of his tongue matching the brush of his thumb over her distended nipple. His other hand shot up under the dress and found the black lace panties.

Desire ripped through her, making her movements jerky as she tried to keep up with his mouth, tried to rub against his hand and encourage him to rush all he wanted. The panties he'd bought her were damp and needed to come off.

She pressed, she ground, she begged with her body for him to take her, make her burst, satisfy this raw need.

Wyatt broke off the kiss and pulled his hands back. As she stared at him, sucking in air, trying to remember where she'd left the condoms, he gave her a gentle nudge.

"Dance with me, CJ." His voice was a little rough, lacking in his standard charming flirtation, but otherwise he didn't look ready to explode, the way she felt.

"What do you mean?" She'd been off the sexual circuit for a while, but she didn't think she was that out of it. Dancing only meant one thing to her, and it wasn't what she wanted to be doing right now.

"Stand up." He nudged her again. "I like this song. Let's dance."

Given a thousand chances to guess what he would say, she never would have gotten that right. "Why?"

"Because I want to." He lifted his thighs so that she was forced to stand or tip onto the floor.

She stood and just stared at him. She had no idea what to say, and was waiting for some kind of punch line, accompanied by thigh slapping and hearty chuckles.

"Don't look at me like I'm nuts." He moved away from the table and held his hand out to her. "I want to dance with you to Frank Sinatra. I want to hold you in my arms." With a wry smile, he added, "Please? It's just one night."

Suddenly she didn't want to be reminded of that. Not when Wyatt Maddock was standing in front of her in a tux, holding his hand out for her. Her. Looking earnest and aroused. Looking like a dream.

CJ put her hand in his and clung to sarcasm for protection. "You'd better not step on my foot. I'm not wearing shoes."

He glanced down, holding both her hands. "Cute little toes."

Which made her want to both blush and slug him. Or kiss the quiche out of him.

"Did you get enough to eat? We rushed dinner, didn't we?"

Dinner? They'd eaten dinner? CJ nodded as Wyatt pulled her closer, snug against his chest, his arms tightly around her waist. "I had two bites of beef and half of the roll I winged at you. I'm good."

Normally she had a healthy appetite, but food was the furthest thing from her mind as she dangled her arms by her side, not quite sure what to do with them.

"Put your arms around my neck," he said, swaying just slightly to the music.

Damn, she'd been hoping to avoid that. Biting

her lip, she did as he asked, and when her chest rested against his, and he dropped a kiss on her ear, she couldn't help but sigh in pleasure. She had offered Wyatt a quick wham-bam, and here he was wining and dining her, giving every appearance of enjoying himself.

Maybe she didn't have him completely pegged after all.

He said in a husky voice, "I always thought you were beautiful."

And she was suddenly damn glad she was wearing the floral foo-foo dress.

Four

Wyatt was trying hard to breathe. Damn, but CJ was hot. She looked spunky and defiant yet feminine in the dress and her bare feet, and even though she rested in his arms a little stiffly, it felt right. Good.

Like he'd found something he hadn't even known he was looking for.

Where the hell had that thought come from?

Scaring the shit out of himself, Wyatt straightened up a little, removing his mouth from the temptation of her cute little ear that he kept wanting to nibble.

"You dance well, White." Her movements were confident and graceful, even if what they were doing was simply swaying, not really dancing.

She smiled. "I went to theater camp every summer from the time I was twelve to fifteen. I had to take daily dance lessons on everything from jazz to tap to ballroom."

"Theater camp, huh? I have a hard time seeing you in a musical." But then again, he was learning there was way more to CJ than met the eye.

"It was a compromise. My mom wanted me to take ballet, to keep me from spending all my time on the soccer field getting muddy and sweaty. But I wasn't about to put on tights and do pliés, so we settled on the theater camp. I actually had fun there."

"Sounds like a better way to spend your summer than I did when I was a teenager. I was washing dishes at my parents' restaurant every night."

Not that it had been all bad. He'd gotten to do what he wanted every day until three o'clock or so; then he'd headed to the restaurant to do whatever was needed until closing at ten. Usually that had been washing dishes, but back in the kitchen, he'd had fun talking and laughing with the busboys and flirting with the waitresses.

"Really?" CJ looked up at him, and he realized that her body had relaxed against his. "That's tough, having to work all the time."

"Yeah, well, we were a family, we all pitched in, but there were good times, too. One night when I was fifteen, Paula Ramsey—who was seventeen, by the way—kissed me with tongue in the deep freeze."

CJ rolled her eyes and he laughed.

"Well, I had my first real boyfriend at that camp. He was from Michigan, and we talked about soccer and held hands, and he was a perfect gentleman. He kissed me on the cheek once and that was it."

"What an idiot," Wyatt said.

CJ frowned at him. "It was cute and polite and showed admirable self-restraint!"

Her breasts were pressed against him, her hands were tickling up into his hair at the back of his neck, her breath was warm on his cheek, and Wyatt saw no need for self-restraint.

"Maybe I'm not cute. Or polite. And I don't plan on showing any self-restraint. But I can make you feel good." He dragged his thumb over her plump bottom lip. "If you want me to stop, tell me now."

They weren't moving to the music anymore and CJ had sucked her breath in on a nervous hitch. Wyatt waited, jaw clenched, hands lightly on her back, for her answer.

"No."

"No, what?" *No, don't ever touch me again, you nasty pervert? No, I don't want you to stop until you've come all over me? No, what?*

"No, don't stop."

Okay, not as good as his imaginings, but still good.

"CJ, CJ," he whispered, before bending over and sucking the top of her breast exposed above the dress.

He'd been waiting, wanting, too long. While he licked and dampened her flesh, his hands dropped lower on her backside, down to cup her firm behind, to pull her close against him so she could feel his cock pulsing on her thigh. The dress molded to her body, and he could feel the heat between her legs, the sharp, tight jerk of her leg muscles as she pinched her fingers in his neck.

No sound came from her, but her head writhed and her lips were white from clamping down so hard. He wanted to hear her, to feel her, to smell every inch of her smooth, fair skin, so he eased her dress up past her knees. Afraid to rip the delicate fabric, he decided not to pull down the top to expose her breasts, but settled for finding her nipple through the dress with his teeth and nipping and nibbling, sucking and pulling, driving himself insane.

Man, she felt good. Hot, willing woman. And wet. He got the dress past her thighs and cupped her, stroking across the panties, relishing the dampness he felt there. Her fingers cut deep into his flesh, and her eyes were shut tight, but she was still quiet, the only sound of her arousal rapid breathing, which she couldn't quite mask.

She was holding back, hiding from him, not wanting to give in to the pleasure and scream out loud. Wyatt wanted her to yell, moan, whimper, to relax with him and share the passion that flared so easily between them.

Shoving the panties to the side, he teased around her clitoris, groaning softly at how swollen she was already. "You're very wet, CJ. I find that really sexy."

There was no answer, just a pink stain on her cheeks that gave away her embarrassment.

He slipped his finger inside her wetness, felt her body clasp onto him and pulse. Her fingers convulsed on his shoulders, and her thighs rocked forward, but still no sound. Everything about her was tight, tense, taut with desire and agitation. He wanted her, but not like this.

Removing his finger, he rolled it around her

swollen nub, kissing her on the swell of her breast, trailing his tongue between her breasts. He stroked over and over, feeling her strain tighter and tighter, and he knew that if she came now, it wouldn't be enjoyable for either of them. CJ was holding back, yet seemed determined to forge ahead, bumping against his finger.

It was like she wanted to get it over with. Without revealing anything about herself.

He didn't want part of her. He wanted all of her. Everything. Every inch and every angle, and he wanted her to open her mouth and say his name with all the desperation that he felt.

Just as her grip got tighter and her thighs clenched, he pulled his hand back, preventing her from having a watered-down orgasm.

"Let's get this dress off," he said mildly, wondering if she knew he'd done that on purpose, wondering if she'd be angry. Or if she thought he was clueless about a woman's body and its reaction, assuming that he had no idea she had been on the verge of coming.

Arms still in the air, even after he stepped away, CJ blinked at him. "I was . . ."

She couldn't seem to finish her thought, her expression so forlorn he had to hide a grin. Wyatt took her by the shoulders and spun her around gently so that her back was to him. He reached for the zipper.

"Shh. It wasn't the right time. You weren't ready."

CJ stiffened and jerked forward so his hand fell off the dress. "Was too," she muttered.

Yeah, but he happened to like his women to

enjoy themselves, not willing their bodies to an orgasm so they could go home.

He stepped toward her and pulled the zipper down in one smooth motion. Greeted with the sight of her back descended to the rounded curve of her very nice ass covered in sheer black lace, he swallowed hard. Then reached inside that dress and covered her backside, caressing along the underside of each cheek, teasing with the leg band and bending so he could dart his hand all the way around to her soft mound and brush across it.

Kissing her shoulder, tasting the fresh, clean scent of her skin, he roamed all over her body, exploring her curves with his hands, noting that CJ was lush, particularly in the chest, but strong and firm, with an athletic build. Her waist dipped in only slightly and her behind was solid, smooth muscle. He wondered idly if she could kick his ass if he gave her a chance.

Nah. But the tussle before he won could be fun.

He found her nipples, played with them, straining the dress to accommodate his big hands. She wiggled in front of him, trying to maneuver his touch more fully on her. Wyatt's hard-on was pressing into her tight little ass, making him want to slip inside her panties and take her from behind.

But CJ still wasn't making any sounds and she felt tight enough to snap in half like a pencil.

With a flip of his fingers, he stripped the dress down her arms and dropped it, the upper half pooling on her waist, caught by her hips. Another tug and it fell to the floor. CJ's shoulders rose and fell, her hair moving a little, swayed by the breeze of the dress dropping. He lifted her hair off her neck and kissed her.

She shivered.

Wyatt stepped back to check out the view in front of him. It didn't disappoint. She didn't turn, didn't move, and he ran a finger along her spine, her flesh hot, a sheen of excited perspiration on her skin. He undid the bra hook, but left it alone, dangling under her shoulder blades.

His head was swimming, his desire so intense he could barely breathe. Shrugging out of his jacket quickly, he tossed it on the floor, next to her crumpled dress. His tie was strangling him, but he didn't bother with it. He couldn't keep his hands off her. Especially not when CJ moved just a little, just enough to make her bra straps fall down her arms.

With a quick Houdini effort that he almost missed, she extracted herself from the straps and the black lace fell to the carpet. Whoa. The curve of her breast on the side taunted him, but Wyatt didn't want to face CJ just yet. She seemed more comfortable staring at his Christmas tree than she did facing him. Her body had relaxed, her breathing more natural, her shoulders dropping a little.

And she had taken off her bra, no matter how much she wanted to be discreet about it. That thing wouldn't have gotten on the floor without some help.

Neither would her panties.

So he helped them.

He shifted to her side, and his tongue followed the descent of the black lace as he drew them down over her thighs. But he got distracted as he caught the first glimpse of her bare flesh, her light brown curls, and her sweet, musky scent. His fingers shoved the panties past her hips and he stretched across her thigh until he could reach her. Down on his knees, he teased between her legs with his tongue, forcing her to step apart to allow him room, her panties straining across her knees.

A raspy little moan jerked from her.

Wyatt throbbed with triumph. Crouching down, facing her as he spread her apart, he took another long, leisurely taste, holding on to her thighs to keep his balance as her moist inner folds trembled beneath his tongue.

Her hands went into his hair, and she said, "I'm going to fall. I can't spread my legs like this with my panties still on."

Looking up the long length of her pale, naked body, past her dusky, damp curls and her flat stomach to the most incredible breasts he'd ever seen, he smiled at her. "You're going to spread your legs a lot farther than this before we're done."

Her eyes squeezed shut. "Oh, God."

Wyatt pressed a kiss on her clitoris, then sat back on his haunches to wait, to think, to watch. Her breasts rose up and down, and he drank in the sight of them, marveling at what those baggy sweaters had been hiding. She was stacked, voluptuous but perky, her nipples rosy, her areolas a deep, ruddy red, and large. He wondered if they would even fit fully into his mouth.

His hard-on pressed painfully against the tux pants, but still he waited, gauging how close they were to the couch. Just a foot or two back.

Once she opened her eyes, he was going to lay

her on that couch and keep her there until she screamed in pleasure. He'd certainly heard sarcasm and disgust come from her. Now he wanted to hear ecstasy.

CJ squeezed her thighs together, her flesh bumping him in the shoulder. Her hands fluttered off his head, and she rocked on the balls of her feet. Finally, her eyes flew open and she looked at him impatiently.

"What are you doing?"

"Move forward a little." Tugging her hand, he dropped onto the couch, sitting on the edge.

She took a tentative step, her belly level with his eyes. Wyatt lay down, mouth wet with need. CJ leaned over him.

"You look weird still wearing a tux tie." Her fingers undid the black tie and stripped it from around his collar.

Her breasts were dangling in front of him, and he clamped down the urge to grab on and suck them hard. Instead, he nudged her up a little. "Put your knees on either side of me."

She did, then leaned over again, like she wanted him to take her nipples. Not wanting to be distracted, he raised his head a little, grabbed her ass, and shoved her toward him until his tongue and her labia collided.

CJ let out a cry of shock before she could stop herself. Wyatt had pulled her onto his . . . oh, help, he was . . .

She was sitting on his face.

Even her armpits must be blushing.

She tried to pull away, to lift up, to evade his tongue, but he was strong and she had nowhere to grab. Her legs were bent awkwardly, preventing her from getting a good grip on anything, and even when she swatted at his head, he didn't stop.

Which was a damn good thing, because despite her embarrassment, it felt good. Catastrophic, sound barrier–breaking good. He was doing all kinds of interesting little things, moving slow and sure, flicking and sucking, and CJ found herself sinking down onto him.

He was holding her firmly in place and though she felt exposed, naked while he was still completely dressed, his touch was so delicious, so erotic, that she couldn't bring herself to forcibly remove her body from his. She sank, sank down, sliding her knees out on either side, grabbing the arm of the couch behind his head for support as heat tore through her.

As he stroked her over and over, randomly dipping his tongue inside her before darting back to her clitoris, CJ couldn't prevent a little moan from escaping. Her body was ready to let go, and she wanted to have her orgasm before Wyatt denied her again. She had no idea what that had been all about earlier, but she didn't intend to let it happen again.

But Wyatt did pull back, just a little, far enough to glance up at her and murmur, "Relax, CJ."

Relax? She was sitting on his chest, her butt resting on his shirt buttons, completely naked, while his tongue swam laps across her crotch, and he wanted her to *relax?*

"I don't know what you mean."

And if he didn't stop talking and get back to work, this position was going to become really em-

barrassing. They weren't filling out office forms.
She was naked.

"You're tense. I just want you to relax and enjoy it."

"I'm enjoying it," she said through gritted teeth.
"Or I was until you stopped."

He sat up without warning, and she would have
sprawled all over him if he hadn't caught her and
flipped her onto her back. She barely had time to
blink before he kissed her, wild and wet, and then
he was gone, down to her breasts, sucking one nipple, then the other.

"What do you want me to do?" she asked, thinking that he had some kind of orchestrated moves
here and obviously she wasn't complying.

What did she know about sex? She hadn't had
any in three years and before that it had been five
years since she'd fumbled her way through a first
time with someone.

Wyatt probably had sex every . . . no, she didn't
want to think about how often he had sex. It would
make her feel inadequate and maybe even jealous.

Moving away from her slick nipple, he said,
"Nothing. I just want you to lie there, soft and relaxed, taking what I give you. I want you to make
noise, let me know how much you like it."

CJ watched Wyatt kiss a path down her abdomen.
She wasn't sure she could give him what he wanted.
It had been hard enough to let go of her control, to
gamble that this night would be satisfying and not
a disaster, and to give in to a wild physical impulse.
But now that she was here, now that her own
clothes were still in the bathroom and the clothes
Wyatt had her wearing were discarded on the

floor, she was enjoying what he was doing, but she felt vulnerable.

If she really let go, exploded with passion the way she wanted to, and screamed his name, she wasn't going to be able to retreat at the end of the night. There would be awkwardness, embarrassment, raw feelings. This way she could still keep him at a distance and walk away with a smile and a sarcastic remark.

But that wasn't taking into account what he was doing to her right now.

Wyatt had descended until he was between her thighs again. He took her left leg and rested it on the back of the couch, spreading her legs wide in front of him. Then with his fingers, he opened her folds, reached forward and sucked her clitoris.

He wasn't making this easy.

But she clamped down on her lips, and the only sound in the room was the slight squeak of the leather couch as she squirmed on it, and their breathing, hers ragged, Wyatt's intermittent as he expelled large breaths before returning to torture her.

It was creeping up on her again, that pulsing, deep ecstasy that she could either fight or give in to. She could either hang on tight and feel good, or let it loose and feel way better than good.

Wyatt's movements had changed, had lost their controlled skill. Before it had seemed as if he was an observer, watching her as he fingered her, giving her pleasure but not taking any. Now, he was gripping her hard, his tongue was everywhere, his teeth grazing her thigh, a groan slipping out of his mouth as he enjoyed.

"You taste so good," he said.

The hard edge in his voice was a turn-on, and she believed him. He was losing his playboy charm, becoming desperate and a little rough, and CJ let go of the last vestiges of her own control. Sinking into the couch, she dropped her thighs even farther apart, let her arms sag above her head, and opened her mouth.

What came out of that mouth would have shocked any FBI coworkers who knew the two of them, and hell, even shocked herself. "Oh, Wyatt, dammit, don't stop. You're so good at this."

He didn't stop. And those perfect, desperate, slick, and out-of-control touches sent her rushing into an orgasm.

As it rocked through her, pitching her forward off the couch and gripping his head, she let out a yell to rival a Superbowl crowd after a touchdown. He held her in place, and his mouth continued to move on her as she shuddered and moaned, clawing at the couch in ecstasy.

"Damn, damn," she murmured as her body settled back down.

But Wyatt was up, undoing his pants, pulling a condom out of his pocket. The speed with which he opened the package and rolled it on himself amazed her. Before she could even move any of her still-trembling muscles, he sank inside her. Which made her groan again, loudly and without restraint.

Wyatt didn't wait for CJ's body to adjust. He didn't

stroke slowly and ease himself inside. He just took, burying himself all the way as far as she could accommodate. He couldn't stop himself, didn't want to. When CJ had finally found her voice during her orgasm, he had thought he would come right then and there. Never had anything sounded so incredible, so desirable. So satisfying.

It satisfied him to satisfy her. But it also made him ache with a throbbing hardness deep in his gut until he had to take her, had to be inside her warm and wet body. CJ's fingernails scratched his chest under his tux shirt, and he resented the fabric between his flesh and hers, but he wasn't about to take the time to rid himself of it, either.

Her knee was still on the top of the couch, and Wyatt pulled it down and pushed it toward her, resting his hand on her kneecap. He did the same to the other leg, leaving her more fully open to him, and he pulled in and out, wanting to go forever but not sure how long he was going to be able to last.

The sight of her, eyes half closed, arms falling back weakly, her body relaxed and pliant, breasts dancing in front of him, was absolutely incredible. He felt a sense of awe that she was there with him, a need to please her, and a contentment that he'd never felt with another woman.

When she opened her eyes wide and said, "Wyatt, I'm going to come again," he didn't think that anything could sound better.

There was a pause where he could feel her inner muscles quivering and he urged her, "Let me see you come, baby."

When she did, with another violent cry, gripping the armrest, he followed her, digging into her knees as he pulsed with her. The feelings, the shudders and the moans, went on and on until finally he laid his head down on her damp shoulder.

"Jesus, CJ, you trying to kill me?"

"If I wanted to kill you, I'd use my gun," came her lazy, satisfied voice.

Her fingers were stroking along his back, nails lightly scratching his skin. He rolled a little onto his side, so he wouldn't be crushing her, and kissed her forehead.

She didn't snuggle into his arms, but she didn't move away, either, and she didn't make any objections to him still being inside her.

"I hope you have thick walls or your neighbors are going to know exactly what's going on here."

"A flight attendant lives next door. She's probably not home." And if she was, let her be jealous.

Sighing in regret, he pulled out of her, but stayed next to her on the couch, running his fingers along her stomach. "I can't get over how gorgeous your body is. You're like a buck-fifteen under all those baggy clothes, CJ."

She stilled his fingers. "That tickles. And what does a buck-fifteen mean?"

"You look like about a hundred and fifteen pounds." He grinned, giving her nipple a tweak. "And most of that is in your chest."

She gasped. "They're not that big. It's just that the bra you had me put on was defective."

He wished he'd gotten a better look at it before he had unhooked it. "How was it defective?"

"It seemed to think that a woman's breasts belong a half inch under her chin."

"Don't they?" he joked.

With her thumb and index finger, she flicked him in the chest. "No, they don't."

Then she undid one of his buttons. Surprised, in a good hell-yeah kind of way, he let her undo another before he said, "What does CJ stand for?"

He had a real hard time seeing her as a Catherine or a Chelsea.

"Nothing. It doesn't stand for anything." She had four buttons down, three to go.

Without warning, her fingers slipped inside his shirt, running across his chest and he felt renewed life down south. If she didn't watch it, she'd find herself flat on her back.

But he was more than ready to ditch the shirt and pants. He wanted CJ's hands on him everywhere. And he had just the place to do it.

"You want to see my hot tub?"

"You have a hot tub?" She said this like he'd admitted to having handcuffs bolted above his headboard.

"It's out on my patio. Very private, no one can see in." The patio he'd spent half an hour stringing freaking Christmas lights around.

While she sat up and peered toward the sliding door out to his patio, she still said, "I'm not just walking out there naked." She gestured to his pants. "You still have your clothes on, it's not fair."

"I could take my clothes off, no problem."

"No, that's not what I meant. Go get me the bra and panties. I'll wear those."

Naked was what he preferred, but at least this way he could check her out in the sexy underwear. It was only when he'd retrieved them and brought them to her that he realized she'd just ordered him around.

In which case, he had the right to put the panties back on her.

Slowly, with lots of detours along the way.

Five

What felt like half an hour later, Wyatt had her panties back on her and CJ was aroused all over again, wet and limp as a noodle.

Lying on her back on the couch, she groaned when he stood up and said, "Now we'll put your bra back on."

"Maybe we don't need to put my clothes back on." She resisted when Wyatt tried to tug her up into a sitting position. She didn't want to move. Ever again.

He came at her with the black lace bra.

"Oh, no, you don't." Trying to wiggle away, she let out a grunt when he grabbed her.

"I'm serious, Maddock. I'll put the bra on myself." She shot him a warning look, but he didn't see it with his head buried between her breasts.

"Why are you so stubborn?" he murmured, between dropping wet kisses left and right.

"Because I don't want you putting my bra on me. It's weird." And intimate. She needed to steer clear of intimate or she was going to be in trouble.

But he was already slipping the armholes of the bra over her, sliding the sheer lace up, while kissing her neck. She was profoundly disappointed that her nipples were covered, but resigned to his stubbornness outlasting hers, she turned so he could hook the back.

Wyatt's fingers fumbled. "These things are harder to put on than get off." He gave a final tug. "There."

CJ turned back to him, caught between wanting to laugh and whimper in pain. "Obviously."

His eyes bugged out. "What the hell?"

CJ did manage a laugh before she grabbed the bottom of the bra and yanked it down. It wasn't doing a thing cutting across the middle of each of her breasts. "You sort of need to lift them into the bra."

"Oh. Sorry." Wyatt studied her chest, confusion clearing, desire sparking. "I'd be good at that."

Help her. She smothered a laugh and swatted his hands away. "Be quiet and take your pants off."

He grinned back. "Bossy, aren't you? But for some weird-ass reason I don't mind." He stood up and dropped his pants to the floor with one push, then stepped out of them.

"You mind at work." CJ tried not to look at his thighs and that big bump in his boxer shorts, but she wasn't having much luck.

"We're not at work. Order me around all you want."

"Really?" That brought her attention to his face.

"Sure, why not? You wore the dress. I can be submissive, too."

Hah. That was a joke. Wyatt would never be even close to submissive. More likely he'd charm her into thinking he was complying, when really he was getting his way all along.

Reaching for the final buttons still holding his shirt together, she said, "Nah. I don't want to order you around. But the next time I tell you 'don't stop,' I expect you to keep going, all right?"

She had the buttons undone and was bending over him.

Wyatt sucked in hard. "Keep going. Got it."

CJ ran her fingers over his hard, warm chest, feeling the smooth muscles, toying with the edge of his boxers as she kissed his salty-tasting flesh above his waistband. Their breath quickened together; then she slowly pulled back.

"Let's go in the hot tub."

Wyatt groaned. "Tease."

"Look who's talking. You spent ten minutes getting me hot while putting my panties back *on*."

"Once we're in the water, they're coming back off."

That sounded like a plan to her. "Promise?"

They stood up, and she was flush against him, his erection pressing into her, his hand on the small of her back, sending her pulse racing.

Wyatt's eyes were dark, and a satisfied smile turned up the corner of his mouth. "I always knew there was a hell of a woman hiding behind those baggy clothes and that frown."

His comment irritated her. Maybe because he had read her so easily, seen her desire for him. Or maybe because somehow she had come to see Wyatt as more than the office flirt, started to picture him as belonging to *her.* Which she couldn't afford to do. Not when she had her son to think about. Wyatt was good for one night, nothing more, and she was going to remember that or force herself to walk away.

"Don't get too cocky there, Maddock. I still hate you, you know." CJ flushed as she heard her own words. That was rude, nothing but plain bad manners.

But Wyatt just laughed. "Sure you do. Whatever you need to tell yourself."

He kissed her—a soft, gentle brush that made her feel about as big as a flea.

She rolled her eyes and sighed. No matter if she choked on it or not, she needed to apologize. "All right, I don't hate you. I actually kind of like you."

He didn't gloat like she expected, or laugh hysterically. Instead, he tossed her hair out of her eyes and smiled softly, which only served to cement her opinion that he was much nicer than she'd ever realized.

Which totally sucked. Because if she wasn't careful, she was going to wind up falling for him. Hard.

Wyatt wasn't surprised at the edgy tone CJ had taken on. He had realized something about her tonight. That she was protecting herself from being hurt. She was attracted to him and she didn't like it because she didn't want to get hurt.

Her ex-husband had left some deep wounds, but Wyatt wasn't an impatient guy. He had the time, the patience, and the easygoing personality to bring CJ around eventually so that she trusted him.

After being with her, sharing what they had, seeing how different it felt, Wyatt knew he wasn't going to be requesting a transfer to Tampa. He was staying put and seeing where this could go with CJ, especially now that she had just admitted that she kind of liked him.

For her, that was a giant leap forward.

"I kind of like you, too. In a dress. Out of a dress. Even in your baggy-ass sweaters."

Before she could answer, sputter, or grab his nuts in a chokehold, he kissed her, feeling his cock tighten in response. He didn't think he'd ever get enough of CJ. He loved that there was nothing phony or overblown about CJ, that she was who she was, and he suspected he was on the verge of acting like a damn fool over her.

Tomorrow anyway, when CJ wanted to stick to their original agreement and he had to explain that he wanted to be with her. That was a conversation he wasn't looking forward to.

But tonight they were in sync.

Breaking the kiss, he reached for the sliding glass door that led to his patio. He had chosen this unit because it was on the corner of the building, and the high brick walls made the small patio completely private.

"The lid's already off, and the water's nice and hot, but it's going to be cold when we step outside."

She rolled her eyes. "No kidding. It's December

and I noticed the foot of snow on my way over here."

Here he was trying to be considerate, and she was being a smart-ass. Opening the door, he grabbed her by the arm and gave her a friendly, helpful nudge outside. Right through a large snowdrift.

"Shit!" CJ bounced out of the snow pile, which had gone past her ankles, and hopped over to the hot tub, her mouth drawn down in a wince. "Maddock, that is not funny!"

The bouncing did really great things to her breasts, and Wyatt watched from the doorway in horny amusement. "Hey, you were the one who got all smart about it. I was trying to be nice."

CJ had bent over in front of the hot tub, brushing snow off her foot. Goose bumps raced over Wyatt as he stood in the open doorway and thirty-degree Chicago winds pummeled him. He needed to get in the hot tub before he froze his nuts off, but he was a little nervous CJ might try to drown him.

She turned right as he strode toward her, risking her wrath in pursuit of hot water. Her arm moved and then a big, wet ball of slushy snow slapped him in the chest. It was so cold it stung, sliding down toward his stomach as he let out a strangled groan. "Dammit, White."

CJ had already climbed into the water and was submerged to her chin, grinning at him. "You can dish it out, but you can't take it, huh?"

He could take it. Oh, yeah, he could take it.

Wyatt jumped over the side and into the water, sending a wave flooding in her direction.

Water crashed over her face and CJ rubbed at her eyes. "Geez, you're like a tank dropping into the water."

That didn't sound like a compliment. "Watch out, I might roll you over."

Wyatt pinned her against the wall and surrounded her with his arms. Her face was pink, water droplets running down her cheeks, her bangs flat on her forehead. As she breathed, her hot breath turned to steam in the cold winter air, and Wyatt was blown away by how beautiful she was.

The bubbles from the jets floated between them and CJ braced her hands on his chest. "You don't scare me."

"No? Because you scare me." He kissed her chin, the corner of her mouth, tasted the coolness of her skin, nudged his thighs between hers.

"How do I scare you?"

Her head tilted to allow him access to her neck, and Wyatt bent over her, groaning when he saw her breasts break the surface of the water, the black lace clinging to her curvy flesh, pink nipples straining against the sheer fabric. "It scares me that I want you so much."

CJ paused, and then her fingers started to roam lower, from his chest to his stomach. "You don't need to be scared of that. Just take me."

There was an idea. A damn good idea. He reached under the water and ditched his boxers. He let them go and they floated to the surface. CJ's breath hitched.

"Your boxers fell off."

"Damn jets."

Reaching around her back, he unhooked her bra. "Oops. It knocked your bra off, too."

She gave him a look.

"What?" He watched the bra float to the left, caught in a jet propulsion. Her creamy pink breasts looked so wet and round, and he wanted to eat her nipple, just suck it until she came.

He was bending over to do that when her hand closed over his cock. "I like the Christmas lights hung around the patio wall," she said.

Wyatt froze in place. His near brush with death by electrocution was forgotten as her light fingers stroked over him under the water.

His response was a cross between a grunt and a roar. He sounded like a sleeping lion being nudged awake. It might have been embarrassing except that CJ's hand moved up and down, slowly, giving him a little squeeze now and again. Embarrassment fell far behind delirious pleasure.

"It looks very cheerful, romantic," she went on casually, like she had no idea she was giving him a hand job. "Thank you for going to so much trouble tonight. This wasn't what I expected."

He was having a little trouble thinking clearly. Her breasts were bumping into him, all warm and wet and round, and her mouth was right in front of him, dewy and plump from his kisses, her damp hair clinging to her rosy cheeks. Her hand moved over and over, squeezing the head of his cock and ducking low to cup his balls.

Though he wanted nothing more than to just

explode under her touch, he saw an opportunity to clear the air between them. "CJ, I only sleep with about ten percent of the women I date, and I never bring them back to my place. The only female in this hot tub before you was my three-year-old niece."

Her hand stilled. "What are you saying?"

"I'm saying that I'm attracted to you, yes. But I also really like you, and I don't want this to be just one night."

Before she could protest, he took advantage of her confusion and sat down on the bench next to her and pulled her toward him. Catching the underside of her breast with his mouth, and giving her little nibbles, he reached through the bubbles and tugged her panties down to her knees.

"Wyatt . . ."

He could hear her saying no in that word, feel her reluctance to believe or accept that they could be anything beyond frigid coworkers or have more than this night together. He never would have imagined he would be determined to talk CJ into his bed and life on a permanent basis, but then he'd never seen the reality TV invasion coming, either.

"The jets knocked your panties off, too."

Through the hot water, he eased his hand between her thighs and stroked across the front of her pubic hair, cupping her mound and enjoying her little lurch forward. Wyatt didn't have all the answers. He couldn't predict how a relationship with CJ might turn out, but he did know he wanted to try. She fascinated him, with her honest stare and her simple, no-frills attitude.

"I'll never ask you to wear a dress again." Wyatt slid his thumb inside her and turned it a little.

"Oooh," she said, grabbing his arms, as her body happily responded. "Can we talk about this later?"

Much later, she figured, when the postcoital lust had worn off, and Wyatt remembered that they had yet to go a day without an argument of some kind. Or at least major eye rolling on her part. When she somehow found a way to tell him thanks, but no thanks, she could not ask her mother to babysit for her every other night so she could dash off and play hide the salami with him until he got his transfer.

Or the fact that she'd never quite gotten around to mentioning that she had a child.

Yep, all that could wait. Because this was her one night, her one chance, and she wanted to wring every last drop of pleasure out of it while she still could, since starting tomorrow she was back to boring underwear and baggy sweaters. Given that reality, there was no telling when she might have another crack at a guy like Wyatt, if ever, before the wrinkles took over and her butt started to droop.

"I'll hold you to that," he said, as his foot stepped on her panties, still caught around each ankle.

While he held the panties in place on the bottom of the hot tub, she lifted her feet out, losing her balance a little as the force of the propelling water rocked her forward. Wyatt pulled her to him, and with no instructions whatsoever from her, her legs spread and wrapped around his waist, until she was cuddled up in his lap. In hot water.

"CJ, I have to get a condom," he said, his hands holding her still, slightly away from his erection, his voice low and tight.

"You should have thought of that before we got in," she teased, sucking on his bottom lip, feeling really damn naughty and not about to give him up even for the two minutes it would take to grab some latex. Not when she'd had her tubes tied three years ago at her ex-husband's insistence.

Sneaking between their wet bodies with her thumb, she stroked him. He moaned and started to nudge her backward away from him. CJ clamped her legs around him tighter.

"Knock it off, White."

"What?" she said, rubbing her nipples against his chest. She closed her whole hand over him and guided her body to his erection.

"CJ!" he let out an alarmed squawk and tried to scoot back. The hot tub wall stopped him.

She sank onto him, allowing herself to moan her gratification loudly, not hold anything back. Wyatt without a condom was beyond anything a reasonable woman could expect to endure for more than thirty seconds without coming.

"CJ, don't, shit, stop. . . ." He tried to push her away, his eyes closed, his lips clamped together in two tight lines.

"Wyatt, we don't need a condom. I can't get pregnant." She didn't want to get more specific right then.

As she moved up and down, savoring the feel of

him, resting her head against his shoulder, he relaxed a little.

"Are you sure?"

"Positive."

He had stopped fighting her, and she moved on him faster, breath hitching. Then without warning, Wyatt responded, giving in, thrusting up inside her so deep she sucked in air hard and gripped his shoulders, feeling every inch of him pulsing in her. The hot water lapped around them and the frigid December air bit across her cheeks. Steam rose between them and CJ watched his face as Wyatt took over, setting a rhythm, pounding into her, holding on to her waist with tight, possessive hands.

His brown eyes had darkened, and his straight teeth were clenched. He rocked her, he held her, and she felt so alive, so in tune with him, fantastically indulged and wickedly sexual. A woman with a man who wanted her, and the feel of him without the condom stroked her sensitive body, reached deep inside her and splintered her with pleasure until she thought she couldn't stand it anymore.

"Wyatt, oh, yes, don't stop. . . ." CJ didn't even know what she was begging for, since he didn't look to have plans to halt anytime soon.

"You're so hot, so incredible," he murmured.

CJ knew she was rushing to an orgasm, felt it building deep inside, felt her hips fall slack, her stomach muscles coil, her head loll back. "Harder," she said, wanting to take all of him, to know that he was strong enough and man enough to understand her and what she wanted.

Some men stared right through her, seeing only the plain hair and shapeless clothes. Others backed down, intimidated by her job or her abrasive manners or her straightforward, no-bullshit attitude. Only Wyatt had figured out a way around her defense wall. Only Wyatt saw inside her, sensed her vulnerability.

Wyatt gave her what she asked for, lifting so hard into her she almost fell over backward. Their thighs slapped together, his grip so tight her skin pinched, her nipples boring into his chest. Their breath mingled together in the cold air, desperate little pants, CJ unable to even moan as he claimed her over and over again.

When she came, raking at his chest, shivering and moaning, her body clamping down on him, Wyatt gave a little laugh of triumph.

"Damn, baby, that's right. Keep going."

CJ locked eyes with him, let him see the pleasure on her face, let him read the freedom she felt with him. The small smile slid off his face.

"Oh, shit," he said, and stopped thrusting, pulsing into her as he came on the heels of her orgasm.

Squeezing her inner muscles tightly over him, she watched his mouth fall open, his eyes drift shut, his breath coming in little strained, frantic groans. His chin sank down as he rode the last waves of pleasure and CJ sighed in contentment.

Resting her forehead on his warm shoulder, his chest hair tickling her, she said, "Hey."

"Hey, yourself."

The bubbles swirled in the water around them, and when CJ glanced up, she saw the stars in the midnight-blue winter sky. His hold had loosened on her, and he shifted her off of him, settling her into his lap, holding her close. It had been such a long time since anyone had held her, since she hadn't had to be the strong one. Her body was relaxed, satiated, and so was her soul.

"I don't want just one night, CJ."

That was the second time he'd said that. The first she had attributed to preorgasmic lust, and not to be taken seriously. This could be postorgasmic contentment, or he could just actually mean it. Damn, she really hoped not. Because she just might be tempted to give in, and that would be a gigantic mistake. This wasn't like eating a whole bag of chocolate kisses, which was regrettable—a sign of weakness and an overindulgence—but easily eradicated through a five-mile jog. Once she let Wyatt in, she wasn't going to be able to get rid of him so easily.

He kissed the top of her head. Her breath quickened and her heart melted like same-said chocolate in the microwave on high. Dammit, she'd already let him in.

"Sorry, that wasn't part of the deal," she said in a mean little voice that shocked even her.

Wyatt stiffened. "You're trying to tell me, sitting here naked and thoroughly fucked in my hot tub, that you don't want me?"

CJ felt her cheeks burn. "There's wanting you and then there's wanting you. I want you but I don't want you."

He snorted. "Oh, well, thanks, that cleared it up."

"You tell me what *you* mean. What do you want

beyond one night? Another night of sex? And another? An affair, is that what you want?" She lifted her head off his shoulder and stared out at his fence, not at all sure she wanted to hear his answer.

"No, I don't want an affair, though I do want another night of sex, and another. I want to date you, be together, for God's sake. Is that so hard for you to grasp?"

Actually, it was. Her anger dissipated. "Wyatt, you just want me because you think you can't have me. I've been a bitch to you for months and it drives you nuts."

"I'm not going to dispute that you've been a bitch." He nudged her with his knee and gave her a smile. "But I think you've got me all wrong, CJ. You know, I date women, I enjoy their company, we talk, I have a good time. But none of them ever ties me up in knots and makes me want to string up Christmas lights. You do that. I feel different about you."

"You strung these lights up for me?" She suddenly felt very small, but very happy, cozy in his arms. She couldn't imagine feeling this contentment with any of the men who had asked her out since her divorce. But that didn't mean she was ready to give it a go with Wyatt, not when she had Sam to think about.

"Yeah, I thought it would be romantic. Didn't do it for my damn health, that's for sure. I may know my way around the firing range, but I don't know shit about Christmas decorations. Nearly killed myself twice."

She smiled against his chest, his damp hair tickling her nose as they hovered in the water together. "I'm glad you didn't kill yourself. And I don't know anything about Christmas decorations, either. I leave that to my mom." Staring up at his scratchy chin, she warned him, "I don't know how to be romantic. To me, you show someone you care by getting the oil changed in their car."

His thumb stole across her lip. "Maybe we can learn to be romantic together."

He was going to kiss her and she was going to cave, to forget everything and pretend they could exist in a heated hot-tub world.

"Let's get out of here, my skin is wrinkling." She stood up and gasped as the arctic wind blasted across her slick breasts. Her nipples felt like she'd taken a cheese grater to them and goose bumps rushed over her arms and neck. Her hair froze.

A shocked howl ripped out of her mouth. Dropping back down into the hot tub, she tipped her head into the warm, frothy water to defrost. Gasping, trying to calm her jolted body, she said, "Oh my God, we're trapped in here forever."

And here she'd been trying to exit gracefully and prevent further intimacies. Having to yell for help so the neighbors could toss them overcoats wasn't going to help her maintain an emotional distance from Wyatt.

Neither was rubbing up against him to steal his body heat. She shivered and showed no shame, wiggling into his warm chest.

Wyatt placed his hand square on CJ's ass and enjoyed her jerky movements, her slippery skin connecting with his in lots of interesting places. He'd been regretting not having thought ahead far enough to bring out towels or robes, but now he was reconsidering. CJ had been on the verge of making an escape, and now he had her in his arms again.

But they did have to get out of the hot tub eventually, and maybe if he played the hero he could earn a few extra points. He certainly needed all he could get. "I'll go get some towels."

He nudged her aside.

CJ shook her head. "You'll die if you go out there naked. I'm serious."

Scoffing, he said, "What's a cool breeze? I'm an FBI agent."

She rolled her eyes right back at him. "So am I, you goof. It's freezing out there."

Wyatt sucked in a breath and stood up, walking toward the step to climb out. The shock of the cold air made him want to moan, but he clamped his lips shut. No way in hell was he going to let her see him squirm. When his feet touched the ground, he moved fast, afraid his skin would stick to the flagstones like tongue on metal.

But he refused to run, refused to bend over, and refused to make a sound, even though it was possible his nuts had just frozen off and dropped to the ground. He sure in the hell couldn't feel them anymore.

When he reached the door, he turned and winked at CJ, who was watching him in awe. Then he ran like hell.

In his bedroom, he allowed himself a much-deserved whimper before grabbing a towel and wrapping it around his waist. He stuck his feet in sandals, then grabbed a couple more towels and the blanket from his bed. He dropped the blanket by the door, braced himself, and stepped back out into old man winter.

"Holy crap, I need to stick a dome over top of this patio," he told CJ as he approached the hot tub, where she waited with only her nose and eyes out of the water.

Her lips broke the surface. "It didn't seem this cold before."

"That's because I was keeping you busy." He stood there, numb in all his extremities, and urged her, "Stand up, I've got a towel."

CJ closed her eyes, then stood up in a rush. She moved up the steps while he wrapped one towel around her, not even taking the time to appreciate that her nipple was level with his mouth. He scooped her up into his arms, losing the second towel in the process, and carried her, dripping, shivering, and moaning, to the door.

Where he promptly tripped over the metal doorjamb in his sandals and tumbled them both to the floor, where they landed on the blanket, naked and wet, looking like they were attempting to enact the Kama Sutra.

"Close the door," CJ said, her face stuck in his armpit.

He kicked it shut with his foot, then grabbed her and rolled until they were snug in the blanket, cabbage-roll style.

"We're in," he said, getting one hand on her back and the other on her smooth, cool behind as they both lay on their sides facing each other.

She blinked up at him, shivering, then suddenly, without warning, she laughed. Her whole face changed, her eyes softened, her cheeks got round, her lips curved, and he saw her small, white teeth.

Wyatt had never seen CJ laugh before. Never. She had scoffed, glared, snorted, then tonight had smiled and moaned and begged, but just an honest light laugh he had never heard. There was joy in her face, in that sound, and wham, it hit him, robbing him of all thought.

Damn, he'd gone and fallen in love with her.

Or maybe the sex had just made him stupid.

"I've never seen you laugh before," he said, as her breath tickled his chin and her fingers danced across his sides, giving him goose bumps.

"You've never been quite this laughable before," she said with a grin.

Nope, it wasn't the sex. He really was in love with her. Shit.

"Here I almost froze to death saving your ass from hypothermia and you're laughing at me? Some thanks." He kissed her nose. "Some parts of me may never work again."

"Which parts?" Her laughter cut out, and she opened her eyes wider, the little witch.

He shrugged. "Just the parts that stick out."

CJ's little fingers started to wiggle under the blanket, moving lower. Oh, yeah.

"Maybe I can warm them back up."

"Maybe you can." Their combined body heat had already taken the chill from his skin and her words about set him on fire.

She found him, semi-erect, and went to work,

squeezing and rushing along him until he fell back and moaned, enjoying the feeling but knowing it was too soon.

"Jesus, CJ, I don't think I can again. . . ." It was embarrassing to admit, but hell, he'd come twice in the last hour and a half. Three might be pushing it.

"It's okay, I just want to play with it."

Fuck. His dick swelled the rest of the way.

And when her head disappeared as she burrowed down into the blanket, he decided he most certainly could come a third time. In just a minute or two.

Her cool lips closed over the head of his cock and she sucked hard. Shudders wracked his body and he muttered, "Damn, I like the way you play."

Her movements weren't practiced or remote, but were ravenous, tugging, like she'd never tasted anything so good in her life and it had him growling, not wanting to burst too soon. His thighs were on fire, her damp body pressing against him, and he lifted the blanket to peek down at her.

The top of her head was visible, as was her little button nose and her pink, slick lips moving over him, shiny and wet, her cheeks collapsing as she drew half the length of him into her mouth.

"Can you breathe under there?" he thought to ask, aware that the temperature in the blanket had risen rapidly.

"Mmm-hmm," she said, muffled, her mouth too full to talk.

Teeth scraped him gently, fingers massaged his testicles, and he lost it. Reaching down to cup her head, he warned, "I'm done, baby, stop."

Devilish eyes met his. She sucked harder, making a suction sound on his cock with her lips, her tongue flicking out to lick the length of him.

It seemed she had loosened up quite a bit since she'd walked in his door earlier.

He was strung too tight, enjoying her too much. He loved her, he really did, and it seemed natural to stay there, to trust her to tell him what she wanted. Her iron grip and smiling eyes told him to go ahead and explode, and so he did, pulsing into her mouth and nearly ripping the wall-to-wall carpet off the floor.

She held him until he was done, lying back spent, and when she pressed one last kiss on his head, he let out a strangled laugh. "CJ White, you are one hell of a woman."

Fingers trailing across her moist mouth, she said, "Your parts seem to be working just fine, not frozen after all."

Amen to that.

Six

CJ was toasty warm, enough so that it didn't bother her when Wyatt let the blanket fall open, his fingers running across her ribs, tickling her.

Just that little bit of contact, along with his lips pressed to her temple, had her body stirring to life yet again. It was unbelievable the sexual glutton she had turned into in the course of one evening. By morning she wasn't going to be able to walk, and her heart was going to thoroughly belong to Wyatt.

If it already didn't. Which she suspected it did.

"Witchcraft" was playing on the stereo. They had never turned the music off and it had just rolled around to play the same Sinatra CD over and over again. CJ would never be able to listen to Frank again without wanting to tear her clothes off.

"Appropriate song, don't you think?" Wyatt murmured, rubbing his chin into her hair. "You've seduced me."

If she could have moved a muscle, she would have shot him an incredulous look. "I think you've got that backward. You with the tux, and the dress, and the dinner—you seduced me, Maddock."

She was big enough to admit it, especially with his hand brushing across her pubic hair possessively.

"I think we just both acted on what we've wanted for a long time."

"That could be true." It felt so good in his arms, snug in the blanket on the floor, the steam from the uncovered hot tub fogging up the outside of the glass door in front of them.

"I want more, CJ."

There he went again. "I heard you the first two times, Wyatt."

"Well?"

She closed her eyes and said, "I'm thinking. It's complicated." Like the fact that she had a child who needed constant care and Wyatt wasn't the kind of guy who struck her as eager to be saddled with that much responsibility. And she would never just parade a man through her son's life unless she knew it was serious, and she honestly didn't know how serious Wyatt wanted this to be.

It was time to tell him about Sam, talk it out.

"Hey, what's this?" His finger slowed down, right at her bikini line.

"What?" Distracted, she glanced down. Wyatt was bending over, studying the puckered skin there.

"This scar, what's it from?"

Whoops. Dread filled her. The time to tell Wyatt

was more than past due. She didn't think his reaction was going to be good. But she had never once denied her son to anyone, and she wouldn't now.

"It's from my C-section." Wyatt had been retreating from the idea of transferring. This might make him reconsider that, which was really for the best.

Too bad her stomach churned at the thought and her heart squeezed painfully.

His head snapped up, wide eyes met hers. "C-section? You had a kid? I'm sorry, CJ."

That confused her. "Sorry for what?"

"Well . . . something must have happened, since you never said anything. Did you give it up for adoption? I mean, it doesn't live with you, you're not a mother." He watched her, his brows drawing together. "Are you?"

She nodded, tongue stuck to the roof of her mouth. "Actually, yes, I am. My son does live with me."

"What?" His expression of horror told her how he felt about that. "How old is your son?"

She had known he wouldn't want to have any part in dating a woman with a child. But hearing his distaste felt worse than she could have imagined. "Sam is five."

Wyatt sat straight up. "You have a five-year-old son and you never bothered to mention it to me? We work together, I've known you for nine months, and you never said a word! You don't have any pictures on your desk or anything."

She stiffened and pulled the blanket over her bare body. "My personal life is just that—personal."

"Oh, man." He ran his fingers through his hair. "This is unbelievable. You're lying here with me, sharing what we did tonight, and you don't even tell me something like that? Damn, I'm an idiot. I should have known better."

And she should have, too. "Look, I didn't lie to you, I just didn't see what that had to do with anything. I came here tonight for one night of sex, then you were supposed to ask for a transfer. None of that has anything to do with my having a child."

He shook his head. "It has everything to do with you having a child. I wanted more, CJ. I wanted you. But I just don't know now."

Wyatt couldn't believe what he was hearing. How could CJ have neglected to tell him that she was a mother? To a five-year-old. He didn't care that she had a kid. In fact, it made her all the more appealing, in his eyes. Some of that crusty apprehension she'd shown had made sense. Who knew what had gone on in her marriage, but clearly she was wary of dating, and intent on protecting her child.

The thought of her cuddling up with a kid made his chest inflate with all kinds of embarrassing emotion.

"I expected that from you," she said coldly, propping herself up with her elbow. "Maybe that's why I never told you."

"Expected what?"

"You to react this way. I can't imagine you wanting to date a woman with a child. It would cramp your style."

He saw red. "I don't have a problem with kids, and maybe if you had fucking asked me, I could have told you that myself, instead of you just judging me. If you think I'm such an asshole, what are you doing here with me?"

Naked, sharing the best sex she'd ever had with him.

"Why do you think I'm here? I came here for sex," she said so bluntly that he was sorry he asked.

His gut clenched in pain, he had trouble swallowing.

"I haven't been with anyone since my ex-husband left, and I had an itch. You scratched it."

"Glad I could help," he said with dripping sarcasm.

CJ's lip was quivering. Wyatt saw hurt in her eyes, and thought to wonder what the hell had happened to the ex. He had an idea. "Your ex blew the kid off, didn't he?"

She took a deep breath, then let it out slowly. Her eyes were fixed on the door behind him. "If you have to know, yes, Scott hasn't seen Sam in three years. When we found out Sam was autistic, he toughed it out for a whole two months, then bolted. He said he couldn't deal with a kid who wasn't normal."

Wyatt heard her pain, felt it shake and shatter deep down inside her, and he reached for her. "Oh, baby, he was just an asshole." He didn't know a damn thing about autism but he knew it couldn't be easy raising a child like that alone.

But CJ twisted out of his reach and stood up. "I can't do this, Wyatt. I can't pretend that we have a future when we don't. I wanted to be free tonight, to just let go for once, and I never pictured you wanting more. But my priority is Sam, and you don't fit what I have in mind for a husband and a father."

If she had been looking for a way to hurt him the most, that was it. It cut so deep, he couldn't think of a single thing to say. It just told him she knew nothing about him. Nothing.

CJ was naked, her skin still flushed, her hair snarled and standing every which way. "I got what I wanted here tonight and I think it's time for me to leave."

He could argue that he was good father material, that he was adored by his nieces and nephews, and that though charming he may be, he was also about as staid and responsible as they came. He didn't drink, he managed his money well, and nothing would make him happier than being woken up on a Saturday morning by warm little bodies bouncing on his bed.

He had just been waiting for the right woman. He had thought he'd found her.

Now he wasn't so sure.

CJ took Wyatt's silence as an indicator that her leaving was fine with him. Turning on her heel, she took off for the bathroom, tears threatening. That had been about as fun as an earthquake, and only slightly less damaging.

She hadn't meant to criticize Wyatt, she just needed him to understand that she had responsibilities that she didn't take lightly. It had been a mistake to come here tonight and pretend otherwise.

Trying not to look at herself in the mirror, she pulled on her own sensible underwear that came up practically to her nose and her baggy pants that were about as big of a turn-on as a stint in the dentist's chair. Likewise for her sweater, and bulky as it was, she decided there was no point in putting her bra back on. It was two in the morning and no one could possibly tell anyway.

The tears were winning the fight and she swiped at them angrily. Pushing up her sleeves, she left the bathroom and headed straight for the front door, scooping her bag and coat up off the easy chair on her way by. She had only one goal—get out before she lost it and blubbered like a baby in front of Wyatt. That would make Monday at the water cooler even better than it promised to be right now.

"Do you really think I'd make a bad father?" Wyatt said, his voice hard but vulnerable, laced with pain.

CJ stopped, her hand almost on the front door-knob. She turned and he was standing there, big and tall, light brown hair falling in his eyes. He was naked except for his watch. His tux and the dress he'd bought for her were still crumpled up in front of the couch and she ached in an agony of indecision.

"No, Wyatt, I didn't mean that." He was a good man, she'd seen that—different from her, but caring, concerned about his coworkers, always wanting to take down the bad guys. He was noble and responsible and she had never meant to hurt him. Couldn't have imagined she even had the power to do so. "I just meant that I can't take any chances with Sam. I can't let you into our lives, then have you leave in six months."

Sam couldn't take it, and hell, neither could she.

And if Wyatt didn't want to leave, well, she still couldn't have any more children since she'd had her tubes tied. Wyatt deserved to have a family if he wanted one, and she couldn't give him that.

"I love you, CJ."

Her heart wrenched. He stood there, hands on his hips, a stubborn set to his jaw as the tears leapt out of her eyes and rolled down her cheeks in twin rivers. Could he make it any harder? Why didn't he just kick her in the knee and steal her purse while he was at it?

How dare he tell her exactly what she wanted to hear—but couldn't.

Without another word, she grabbed the dress off the floor, opened the door, and bolted.

When she got home and she checked on Sam, watching him sleep so peacefully, more tears fell, rushing and anxious, blinding her. She was turning on the shower, intent on washing the smell and feel of Wyatt off her skin, when she heard her cell phone ringing in her purse.

Startled, she moved into her bedroom quickly and fished it out, tossing the floral dress aside. She wasn't even sure what had made her grab it. "Hello?"

"It's me." Wyatt's voice sounded gruff, but the sound still raced along her spine, causing goose bumps. "I just wanted to make sure you got home okay."

A sob tore loose. Wyatt was so . . . *nice,* and she had screwed this whole thing up from start to finish. "I did."

"Good." He sighed. "G'night."

He wanted her to say something, she sensed it

in his voice, a pleading, but she couldn't do it. She just couldn't, not when her heart was already shredding. If she allowed herself to think there could be something between them, when she knew there couldn't . . . well, she just might not ever recover from that kind of disappointment.

"Good night." CJ hung up the phone and stripped off her clothes with trembling cold fingers.

When her pants hit the floor, her mother's condoms fell out of the pocket. CJ figured she'd give them back in the morning. Her mother would need them before she would.

She was never having sex ever again.

Any guy after Wyatt would be anticlimactic. Literally.

Seven

Wyatt's week of self-pity culminated in his getting shit-faced in Pete's Bar on Friday after work with Derek Knight, an agent he'd previously worked with.

"See, the thing is, when I told you it was stupid to fall in love, I had no idea how right I was," Wyatt said, reaching for another pretzel. "I suspected I was right, you know, but damn, was I right. It's like every piece of my body just hurts. I'm in *pain*."

Derek raised his eyebrow and shifted on the stool next to him. "So talk to her."

"I have. I said good morning to her and she ignored me, then I asked her to go to lunch with me and she said she had packed her lunch. And when I leaned over her desk to get a pen, she fell out of her chair trying to back away from me."

He'd never been one at a loss for words, but when confronted with CJ's icy dismissals, he was about as articulate as a golden retriever. He had thought through their conversation over and over again and was left more baffled than before. If anyone had the right to be pissed, it was him. She'd lied to him. She'd forgotten to mention that she had a kid, yet she was the one acting like he'd done something wrong.

For five days his confusion had been growing, and the beer wasn't helping. Now he wasn't just confused, he had to take a leak, too.

But one thing hadn't been in doubt since Saturday, and that was that he did love her. He wanted CJ, and he knew he could love her child just as much as he did her. He could even understand her reasoning for not telling him. Sort of. And he was willing to forget about it if they could just move forward.

If anything, he loved her more knowing all she had been through. Here she had been worried about her child, trying to seek help for him, and her shyster husband had up and left her. Any man who couldn't love his own flesh and blood just because the kid wasn't perfect didn't deserve to be a father.

"You shouldn't talk to her at work, Wyatt, it probably makes her uncomfortable. Go to her apartment, catch her off guard." Derek grinned and took a swallow of his beer. "Then if CJ doesn't want to talk to you, she'll let you know. Probably with the barrel of her gun."

The thought of that made him laugh a little. "She is kind of a stubborn hard-ass. She likes to take care of herself, and doesn't like help. Maybe this is just her being stubborn."

"Man, I don't know how you can even consider throwing yourself at the mercy of CJ. She scares me a little."

"You should have seen her in a dress." Wyatt got hard just thinking about it. "She's gorgeous."

Derek snorted. "I can't believe you got her in a dress."

"I got her to do a lot of things." Sweat broke out in his armpits.

"Hey, I don't need to know that kind of detail, okay?" Derek held his hand up. "And look, I like CJ. She's a great agent and a loyal friend, but she's not easy to get close to. If you want a future with her, you're going to have your work cut out for you. It'd be easier to just give up, pursue an easier target."

Easy for Knight to say that. He was going to marry the woman he loved.

"I can't do that. I'm going crazy wanting her. And she started wearing these tight sweaters to work, and I look at her looking right through me, and I tell you, man, I'm just gone." The beer had made him maudlin.

"Then go for it. Don't take no for an answer."

Well, that made sense. If Wyatt could corner her, kiss her, coax her, explain carefully how all her arguments were stupid and had no bearing on reality, she would see they should be together.

If her big concern was that he wouldn't stick around, well, he'd just have to prove to her that he could stick around. He'd be so stuck he'd be goddamn glue.

"Thanks, Derek."

"No problem, buddy."

                              *   *   *

It had been a mistake to put the dress on. CJ
winced as she stepped into a pair of heels she'd
borrowed from her mother and rushed past the
mirror. But she couldn't help but stroke the fabric
across her stomach and remember the look on
Wyatt's face when he had seen her in the black
dress he'd gotten for her. She didn't think a man
had ever looked at her with so much frank appreciation.

Annoyed with herself for letting her thoughts
fall back to Wyatt for the eleven millionth time in
six days, she started down the hall, her toes pinch-
ing in the shoes. She didn't want to go to this wedding alone, but it was her college roommate's,
after a long five-year engagement, and CJ couldn't
justify staying home and kicking her boxing bag
like she really wanted to.

She was cutting through the kitchen to yell out
the window that she was leaving when the doorbell
rang. Distracted, she watched Sam tumbling in a
snowdrift behind the apartment building, her
mother standing next to him, before she went to
the front door in irritation. It was probably the
neighbor's kids selling chocolate bars for sports
fund-raisers, and Lord knew she didn't need any
more chocolate. She'd eaten a bucket-load in the
past few days.

And whoever said chocolate was better than sex
had never slept with Wyatt Maddock.

CJ pulled open the door, shivering as the cold
air rushed in, and her smile froze. It wasn't the

neighbor's pudgy ten-year-old. It was Wyatt, in jeans and a black leather jacket.

Speaking of sex.

Mama. He was so damn hot, drool instantly puddled in the corner of her mouth.

"Hi," he said, giving her a smile that would have a lesser woman flinging her dress to the floor.

She was made of stronger stuff. Her nipples only headed. "Hi. What are you doing here?"

"I'm here to beg. It's Saturday night and my hot tub is just sitting there, unused, lonely without you. I've got towels and two robes all ready, just waiting for us. . . ." Another slow smile.

Her bones sagged and her inner thighs lit up like a pilot light. There was a reason she couldn't go with him—now, what was it? Oh, the wedding. And her dignity, sanity, and somewhat damaged, but not yet completely obliterated, heart. Another romp in the hot tub would take care of that.

"I have a wedding to go to." She turned around, wobbly in more ways than one, and walked back into her living room. It occurred to her that anything short of slamming the door in his face probably wasn't going to dissuade him.

It didn't. He followed her, juggling two packages in his hands. "I could go with you. I have a tux, you know. Nice dress, by the way."

Then the bastard actually winked. She wanted to string him up by his nose hairs. She had spent all week with her guts feeling like they'd been pureed in the blender, and he was just missing the good sex? "If you're looking for a good time, Wyatt, I'm sure there are plenty of women who'd eagerly jump into bed, and the hot tub, with you. Maybe Agent Dempsey's not busy."

His grin fell off his face. "But I don't love them. I love you. And I'm going crazy. Explain to me why this can't work out, CJ, because I don't get it."

Wyatt set down his packages—which were wrapped presents, if she was seeing them right—and came toward her, intent to touch her written all over his face.

Did she have to wear garlic around her neck to keep him away? Geez, almighty.

Backing up, she maneuvered until there was a couch between them.

It wasn't fair of him to use the L-word. It really wasn't, because given her need to cry into chocolate all week, and the sudden seizure of emotion she'd experienced on seeing him at her door, it was a safe bet she felt the same way. In an impractical world, love would be enough. In the reality of her complicated life, it wasn't.

"Oh, let me think. Because we work together. Because I have Sam, who on the best of days can't be called easy. And because I can't have any more kids."

He moved around the couch, determined, eyes soft, expression serious. CJ backed into a corner, her butt hitting the wall with a thump, knowing if he touched her, she'd cave.

"Why can't you have any more kids, baby?"

Swallowing hard, she stared at the collar of his jacket. She could smell his aftershave now, and his knee brushed against the skirt of her dress. "Because when my ex found out what was wrong with

Sam, he insisted I get my tubes tied so we didn't have any more kids like Sam. I did because I wanted to save my marriage."

Wyatt swore, an ugly, nasty sound made all the worse because he whispered it. "That's why we didn't need to use a rubber."

CJ nodded. "This is just not going to work out, Wyatt."

Wyatt wished she would get it through her thick skull that he didn't care about anything but being with her.

"CJ, I'm not perfect, and I'm going to make mistakes, but we'll never know unless we try. I don't care that you can't have kids, and I'd love to meet your son, but only when you're ready." He took her hand, caressed it, felt her tremble. "It could be good between us."

Leaning in, he trapped her with his arms, breathing in the light floral scent she was wearing. "I promise."

She gave a little gasp when he kissed her ear, dipping his tongue inside her. He spanned her waist with his hand, bringing her closer to him.

"You know I hate you," she whispered.

He grinned against her soft skin. She always said that right before she kissed him.

"Whatever you want to call it." He pressed his advantage and took her mouth.

Her lips were soft, pliant, and he flicked along her bottom lip with his tongue until she groaned, then wrapped her arms around his neck. She opened for him, and he dipped inside to taste her, sighing against her sweetness. He gathered her into his arms, held her tight, never wanting to give her up.

"I love you," he whispered, brushing his lips along her jaw.

"Shit," she said, quite clearly.

She opened her mouth to elaborate when a cheerful voice called out, "Christine, do you have another pair of gloves for Sam? Oh! Sorry, I didn't know you had company."

CJ made a squawking sound and tried to move away from him. He tucked her into his side and turned around. A woman he assumed was CJ's mother stared at them in astonishment, before she recovered and pasted a smile on her face.

CJ continued to tug away from him, but he held her fast and smiled back at her mother. CJ may be strong and in great shape, but he had the advantage of height and determination.

"Hi, I'm Wyatt Maddock."

"Wyatt, how nice to meet you! I'm Judith Nolan, Christine's mother." She smiled at him and shot CJ a curious look.

"Christine?" Wyatt murmured to CJ, enjoying the pink staining her cheeks. "You said your name wasn't an abbreviation for anything."

"Do I really look like a Christine Judith?"

She had him there.

A boy walked in behind CJ's mom. He was bundled up in a winter coat and hat and he was peeling soaking wet mittens off. His nose was bright red, and his brown eyes were round with curiosity. "Who's that?" He pointed at Wyatt.

"Sam, say hi to Wyatt," CJ said.

"Hi," Sam said, clearly losing interest as his eyes darted around the room.

"Hi." Wyatt smiled at Sam and marveled that he could see CJ in Sam's features. CJ was a *mother.* Damn, that was sexy.

"Are these for me?" Sam dropped his mittens on the floor and walked over to the presents resting on the coffee table.

"Sam, your mittens don't belong on the floor. Pick them up, please," CJ said in a gentle voice he'd never heard from her.

A voice that convinced him he'd stand here all damn day until she admitted that they belonged together.

Sam stopped, backtracked, stuffed the mittens in his pockets, then went right back to the presents.

"One of them is. The round one. The other one is for your mom." Nervous, he turned to CJ and whispered. "I read about autism, and the books all said that they like simple, repetitive toys that won't frustrate them. I got him a ball. Is that okay? I guess that's kind of a stupid present for winter, isn't it?"

CJ stopped trying to get away from Wyatt and stared up at him, her eyes starting to sting. He had gotten her son a ball. He looked worried. He had read up on autism, even after she had walked out on him after tossing off some pretty cruel comments Saturday night.

"Yeah, that's okay." Everything was okay. Everything was right. She owed it to herself and she owed it to Wyatt to give their relationship a chance.

Any man who bought her son a ball and could give her an orgasm in a hot tub was a keeper.

"Thanks." Sam ran out the door, new red rubber ball in tow, and promptly tripped with a splat on the front step. The ball went rolling into the bushes. Sam stood up, adjusted his hat, and ran after the ball.

Her mom headed out after him. "It was nice meeting you, Wyatt. Have fun at the wedding, Christine."

"Cute kid," Wyatt said, turning to her, his thumb running over her wrist. "He looks like you."

"Thank you." CJ didn't know what to say, where to start. So she blurted out, "I probably love you, too. There, okay? I can't help it, you're just such a nice guy."

Wyatt grinned. "You say 'nice guy' like it's a bad thing."

"I always thought you were a smooth operator, you know, or maybe I just told myself that so I wouldn't fall for you." Too late on that one. "But I have and I'm sorry for all the things I said the other night. I get defensive sometimes."

"You think?" He brushed her hair back. "I love your hair loose like this. It's so pretty and soft. I know, you're one tough cookie, and you can take care of yourself, but that doesn't mean you have to freeze everybody out either. Or hide your body."

Damn, he did not want her to hide her body anymore. He liked the dress, but he'd prefer naked even better. Now that she had admitted her feelings for him and saved him from going gray with the stress of waiting, he wanted nothing more than to take her home and love her all night.

But she was a mother, with responsibilities, and couldn't just spend the night with him any time she felt like it. He had the feeling he was going to have to get creative with their sex life. That thought made him go hard in his jeans.

"I'm working on it," she said, her face muffled against his jacket.

"We'll work on it together. We'll take it slow, all right? And you let me know how much or how little I can be in Sam's life."

Her eyes searched his. "You don't mind that I can't have any more kids? At least not without an expensive reversal."

Maybe a little, but it wasn't important right now. Hoping to reassure her, he gave her a grin. "Hey, that way none of your personality traits will be passed on."

CJ didn't laugh at his joke. She pulled away from his chest. "Take a step back for me."

"Why?" He was comfortable where he was, with her snug in his arms.

"So I can beat the crap out of you," she said quite clearly.

He laughed. She was going to keep him hopping and he was looking forward to it. "I'm kidding. Kidding. Seriously, we'll cross that bridge if and when we get to it. I just want to be with you."

CJ studied his face for a second and decided he meant it. She kissed him and sighed. What more could she ask for? Wyatt understood her, when to tease and when to be serious, and he never backed down, and somehow she knew he had staying power. Beneath the charm and the grin, he was a man of his word.

"Sounds like a plan, Wyatt." She remembered the package on her couch. "Hey, that other gift is for me, right?"

"Nah, I changed my mind."

Wyatt was running his hands over her behind, squeezing her cheeks and making her panties grow moist. His mouth was kissing a path across the front of her dress, sucking her nipple through the slippery fabric.

"You can't change your mind." CJ ducked out from under his embrace and lunged for the present. "Nice wrap job, did you pay someone to do it?"

"I did it myself," he said as he caught hold of the other end and tugged it away from her.

"Give it back, Wyatt." CJ laughed and pulled harder.

"I love your laugh," he said, looking so besotted it was damn adorable. She tugged again, thinking he deserved a nice, grinding kiss.

Then Wyatt suddenly let go, and she stumbled backward. He grinned. "Gotcha, Christine."

She whacked him with the gift on his arm. "Don't call me that."

Disposing of the wrapping paper quickly and tossing it on the floor, she started to open the box.

"Wrapping paper doesn't belong on the floor, Christine."

"Very funny." She opened the box and found the black Band-Aid bra and panties nestled in tissue. "This isn't a gift. A pain in the ass isn't a gift, and these are about as comfortable."

He shrugged. "Once I fished them out of the hot tub, I had to do something with them. I slept with them the first two nights, then figured I might as well give them back to you. You look so good in black lace."

He looked like he was kidding, but you never knew. The thought of Wyatt snuggling up to her underwear was oddly satisfying.

"And as long as you wear the sexy underwear from time to time I'll never ask you to wear a dress again. And actually, I don't care what you're wearing, I just want you with me."

She pulled the bra up and dangled it in front of her. "It will be like our little slutty secret, me wearing sexy stuff under baggy sweaters."

His jeans looked a little tight, and his eyes had darkened. "I like the way you think."

"Of course, a dress once in a while isn't so bad."

"I'd especially like to see you in white."

Though her heart did some weird kind of gallop-jump thing in her chest, she was going to ignore that one for now. "Let's go get your tux and get to this wedding." She thumped him in the chest with the bra. "I'll go put this on first."

His answer was a groan. "Don't torture me."

"What? The sooner we get there, the sooner we can leave. And as long as I'm home by midnight or so, it'll be fine."

He caught her by the arm and slid his lips across hers in a possessive kiss. "Maybe this time we'll actually make it to the bed."

She shivered and licked her lips in anticipation. "After the hot tub."

Wyatt smiled. "Now, that sounds perfect, Christine Judith."

That it did.

LAST CALL

Morgan Leigh

One

Fletcher Graham leaned back, elbows propped behind him on the polished slab of mahogany, his heels hooked on the bottom rung of the bar stool as he stared across the smoky room. The woman on the small stage was the center of attention, and she had his like a pit boss watches for cheats in his casino.

She sang a bluesy tune; her long, straight chestnut hair shielded her features every time she looked down and stroked the keys of the baby grand, one of the things the proprietor had slapped down big bucks for when he converted the old honky-tonk into a piano bar.

Her song was one that Fletcher played when no one was around to hear. He was a dyed-in-the-wool Southerner, but liking contemporary music—blues, jazz, and soulful ballads—made him an odd duck in the heart of Dixie. Country music was like breathing down here; you couldn't do without it. And in Justice, it was as sacred as the hymns that could be heard from the Southern Baptist choir every Sunday morning during church services. Listening to this stranger sing one of his favorites was refreshing.

Fletcher was glad he'd stopped by The Last Call before heading home to tons of paperwork, and infomercials to break the silence. He couldn't take his eyes off the woman. Fantasies filled his mind of that hair, dripping wet, sticking to her skin as her hands stroked *him* and urged his body to a shuddering crescendo.

His cock responded immediately to the erotic image, but he tamped down the thought as best he could. If anyone looked around from one of the tables scattered throughout the room, they'd stop the presses at the *Daily Justice* so the morning exclusive would tell how their illustrious mayor had been seen sporting a woody while downing a few at the local watering hole the night before. Slow news days in these parts meant politicians were coveted Big Game. Any transgression that made the front page would have the same effect: his head mounted on a reporter's wall, a quick death to his political career.

"Coop." He motioned the bartender over, nodding his head at the stage when his friend leaned over the bar from the other side. "Who's the new talent? She's somethin'."

Somethin' didn't begin to define what Fletcher considered the most incredible voice he'd ever heard. She captivated her audience with her rendition of "Shameless" now, and though he'd heard both the mainstream version and the country hit, the way she sang it, he felt it like a seduction. He watched her pouty lips move, her tongue dart out and lick over them as the words registered in his lust-filled brain.

"*I go down on my knees. I'm shameless.*"

The hairs on the back of his neck stood on end and his arousal grew to what felt like such mammoth proportions that he had to cross an ankle over the opposite knee. He couldn't hide his growing erection after *that* line. When two men had performed the song, he'd heard it for what it was: a committed lover, willing to grovel if need be for the woman he loved. But this time it was a woman crooning it. *That* woman, and the words took on a whole different implication.

Suppressing a growl of need, he turned his head when Coop chuckled next to him.

"Well, who is she?" he asked, obviously more than just idly curious now. The way he was sitting couldn't hide the effects that voice had on him, either.

"That, my friend"—Cooper Jones pointed a beefy finger at the woman, then back at Fletcher, his tone low with warning—"is more trouble than you want at the moment."

Fletcher shot him an annoyed glare. He and Coop had gotten into more scrapes together in their youth than most siblings did. Coop was a big, burly guy, even taller than Fletcher's six-feet-two, but most everyone in Justice knew he was a fair, honorable man, and despite their reputation as bad boys when they were young, both he and Coop were now two of the most respected men in town. For him to warn him off one of his own employees was odd, but it just fired Fletcher's blood to find out why.

As he turned his attention back to the stage just as she looked up, her gaze connected with his. His lip curled slightly as she stumbled over the words, and he winked at her before she got it back on track; she flashed him the same look he'd just given her boss, and dropped her eyes down to the keys. "Damn," he growled low. "It's got nothing to do with want, buddy. More like . . . need."

"It's your funeral, Fletch," Coop said in amusement, shaking his head and setting a cold beer on the bar by Fletcher's elbow.

"No, really. What's so bad about my interest in her? Unless—?" Fletcher tipped his head, his brow rising in question.

"No. You wouldn't be trespassing, so don't worry about that," Coop assured him. He grabbed a clean, wet glass, absently swirling the cloth around and in it, then stacking it with the others lined up, ready for the next drink order. "But after the disaster you called a marriage, I swore I'd never interfere in your love life again. I'll be apologizing for my part in *that* one for a long time to come."

Fletcher winced, recalling his ancient history. Coop had been the one to introduce him to his now ex-wife, Jane, when he'd moved home after graduating college, and saw her one night at the bar. They were so wrong for each other, and their marriage shocked everyone. Himself included. Fletcher knew almost from "I do" that it was the worst mistake he'd ever made.

At first, the signs weren't in-your-face obvious. She didn't come right out and say she wasn't cut out to be a small-town wife, that she craved a more elaborate, jet-setting lifestyle. But as he settled back into the life he'd missed while he was away at school, and he made it clear that he had no interest in using his degree in business to become a player on Wall Street, had no intention of ever leaving Justice again, in fact, she'd become distant, emotionally and physically. Things just went downhill from there. Jane went so far as to accept a consulting job that took her out of town on too many occasions. And never once did she ask her husband to join her, though he'd cleared his own schedule at the fledgling building company that employed him to be able to accompany her.

He'd had his suspicions, but she confirmed them when she came home one morning after a trip to the coast, and announced she was pregnant with some other poor sucker's child, and she was filing for divorce to be with the man. The fact that the guy had more money than Donald Trump was all Fletcher needed to know. He just thanked his lucky stars that a child had never resulted from their union before she pulled her entrapment stunt on the guy. He took his responsibilities seriously; he'd have demanded custody in a divorce. He wanted kids one day, but with a wife who shared the same values, and the same love of the town where he was born and raised.

Being reminded of that nightmare gave him pause; the woman up on that stage was in a profession that could take her all over the countryside to different clubs and bars, but somehow, he dismissed the similarities. His ex-wife was a money-grubbing gold digger, while this woman was working class, *earning* a living to feed that petite frame he could barely see behind the piano.

And just like that, his mind was off the troubles of the past and back on the delights of the present. But he wasn't totally enraptured. His memories of that black period suddenly made him more cautious than even being the mayor did.

"She's a thorn in your side," Coop said as he leaned over the bar again, speaking quietly in his ear but keeping his gaze on his employee.

Fletcher tore his eyes from the stage and her sensual take on "You Don't Know Me" to look at his friend. "What's the word, buddy?" he asked, a certain warning inflection to his tone.

Coop also met his gaze and said, "Anonymity."

"What the hell is that supposed to mean?"

"It means, don't tell her what your day job is until you get to know her."

Fletcher knew that the way he looked at the moment, no one would mistake him for the head of Justice, North Carolina. He glanced down at his old, threadbare jeans, the knees and legs dark with grease and dirt, and the scuffed cowboy boots that were the most comfortable he owned.

His T-shirt wasn't anywhere near the white it had been when he'd gone over to Toby's after work. They were restoring a classic car to its original condition, and tonight they'd been working on the engine, a filthy, hot job since there were only fans in Toby's garage to cool them off on one of the notoriously hot nights of summer in the

South. The only thing the fans had managed to do was circulate the heat, and Fletcher knew he probably smelled even worse than he looked at the moment.

But he was well known in the community, and he found it amusing that most called him "Mayor" only during working hours, and even then it seemed to come as an afterthought. He'd been elected over a year ago to an overwhelming margin, but it seemed to stun some people that he, the boy who'd trespassed on every piece of property in Justice, had played every prank that could be thought of by a precocious youth, had automatically been given a title with their vote. He didn't take offense. He was glad they demanded that he earn their respect, but had enough faith in him to give him a chance. If they never called him "Mayor," he wouldn't care. They knew that no matter how disheveled he looked, or how unruly, he had their best interests, and that of the community, in mind whenever he made a decision or signed an ordinance.

He couldn't suppress a sinking feeling as he turned his eyes back to the woman. He didn't even know her name and already thoughts of betrayal were like a knife twisting in his gut. "Tell me she's not like Jane, Coop," he said, knowing no matter how cryptic his friend was being about her identity, he wouldn't steer Fletcher wrong again.

"Nope. She's nothing like that social-climbing bi—" he said, cutting off his diatribe as Fletcher turned his head to give him a pointed look. He cleared his throat. "Sorry. But no, that woman and your ex couldn't be more different if they'd been born on opposite poles. Pride and self-respect alone set the two of them apart." Coop nodded his head, motioning out at the stage as the crowd's applause died down and she took Fletcher on another sensual ride, singing "Sweet Dreams." He imagined her song was just for him.

Coop's voice interrupted his thoughts once again. "She's got more damned pride in her little finger than Jane had in her whole body."

"So what's wrong with her?" They'd come full circle, back to his original question, and Fletcher felt his annoyance level kick up a notch.

"Let's just say that, for you, she's trouble with a capital T."

"Oh, right here in River City?" he asked sarcastically, laughing at Coop's menacing tone.

"I'm serious, buddy. Be careful. She's a good woman, but you won't know it if you let other things interfere."

He craned his neck farther around. "Who are you, The Riddler?" he asked.

Coop shrugged. "Just remember what I said, Fletch."

He'd had enough. "And on that note, I'll be headin' out." Sliding off the bar stool, Fletcher threw some bills on the bar.

Coop just as carelessly threw them back at him. "This is your place, too, pal. Silent partner or not, your money's no good comin' from that side of the bar."

"Then take it for the advice, though you didn't tell me a *damn* thing," he replied, grinning, but it slid off his face as Coop's jaw clenched, and

Fletcher realized it was the first time his friend had ever kept something from him.

Fletcher glanced at the stage one more time, and the woman whose eyes conveyed her disappointment that he was obviously leaving. He liked that. He grinned, and dipped his head, pulling his fingers down on the brim of an imaginary cowboy hat. He turned back to Coop. "You're keeping a secret for her."

"Not for her. For you, *Mayor*," he said quietly, his emphasis on the last word unmistakable.

"I'll see ya, Coop," Fletcher said, too tired to decipher his friend's encoded messages and needing a little distance from the very distraction they'd been discussing. Even when she didn't have his undivided attention, her voice still managed to skitter along his spine, traveling around to keep him hard and aching. He needed air. Even if it was the hot, humid kind that he knew he'd encounter the second he walked outside.

"Take it easy, buddy," his friend called over his shoulder as he took a drink order from one of the patrons who stepped up to the bar.

Before Fletcher stepped out, Coop cast a meaningful look in his direction. Why couldn't Coop just tell him? Fletcher wondered, but left the noise and smoke behind, the quiet, black night hitting him like a wall of heat as he pondered what his best friend was trying to hint at. They'd never kept anything from each other in all the years he'd known him. Why the hell would Coop clam up now when it was obvious that Fletcher had an interest in the lovely singer? It was mind-boggling, and more than his taxed brain cared to figure out tonight.

Fletcher spotted the car with New York plates in the parking lot. Not giving himself time to think about how he should be home, going over papers for Tuesday night's town meeting, he turned back to the bar, using his key to the back door, and ducked into the men's room to rinse some of the filth from his dark blond hair, face, and arms. Nothing could be done about his clothes, he thought, but at least he wouldn't smell like yesterday's trash.

From there, he went to the office he shared with Coop and occupied himself by looking over the accounts that he'd neglected in the past month or so, watching the clock until the bar closed. When "Last Call" was shouted above the din, signaling that the bar was clearing out, Fletcher waited another twenty minutes or so, then straightened up the desk and left the building the same way he'd come, quietly and unnoticed. The odd thing was that there was nothing in the office that mentioned that woman's name. Not a W-2, not a pay stub, nothing.

While he made a mental note to discuss that with Coop—the labor board wasn't to be messed with—he decided that he'd just wait and find out for himself a little more about this woman. If his friend wasn't willing to reveal her secrets, then Fletcher was just going to have to go to the source to get the information he was looking for.

* * *

Tess capped her water bottle and tossed it into her backpack as she left the bar through the back door, shutting off lights as she went. She was still thinking about the man who'd watched her so intently while she sang, and how disappointed she was that he'd left before she could meet him. After her last set, she'd gone up to the bar as she always did and asked Cooper the man's name. He told her, and said he was his best friend, but he was sketchy about any more details except that he was single, and not involved at the moment. She'd been here a month and she'd never seen him. But Tess knew her work hours were strange to most people, so she didn't give it much thought.

Coop's endorsement was good enough for her. She just wished she'd been able to get closer than twenty feet from the man. A whole room away, he'd made her skin tingle; his eyes skating over her had felt like an actual caress. She sighed, wondering what he'd be able to do to her with only a breath separating them. She made a cooing sound deep in her throat as she considered the possibilities. She definitely wanted to find out.

She rounded the corner of the building and stopped short. The mystery man himself was leaning on her car, looking way too delicious in his messy T-shirt and jeans.

He must've washed some of the grunge from himself in the men's room. His dark blond hair still had streaks of grease through it, but it wasn't as mussed as it was when he'd been in the bar. His face was clean, but oh, his jaw was rough with stubble. Those powerful forearms were crossed over his chest, scrubbed free of grime as well, as he leaned casually against the driver's door, effectively blocking her from her car. Her mouth quirked up in a half smile; he was trying to look presentable and less threatening when nothing but a hot shower and a change of clothes would do that. But Tess was charmed anyway. And she was well aware that even if he were in black tie and tails, he'd still look a little bit dangerous and devilishly sexy.

When she reached the car, she flipped her long hair out of her eyes and tipped her head up at him. "Stranded, are you, Fletcher?" she asked, struggling to keep her composure. She couldn't let him know just how hot she was at the moment. And it wasn't the sweltering humidity that hung so heavy in the air. He'd waited for her! She'd never felt the instant attraction she did with this man and she didn't want to blow it. The urge to lower her voice seductively and entice him, as he'd so easily done just by looking at her during her set, was a temptation.

But a spark ignited in his eyes and almost sucked a whimper from her throat. Those looks were going to be lethal to any resistance she might harbor.

"You know my name," he said quietly, almost a whisper, but she heard, and damn if she didn't feel that voice dance down her spine.

Not only that, but Tess heard the arrogance that brought out her own challenging nature. She rose to the bait. "Not many men can make me lose my way through a song. It seemed prudent to ask

about you. But Coop didn't tell me much—just
that you work for the town."

His brow rose in question.

Oh, this was a bad boy if she'd ever seen one!
"Uh-huh. When he said that, I'd already figured
you work with your hands, so I know that you're
the mechanic for the town vehicles."

His mouth curved. "Is that right?"

Was that a glimmer of amusement in his eyes?

She shrugged, hoping she appeared nonchalant. "I asked for details, but he said it would be
more interesting to ask *you* if I wanted to know
more." She stepped closer, gazing up at him, and
his breath fanned her lips as he stared down at
them. Oh yeah, she had his undivided attention,
all right.

He didn't budge as she leaned a little closer—
only his eyes moved; they lifted to hers and she almost gasped at the passion that lurked in those
dark green eyes. His blond-tipped lashes were
long, and Tess imagined them brushing her cheeks
as he whispered naughty things into her ear.

Whoa, there! She slammed on the brakes, knowing she was getting a little ahead of herself. She
wished she felt those alarm signals that always went
off in her head when she was ready to do something foolish. But although she was practically un-
dressing the man with her eyes, those warning
bells remained silent. He made her pulse race,
and she worried that her inner radar might be out
of whack, but only a stupid woman would ignore
his sexual energy. The day she'd found out about

that snake Jacob's infidelity was the day she stopped being stupid. "Tell me more, Fletcher."

He opened his mouth to say something, but his eyes clouded a little, like something had just occurred to him. Instead, he lowered his head—that stubble she'd imagined the feel of was softly abrasive—sending shivers up her spine as his lips kissed the shell of her ear. "You first," he breathed.

"Huh?" Tess couldn't think when he was this close. He still looked grubby and rugged, but he smelled of soap, a hint of sweat and hard work, and some lingering cologne that she suspected, when it wasn't masked by the other harsher scents, would be too powerful for her to resist.

He grinned against her cheek. "Tell me your name, darlin'."

"Oooh," she sighed, leaning ever closer, but not quite touching. His jaw grazed her skin, his hot breath turning her knees to jelly. "It . . . it's . . . Tess."

He pulled away so abruptly that she almost stumbled, and she looked up at him in surprise. The shock on his face didn't diminish his rugged good looks, but it sure snapped her out of the haze of lust he'd immersed them in. Like a bucket of cold water!

Two

"What's the matter?" Here she'd been worried that the heat this man generated would make her do foolish things, and now all she wanted was to see that lazy smile again, the casual stance. Without even touching him, she sensed that he was coiled tighter than a spring. Why?

"Tess Braeden? Roy Braeden's granddaughter? The woman who—"

"Keeps phoning city hall, putting in repeated requests for an appointment with your mayor? The one who, by his secretary's definition, borders on harassment? Yeah, that's me. My reputation precedes me, I see," she said dryly, the cloud of lust completely cleared now.

Man, she thought. Word really did get around in a small town. Even the mechanic knew her name. Despite acceptance from her own boss, she wasn't scoring many points with the other people who mattered in the community. Not the board of the historical society, which refused to give her some time; not the mayor, who was like a ghost— never available, always in one meeting or another; and now, not with a man who made her want to pull his mouth down to hers and taste that bead of sweat on his upper lip. She'd never taken so many wrong turns in her life!

"I was going to say the woman who inherited that broken-down old house on the corner of Main and Elm, but okay, let's go with your answer and discuss that."

"Let's not," she sneered, and stepped back, giving him room. "Now, if you'll excuse me, I'll be on my way home to that broken-down old house."

"I'm sorry, honey, but it *is* a wreck." His chuckle and teasing grin mocked her.

Tess shrugged and looked away, but her belly fluttered at the endearment. She liked the way everyone down here was "darlin'" or "honey." In the city, she'd probably clock some guy if he called her that, but with this man, in this place, it felt good, even when it didn't mean a thing.

And she couldn't really argue the point about the condition of her house. The damn thing *was* an eyesore, but it wasn't her fault. It had fallen into disrepair when her grandfather passed away. She didn't even know she *had* a grandfather until two months ago. But after the two years it took them to locate her, the place was barely livable. Not just structural repair, but so much wiring and pipe replacement were needed to bring it up to code that she almost shuddered, thinking of it.

Back taxes and outstanding loans were owed on the Victorian, which must have brought glorious charm to Justice in its day. She couldn't touch a thing until she coughed up the dough to claim it legally. She felt like a squatter in her own house.

It hurt that it wasn't really hers yet. It was in a type of foreclosure limbo. She needed to pay off the debts, and she only had two months left to do it. Because it was old enough to be marked for historical status, the house and property would revert to the town instead of the bank if she couldn't come up with the money. While she was grateful for that loophole that kept the place protected, the looming deadline was creeping up on her faster than she could formulate a plan to keep it. But this was her chance to have a normal life, to be settled, and she wanted it more than anything.

"As for moving so you can get in your car and drive away, forget it."

Her eyes shot to his. Who did he think he was?

He bent his head to her again, so close she could almost taste his breath mint as his mouth hovered near hers. She wouldn't be the one to back off, though she knew she should. Something about him made her want to be daring, a little bit brazen. And in a town like Justice, where gossip was dished out with the best apple pie at Loretta's Diner, she couldn't afford any more rumors or speculation being bandied around about her. She was aware that most of the patrons started coming to the bar not to hear her sing, but to see who that city girl was who'd staked a claim in their quiet little corner of the world.

Oh, if they only knew!

Fletcher made it increasingly hard to concentrate as his thumb skimmed along her jawline and his gaze pinned her in his sights. Distraction was good. And he was a pro.

"We made a connection the second we looked at each other, Tess, and that hasn't happened to me in a long time."

She swallowed a moan that built in the back of her throat and willed her eyes to remain open. God, she wanted him, and she'd only just met him! But he was right about their connection. She remembered seeing him at the bar. She'd even sadistically drawn his attention back from Coop when they were talking by putting a little more sensuality into the words than she normally did. But if he hadn't winked at her when she screwed up, she wouldn't have felt the need for payback. Well, *probably* not, she mused. The warm liquid pooling between her thighs when his eyes settled on her might have had something to do with her teasing behavior. She liked being watched and desired by him. While she was singing, she'd imagined his lips sliding against hers, exciting her, making love to her. And somehow he knew what she'd been thinking.

Oh, she hoped he was just as astute now. Tess tore her eyes from his and focused on his lips.

He tipped up her chin. "I like a woman with determination. But I don't see how the mayor can do anything for you."

Damn! Not as quick as she'd hoped. In her mind, they were already naked and needy, but he was back to the subject of the mayor. "What are you talking about?" Tess shook her head, putting a cap on her desire to concentrate, but it made her testy, impatient. And she didn't like standing in the empty parking lot, late at night, letting this man turn her stupid with his looks and teasing strokes along her cheek when he clearly wasn't on the same page.

The only reason Cooper knew about her situation was because she listed her address at the Old Vic, as she'd dubbed her house, on her application for employment at The Last Call. He knew about the money owed on the place. But for that one exception, she never discussed her personal business with anyone, so she wondered how Fletcher seemed to think he could pull it out of her effortlessly. "You have no idea what the mayor can do for me, Fletcher," she said bitterly, stepping back from the temptation she'd lost herself in for a short while. "If he'd see me, he'd learn that I could do something for him, too."

Fletcher knew his whole body had gone rigid, and his teeth clenched in a rage he fought to suppress. Did she think she could bribe a city official? *Him?* Feelings he hadn't had since his ex-wife screwed his life over began to rise like bile to the back of his throat.

She'd thrown him for a loop when she told him her name, but he'd recovered quickly, knowing there was more to Coop's warning that he not tell Tess that he was the man she was so desperate to see. For a guy who said he wouldn't mess with Fletcher's love life again, he'd done a damn good job of it without even saying a word. He trusted his friend, but he couldn't ignore Tess's last statement.

His eyes bore accusingly into hers, his voice rough, almost menacing, as he tested the waters. "I hope you're not implying what it sounds like you are, Tess. Not only is it illegal, it's immoral. And I would hope that you'd have more respect for yourself than that."

She squared off with him, and he was able to see her eyes. They were hazel, he determined. But flecks around the outer rim turned them the color of honey. Sweet, golden honey that made him ache, wondering if she'd taste like honey, too. He'd never let himself find out if Coop was wrong and she'd do anything, even degrade herself, for a piece of property.

"First, I'm going to let that remark go, since we've only just met. Second," she said, ticking off her list on her fingers, "I've bent the law a time or two—speeding up at a yellow light, knowing it'll turn red before I get completely through the intersection—but I've never actually broken one in my life. And the places I've been, there have been plenty of opportunities. Take my word on that."

Fletcher's muscles began to relax. Her indignation almost matched his disgust for what he assumed she was saying without actually saying it. He was relieved she wouldn't use her wiles to get what she wanted from the mayor. From him.

Her finger poked his chest. "And lastly"—her

eyes lost some of their luster—"I like you, Fletcher. And you're right—we did make a connection—"

She flattened her hand on his chest, using the other to slide up his neck, into his hair. He wasn't prepared for her to pull his head down, or for her scorching kiss, for the way her tongue felt sliding deliciously along his. Gawd, she tasted sweet! Like honey, just as he'd suspected.

With a groan, he deepened the kiss, his hands moving around to cup her heart-shaped behind, pulling her closer against his growing erection. He wanted her with a passion he hadn't felt in so damn long! But when he turned them, pressing her against the car, she surprised the hell out of him again.

She broke the kiss, saying throatily, "As I was saying. We did make a connection, Fletcher." Her tongue licked over her lips. Reaching behind her, she opened the door. He took a step back when she pushed against him insistently, maneuvering around and slipping into the driver's seat. She gazed up at him through the open window, turned the ignition, and looked at his confused expression. "But now you're gonna have to work for it."

It took him a minute to gather his wits to understand what had just happened. *She'd turned him on, then just as quickly, shut him down.* A smile spread across his face, and he laughed harshly, ignoring his painful erection. *I've been put in my place, good 'n' proper,* he thought. Oh yeah, this one was worth the chase.

Taking a deep breath, he tipped his head, grant-

ing her the point in their little teasing game. "I'll
see you tomorrow, Tess."

"Tomorrow's my day off. Saturdays are still tra-
ditionally wild country nights at Last Call."

He just grinned at her. "I know." His eyes full of
meaning, he repeated, "I'll see you tomorrow,
Tess."

He tapped on the roof of the car, and his groin
tightened again as she let out a mewing sound as
he walked away. He didn't have to look to know
she was watching him; he could feel her eyes burning into him as he turned the corner of the building to where his own car was parked.

Yup, he thought. He'd see her tomorrow, and
every day after that, until he knew what she wanted
with him as the mayor, and what she might need
from him as a man. That last part he anticipated
like a kid on Christmas Eve.

But damn! *She* was Tess Braeden! Why did it
have to be this complicated? He shook his head,
her words coming back to him as he pulled his
keys from his pocket, *Now you're gonna have to work
for it.*

Well, that was true, he figured. The best things
in life came from hard work and planning. And
he'd work for it, all right. That kiss had singed his
nerve endings, but it was way too brief for his liking. A mere prelude to what they'd experience together, if he played his cards right.

He needed more of that connection, but
Cooper was wise to tell him to be careful. Finding
out what her angle was had to take precedence

over his lust. He didn't know what she had in store for the mayor, but for the good of the citizens of Justice, and for his own peace of mind, he planned to find out, *before* he took her to bed. He had no doubt that that was where they were headed.

Three

Tess stumbled from the bed, shaky and groggy from what little sleep she'd gotten and being abruptly pulled from it. One eye open, she raked her tangled, mussed hair out of her face, spying the clock on the table as she headed down the hall to put an end to that incessant pounding. Who the hell would have the nerve to darken her doorway at seven o'clock on a Saturday morning?

She hit the bottom landing of the stairs, and her curiosity grew along with her agitation. Whoever the potential homicide victim was, he was at her back door, and by the time she got to it, she almost wasn't kidding.

Opening the door, and squinting against the bright, early morning sun she made a point never to see, she shouted, *"What?"*

Despite her cranky attitude, the answering chuckle sent shivers up her spine. Then Fletcher's voice penetrated the door-banging still reverberating in her head. "Well now, that's a good tip. You're not a morning person. I'll keep that in mind, darlin'."

She still squinted, but seeing him standing there, in a clean T-shirt and jeans, a tool belt hanging low on his hips, even to her addled brain he looked mouthwatering.

She wasn't awake yet, or she'd have attempted to be more pleasant. But that knocking put him on her shit list. "Not until I've had at least four hours' sleep—which you missed by sixty minutes, by the way—and about two pots of coffee," she groused. "Besides, who the hell comes calling this early?"

She couldn't focus with the morning sun pouring in around his big body. She was thankful he at least blocked the blinding light a bit. She got migraines, getting up this early and trying to think.

"Calling?" He chuckled. Then to add to her ire, he made fun of her, exaggerating his southern drawl to sound like a true good ol' boy. "Why, ma'am. The man who's gonna patch up your leaky roof. Now, I know it's sunny, but they're predictin' rain come late day, so I reckon I better get started early, to beat the storm, don'tcha know? In these parts, you only have to wait a little while, and the weather will change faster than a chameleon tryin' to avoid bein' dinner for some predator."

Tess didn't mean to sound condescending, but he wouldn't let her get away with it, regardless. "Okay, I got it!" She laughed. "Stop talking like that. But I swear, if your nickname is Bubba, this conversation is *over*."

He didn't dignify that with a response. Instead he said, "You look incredibly sexy this early, honey."

That got her eyes open. Wide. She looked down, horrified that she stood there in nothing but a cropped tank top and high-cut white panties. "Shit!" she shrieked.

"Wait—" Fletcher said, holding up a hand, but the door swung shut, and she raced back down the hall. Turning the corner at Mach speed, she scrambled up the stairs to grab her robe from the back of the bedroom door.

No one had visited her since she'd moved in, and she couldn't afford anything more than fans in the house, so it was too hot to sleep in anything more than what she had on, she justified to herself. She'd considered sleeping in the nude, but this was an old, rickety house, and it needed an electrical overhaul. She wasn't psychic, but she was smart enough to know that if the damn place caught fire, it would go up like tinder, and she had to have *something* on, just in case she had to get out quickly.

But answering the door like that was just asking for trouble. And Fletcher was trouble, all right, she thought. Trouble to her libido, dangerous to her heart.

If he'd had the decency to wait a few hours, her head wouldn't have been so fuzzy, and she'd have remembered to throw on her robe. It was *his* fault. She hardly knew the man, but she knew he wasn't a bit contrite. Just like last night, when she'd looked right into his eyes and forgotten the words to her song. No, Tess concluded, he *liked* her to be a little off-kilter.

She brushed her teeth quickly, but didn't bother to do anything with her hair. He'd already seen that she looked like the Bride of Frankenstein when she'd answered the door. She was too anxious to care that she had bedhead and looked a mess. She wanted to know the real reason why Fletcher was there at such an ungodly hour.

With her heavy terry robe on, the belt securely fastened around her waist, she started down the stairs again.

She could hear him puttering around down there, and oddly, she didn't feel a bit of angst that he'd come on in, making himself at home in her kitchen. She hadn't paid any mind to the bag in his hand when she'd opened the door; his body was too distracting to notice anything else, except that tool belt. She loved a man who worked with his hands, and she'd just bet that hard, sweaty work came naturally to him. He had broad shoulders, hard pecs that she imagined tapered to washboard abs and into his slim hips. His biceps stretched the sleeves of his T-shirts. Not like a bodybuilder, but more like a toned athlete. His hair was a dark blond, like fresh wheat, and she itched to run her fingers through it. Maybe when he came down off her roof, she thought, grinning to herself. Staring at his butt when he'd walked away from her car last night had been a veritable feast for her eyes. She knew wondering what he looked like naked would pale to actually seeing him. She had a pretty vivid imagination, but Tess equated it to viewing the sculpture of David fully clothed. It just wouldn't be the same.

Her attraction was building like an unstoppable

force, and she didn't even try. That should make those alarm bells go off again, but just like last night, they remained silent.

Her last boyfriend had cheated on her, and she'd had an inkling beforehand; her instincts were more attuned to trouble than she was. She wished she hadn't had to go through all that drama, but it gave her confidence that this time, she was interested in a man who could be trusted.

The delicious aroma of coffee and biscuits wafted up as she paused on the stairs, listening as he hummed a song she'd sung last night. Tess covered her mouth to hide the giggle that she very nearly couldn't suppress. She was pleased that she'd made an impression on him, just as he had on her. Too bad he couldn't carry a tune in a bucket, she mused.

Then the smile faded and her breath caught, as she recalled the exact impression he'd made on her the night before. She'd kissed him in the parking lot, and she'd carried those incredibly erotic feelings he evoked with her into slumber.

She'd had truly decadent fantasies in the night; he was the man who'd brought her ecstasy in her sleep. No wonder she'd awakened time and again, hot and breathless, despite her scant attire. In her dreams, Fletcher's lovemaking was hungry, primal, and voracious. Tess hoped that in the near future, he'd take her to those heights of pleasure for real.

She looked down at herself and hunched her shoulders; there was no mistaking that her nipples were hard, visibly aroused even through the layers of clothing. She rounded the corner and glanced at the mirror as she passed it. There was no help for her flushed skin, either. She'd chalk up her appearance to her mad dash to cover herself. No use scaring him off, looking like a complete tramp, she thought. But she'd have no excuse for the moan that threatened to escape her lips as she came up short at the entrance to the kitchen. Fletcher was there, one hip cocked as he leaned over the table, one palm flat on the surface as he sipped his coffee, staring down at the lyrics she'd tried unsuccessfully to concentrate on last night. His image had kept fogging her mind and she couldn't put two words together, let alone put them into verse, and she'd finally given up at four A.M. to go to bed. Which was why seven A.M. was way too early for anyone to expect her to be polite.

She bit down hard on her lip, keeping silent as she leaned against the doorway, watching him pick up the paper, his expression perplexed as if he were trying to figure out a deeper meaning than the one she'd written.

His head jerked up when he spotted her out of the corner of his eye, and the lust was there, but so was the disappointment. "Aw, honey. I liked your first outfit better," he said, casting her a sad, pathetic look.

"I'm sure you did." Pushing away from the door, she reached for the cup he offered before settling back against the frame. "But I usually save that for the mailman. I like to give him a little thrill a couple times a week, ya know?"

"Cute," he said, but tipped his head, his voice filled with warning. "Do be careful, though, Tess. Justice *is* a small town, but occasionally we have our share of drifters pass through."

Her mouth tipped up in a grin, and her belly warmed with his concern, but she was a big girl—a city girl at that. She could take care of herself. "Most drifters don't beat down your door if they want something, Fletch. And if I hadn't unlocked the door, you wouldn't have gotten in. I made sure both of them and all the windows were secure when I took up residence." She shrugged. "A condition of my life in the city."

"Right. Sorry. I know you're an adult, but if any other man had seen what I just did, he wouldn't have been able to control his lust."

"You controlled yours," she pointed out.

His deep growl and the way his eyes raked over her made her shiver in delight. "Barely. If you hadn't slammed that door in my face, I might *not* have. And you didn't relock it before you made your escape," he countered.

"Maybe subconsciously, I didn't want to lock you out."

He groaned, taking a deep breath. "It's a good thing I'm an honorable man, Tess. Words like that could get you into trouble." His brow raised in warning.

"If I didn't trust you, I'd be locked in my bedroom, on my cell, waiting for the sheriff to get here and haul you off to your own cell—in jail. Trespassing is against the law. And though you wouldn't be breaking in, I'm pretty sure entering without permission would be considered illegal."

"Good girl," he said, his face conveying his admiration for her confidence and common sense.

His smile nearly knocked her to her knees,

though. She was no shrinking violet, despite her mortification at being caught nearly naked answering her door. She was glad he wasn't the type who saw women as weak, needing a man for protection. She appreciated his warning, but she didn't *need* it. Now . . . other needs, she thought wryly. That was a whole different story.

Tess was enjoying their banter. The kitchen was cozy, heating up as they went back and forth, bringing the conversation around to the passion they both felt, but only subtly spoke of. Sidestepping their desire would get old quick, but she was glad he could contain his lust until she was comfortable with him. She only hoped she could control her own!

She gave him her full attention as he put her papers and his coffee cup on the table, and in that slow, sexy gait strolled across the room to take her own cup from her, setting it on the counter beside her.

How he was able to get her under his spell so easily, she didn't know. Maybe she *did* need his warnings, because when he stepped close, looking down at her, his chest brushing hers, she knew she'd do anything he wanted.

"Kiss me again, Tess," he said in that low, gravelly voice. She felt the rumble in his chest, sending tingling sensations to her taut, aching nipples, and as she looked up into those deep green eyes, she did exactly as he asked, one hand sliding up into his hair, the other gripping that tool belt as she rose on her tiptoes to reach his lips, desperate to feel them touch hers again.

He dipped his head and met her halfway, his

mouth crashing down on hers and swallowing her sigh, avidly coaxing her to open wider for him. He took complete possession of the kiss, and she let him, delighting in the taste of the coffee on his tongue as it darted into her mouth and tangled with hers. What a delicious way to get her caffeine fix!

He changed the angle of the kiss, but she was able to take a quick, excited breath before his lips fused with hers again. He pushed her hand away from his tool belt, unbuckled it, and dropped it to the floor with a thud.

Pulling her flush against the hard angles of his body, his hands went to her rib cage and he lifted her, pressing his arousal tightly to her cleft. She heard him shudder through his own breathing as she squirmed between the door's frame and his. Her robe opened and her fingers dug into his shoulders, getting as close as she could, one leg sliding along the rough denim of his jeans, the friction so sensual she moaned into his mouth.

Every inch of her flesh was stimulated, and as his lips left hers to lick and suckle at the column of her throat, she couldn't stand the feelings anymore. She cried out, and her entire body tensed. His answering groan and the insistent rocking of his hips brought her orgasm on like a freight train barreling into her, and she shuddered, her head gnashing against the wood as she ground herself down on his powerful erection.

"Be still, darlin'," he said, his voice strained and harsh. "Tess, honey, you're gonna make me—"

But she didn't listen. Her passion had a grip on her and she wrapped her feet around his calves, the pulsing throb of his arousal prolonging her pleasure.

A joyful laugh of sweet satisfaction resounded through the room, but his groan was louder and longer as he buried his face in her neck. Sliding his hands down to her buttocks, he pulled her hard against him, and she felt the unmistakable signal of his approaching climax.

Her hips rolled, her thighs flexed, and she deliberately dragged him over the edge with her. Fletcher shuddered in her arms, his breath rushing fast, then stopped altogether as he let himself go.

The slim doorframe dug into the length of her spine; she knew their early morning coupling might leave a bruise along her back, but he sighed her name, his hot, wet lips gliding over her throat to the upper curve of her breast as he savored his release, and Tess had never felt more alive than she did in that moment. *What a rush!* She closed her eyes, and he held her weight as she slumped between him and the doorframe, spent and sated. For the moment. Where the *hell* were those alarms bells in her head?

"Wowza. Good morning to you, too, Fletcher," she whispered. Wrapping her arms around his head, she kissed the top of it, combing her fingers through his thick hair as he caught his breath.

Four

Fletcher trailed his kisses back up to Tess's lips. He couldn't get enough of the taste of her! Maybe the idea of warm honey filled his head when he thought of her, or looked at her, but he'd swear that even with the hint of minty toothpaste on her tongue, he could taste the sweet essence of the natural confection.

He lowered her, her belly riding along the now-wet spot on his jeans, and aftershocks of pleasure still flowed through him. Her plump breasts were sensitive as they grazed down his chest, and her own body wracked with the same sensations.

Damn, but he didn't mean for this to happen!

She looked up at him expectantly, but he was too stunned to offer an explanation, or even an apology.

"Oh no, you regret it already, don't you?" she said, disappointment etched all over her face.

As much as he hated himself at the moment—
he'd let himself down as well as the people of this
town who counted on him to make sound, rational
decisions—Fletcher hated the look on her face
even more. He shook his head, turning away from
the temptation.

Raking his fingers through his hair only reminded him of how her fingers felt when she did
it. He covered his face, then propped his hands on
his hips, dropping his chin to his chest. *Get a grip!*
he warned himself. There wasn't any divine inter-
vention to get him out of this down there on the
floor. *Better face the music.*

He brought his gaze up to meet hers. She stood
there, her robe still hanging open, just as he'd left
her, teeth sunk into her lip. The glint of a belly
piercing drew his focus south; he hadn't paid any
attention to it, but it was a damn sight better than
looking at her face, her hopes sinking deeper with
every second he avoided the issue.

"The only regret I have is that it was too fast."

She sighed in relief, and he wanted to take her
in his arms, assure her that he wanted her again,
and again, but he didn't dare. She was flushed and
he'd left marks on her pale skin.

She glanced down at his jeans, and the mess
he'd made with his stupid lust. She caught his eye
again, and put up a finger, going to the door off
the kitchen.

She came back with a pair of dark sweatpants in
her hand. "These are huge on me, but they're
clean. I usually wear them on cold nights, but it's

been too hot. I only just unpacked them yesterday to put them in storage until winter, but you can borrow them while I wash your clothes."

"Tess, you really don't have to do that—I'll be fine." Fletcher picked up on what she said. She was staying? *Until winter?* That was months away. The puzzle was more complicated than he first assumed.

"You'll be uncomfortable, and it'll give us a chance to talk while they wash. I need to explain some things to you."

It was the opening he'd been hoping for. He'd come to help her with the roof—Coop said she had buckets all over the place when it rained—but he really wanted to know what she planned to do. It was an opportunity he couldn't refuse. He still wouldn't tell her who he was. Not yet. But at least he'd know where she stood, and where he fit in, as the mayor, and as a lover

Taking the clothes from her, he went into the same room to change, and Fletcher shook his head, his mouth turning up in a grin as he saw her close her robe again and tie a double knot in the sash this time. "That's kind of like closing the barn door after the horses have already left, darlin'."

"Well, I didn't expect that to happen, and I'm not sorry for it, either, but I won't flaunt myself in front of you. I'm no tease."

Fletcher changed into the sweats that fit him perfectly, wondering if they'd belonged to a previous lover. The thought made his gut tighten. He didn't want to know about other men in her life. But he didn't delude himself into thinking she hadn't had any. She was the hottest thing to hit Justice in years.

Jane was the last one. *Okay,* Fletcher thought. The memory of his ex-wife put his lust in an icy-cold lake. Problem solved.

She came up behind him and took his clothes, throwing them in the washer as he crossed his arms over his chest and leaned against the dryer, watching her. Coop was right. Jane and Tess were two very different women. His ex wouldn't have cared if Fletcher was uncomfortable or not. But Tess didn't even give a thought to saving him the embarrassment of walking out of here with a stain on his jeans. And she didn't even know why the prospect might bother him. He felt like a horny teenager, but the outcome didn't bother him at all. And no way would Jane have engaged in a quickie before her hair was brushed, and she was dressed, and had had her breakfast. He tamped down the bitterness he felt for the woman who'd wronged him and focused on the one who'd pleasured him. He liked a woman who was spontaneous, and Fletcher liked Tess more and more by the minute. He tucked her long hair behind her ear. "Any other time, I'd say feel free to be comfortable in your own home, but you're right. Walking around without the robe on wouldn't be wise, given our lack of control. And we should talk. Me first."

"Let's sit down, then. I want some more coffee, and I think I smell biscuits."

He grinned. Yup, this was the woman for him, he thought, as he watched her sit down and dig into the food he'd picked up at the diner on his way over. She was a tiny thing, five-foot-five maybe, and willowy thin, but not from lack of appetite. She ate two biscuits before leaning back, one hand over her belly and the ring in her navel, now obstructed by the robe. Gawd, he wanted another look at it!

She drank the rest of her coffee, setting the cup on the heavy oak table in front of her, and licked her lips. "Okay, you've fed me, and I've had at least a minimum of caffeine. What do you want to talk about?"

"All right, I believe in straight shooting. What do you want from me, Tess?"

She tipped her head. "From you? I thought I made myself clear last night when I told you I liked you. I couldn't have *been* more obvious. Not to mention what just happened against that wall," she replied, pointing across the room.

Fletcher's jaw clenched. Damn, he'd almost blown it! He meant to ask what she wanted from the mayor, but he'd been distracted, watching her settle back in the chair, shadows darkening the kitchen as the storm clouds he'd warned of began to block out the sun.

"Point taken. And I like you, too, darlin'." His eyes slid to the washer, now on the spin cycle. "Obviously."

She very nearly purred as she sat up, folding her hands on the surface of the table. "What you *really* want to know is, does wanting you have anything to do with your mayor, since you work for him, right?"

Damn, he hated being put on the spot. And he

didn't like knowing that his assumptions last night had stuck with her. "Tess—"

"No, it's okay. I understand. But I'll explain what I meant last night, and then you'll know that the only interest I have in you is on a personal level."

"I don't think you'll use me, Tess. I won't let you. But I'm sorry that this is between us."

"Please, Fletcher?" she said, covering his hand.

There was that connection again, that gut-twisting feeling that he couldn't shake. He was pretty sure she wouldn't screw with him like Jane had. But if he wasn't careful, when she learned his secret, he could hurt her enough to drive her away. He'd gone to bed with her kiss on his lips, and erotic dreams of her made him awaken, hot and hard. No, he didn't want to scare her off.

Since he'd won the election, sex was merely a relief of the tension, a mutual session of give-and-take. It didn't mean anything but the physical satiation he and his partner derived from it. His job had become his mistress. But with Tess, it was more. She made his blood surge hot, and his cock hardened like a rock whenever he thought of her. Hell, they hadn't even undressed, and already, they'd both come. From a kiss, no less! He had a constant hard-on, even after that explosive climax. But that wasn't what kept his butt in the seat. It was his desire to discover her secrets and, eventually, come clean with his own.

He turned his hand up, lacing his fingers through hers. "Tell me, then."

She nodded, and squeezed before letting his

hand go. Padding over to the sideboard, she pulled a stack of documents out of a drawer.

Fletcher couldn't take his eyes off her. *God, she's beautiful*, he thought. She walked with the grace of a dancer, and she didn't even realize how sexy she looked when she flipped her hair back, which she did all the time.

She turned the light switch on as she came back to the table, setting the papers in front of him, one hand resting on his shoulder and her breast just inches from his cheek. If he turned his head . . . *no!* He needed to get a grip!

He forced his eyes to the papers, and his own signature staring back at him. Jesus! Good thing he was sitting down! Thank God he was known by his middle name—everything he signed was as G. F. Graham. He swallowed hard.

Tess didn't seem to notice. "Now, these are the letters I've gotten from Mayor Graham when I wrote to him from New York. I'd already set up a job with Coop when I sent him a download of a demo I'd done. I was thrilled that he has a state-of-the-art system, and I was able to audition via the Internet."

"Tess . . ." He was going to lose patience before long.

"Right. Sorry, I got off track. Anyway, when I told him that my grandfather was Roy Braeden, he gave me a little information when I asked him why there was the lien and a deadline on paying off my house. The lawyer tried to give me a song and dance, but he only handled the estate, and he's not from Justice, so none of the gossip had reached him."

Fletcher took a deep breath. *Wouldn't interfere with my love life, my ass! Coop is neck-deep in the middle of this!*

"I know he's a busy man, but I thought that once I got to Justice, the mayor would make time to see me. I don't know why he's avoiding me exactly, but if he'd hear me out, then he'd know that I can solve his problem with his father and the historical society and landmark committee all together."

"How do you figure that?" Fletcher asked. The heat of her body seeped into his back as she leaned over him to look at the documents, but it was the fact that she knew a lot more than he thought that had him sweating like a condemned man on death row whose number just came up.

"Well, Mayor Graham's father is the fire chief here, and he wants to tear down the house to build a new firehouse on the property. And while Justice needs one, according to Coop, what Chief Graham wants in design and structure is awful, and will ruin the charm that Justice prides itself on."

That was true. Fletcher and his father had been going round and round on the issue for months. And he was his father's son—he'd lost his temper a few times. But there was no way he'd allow that monstrosity to be built on this land. It was too modern, and it would be the first thing anyone entering the town would see. He wasn't willing to let his constituents down. They expected him to make decisions that were beneficial for them and their town. "If he changed the look of it, and the location, like behind the schoolyard, then maybe it would be approved, but you're right. This isn't the place for a fire station. He's just not willing to budge, and he's biding his time, hoping that the house won't be granted historical status."

"It won't be."

His head popped up, his cheek pillowed on her breast as his eyes met hers. "Come again?"

She snickered.

Fletcher rolled his eyes, wishing he'd chosen a different turn of phrase.

She ignored the comment and explained. "They can't have it if I pay off the monies owed on it," she said, her excitement growing as if she were telling a fascinating story, full of twists and turns.

Oh, if she only knew! Fletcher thought. He found her enthusiasm catching; he wanted to know exactly how she could get him out of the tug-of-war he'd found himself in. "Tell me," he said quietly, turning his head a fraction to rub his cheek softly against her breast, needing the contact like air.

Her breath caught, and her nipple, so close to his lips, tightened as his hot breath fanned over it through her robe. He knew it was lunacy, but he wanted her again, all naked and slow this time, a leisurely exploration of her body. His cock hardened painfully under the table.

Fletcher was just about to reach for her again, thoughts of foreclosures, back taxes, liens, and disputes fading fast from his mind, but Tess pulled out the chair next to him, wisely sitting down and putting a bit of distance between them.

Her knowing grin was too much. He laughed

out loud. "Sorry, honey. I lost my train of thought." Trying to look sheepish didn't work. She knew he wasn't a bit sorry.

"So I noticed."

Fletcher shifted in his chair, and cleared his throat. "Okay, I'm back with ya. I promise. So, if you have the money, then why haven't you paid off the debts already and put it on the market to make the profit?"

"Because I don't have the money yet."

Fletcher cast her a sideways glance. If she didn't have the money, then . . . "You've lost me again."

"The only thing I can afford to buy right now is time."

"So where are you planning to get the money? Everyone in this town knows Roy died without a plug nickel to his name."

"Yeah, and I only found that out when the lawyer came to settle the estate. I've tried to get a loan the regular way, but since I don't think I've ever had more than a hundred dollars in my checking account at one time, and no savings to speak of, they won't give me a penny. The highest limit on my credit card was five hundred dollars, and since I was going out of town so much, I was late on the damn payments more often than not." She sighed, then shook it off, saying, "But I got a job offer to open for a well-known artist in Vegas. And if I sign the contract, I can arrange an advance on what they'll pay me."

"Las Vegas? Sin City? As in Nevada?"

Tess sneered at him. "Yes, Sin City. I've worked there before, at one of the casinos on the strip. Believe me, I don't want to go back, and it's a one-year gig. But if I can get my foot in the door, then I stand a better chance of doing what I really want."

"And what might that be?" Fletcher's throat closed, and his voice sounded gravelly to his own ears. His skin chilled, despite the heat of the small kitchen. She was going to tell him that she wanted to be a singer, making money hand over fist, and giving her status, prestige, recognition. Of course, the reason he'd avoided her all this time was because forfeiting the house would leave her free of legal obligations. And she'd be able to use that fantastic voice to be the star he knew it would make her. He could remind her of that, but he wasn't going to help her screw up his life when it was becoming obvious that she didn't want a role in it.

It wasn't the fact that his life was about to get more complicated by having to make some decisions he'd put off these months. He knew the time would come for that, sooner or later. No, he thought. It was the fact that it was Jane all over again; he wanted to stay, and she wanted to go. And that made his chest squeeze. From the minute he'd seen Tess, he'd actually imagined this woman as part of his future.

How could he have been so wrong? He'd awakened Coop at the crack of dawn to force him to spill his guts about their newest resident. And after the few details that Coop was willing to divulge, he'd confided in his friend that he would be careful, that he didn't want to blow his chances with Tess. He'd even admitted that he could see himself falling in love with this woman. Coop maintained that he wasn't getting involved, but damn! They

were best buddies. Coop was supposed to warn
him when he was about to be blindsided!

There was no way he was going to be fooled
again, he determined.

"Earth to Fletcher?" Tess snapped her fingers in
front of him, and he was pulled back to the reality
he didn't want to face.

"I have to go," he said angrily, getting up and
putting on his boots. Looking ridiculous in the
sweatpants, he picked his tool belt up off the floor.
"I'll stop by The Last Call on Monday night to get
my clothes."

She appeared crestfallen at first, but her face
turned hard, and she sneered at him. "Oh, I see.
I'm okay to nail against the wall, but the minute
you find out that my ultimate plan is to settle in
Justice, you're as skittish as a snake."

Fletcher was pissed, but he barely hid a grin. He
wanted to tell her that if she was going to lambaste
him, she should get her euphemisms straight.
Then the last part sank in . . . settle in Justice—?
"Wait. Say that again?"

"Never mind, Fletcher. You can go. I can see
that outsiders aren't as welcome as I thought. No
wonder the mayor won't see me. He probably
thinks the city girl might bring lawlessness to Justice. I—"

Fletcher wished he'd paid attention instead of
letting his bitterness drown her out a minute ago.
Then he'd know where the hell that nonsense she
spouted was coming from. But he knew his ears
weren't playing tricks on him; she wanted to stay,
and that was all he needed to hear.

His mouth covered hers before she could sput-

ter any more absurd notions. He smiled against
her lips. She was as glad as he was that he'd
stopped her barrage; she melted into his arms, her
whimper of need filling his mouth. He pulled away
slowly when he'd had enough of her taste to sus-
tain him for a few minutes. Or at least until he'd
unraveled the mystery of this woman and her role
in his life, personally and politically. He concentrated on catching his own breath, her kiss as po-
tent as a shot of whiskey to his gut.

Sweeping a hand over the soft curve of her buttocks, he tapped a finger to her lips with the other,
hushing her. "Cease fire, honey," he murmured
quietly. "I was wrong. Okay?"

She nodded, her eyes glazed over, but still, a
spark of distrust lurked in their depths. If the desire weren't eclipsing it, he'd be worried. By rights,
she shouldn't trust him at all, but she didn't know
that. He felt like a sneaky bastard.

Her nipples were hard pebbles of arousal, the
pulse in her neck pounding a rapid beat. He
kissed the tip of her nose and took her hand, walking back to the table, but instead of guiding her
back to her own chair, he sat in his and pulled her
into his lap. "And never insinuate that you're
cheap again. I wouldn't ever think that. In fact, all
I *can* think about is how you'll make me work
for it."

Tess chuckled under her breath, relaxing in his
arms. Good. He didn't ever want her to be uncomfortable around him. Especially since he was seriously contemplating ways to help her to stay here
in Justice. Here with him. Tell me again about
you wanting to settle here?"

She wriggled, getting more settled on *him,* easily forgiving him, which he didn't deserve. And if she didn't start talking soon, her little lap dance was going to distract him again so that no matter what she said, it wasn't going to register past the rush of arousal. He growled warningly, "You were saying?"

A sultry, devious grin spread across her face. "Are you ready now?"

He clamped down on the urge to grind her down on his cock. "I'm getting there, honey."

Her soft, musical laugh washed over him. Even when she didn't try, she got to him. She kissed his neck, but slid from his lap, resuming her seat in her own chair before he had the sense to get a firm grip. He felt the loss immediately, wanting her back in his arms, where she belonged.

He'd gone home last night, painfully aware of her sexual lure, gotten up this morning admitting to himself that Tess was like a warm, fresh breeze blowing through his life, one that he wanted to feel over and over again. Just now, he was picturing himself with her exactly like this thirty years from now, sitting in this very kitchen, teasing her and trying to coax her onto his lap for some early morning play. With Jane, he never saw beyond the end of the week. He focused on Tess, determined to find a way to make that vision a reality. She was the one. He knew it as sure as he knew his own name.

"I want to stay in Justice, but that's not possible unless I can cough up the cash. I sent demo tapes to some record companies, but I haven't heard anything yet. I've been a pain in the ass to some of them, and I think they'll have me arrested if I show up in person." She arched her brow and tipped her head.

He knew that would never come to pass. One look at Tess, and they'd be scrambling to sign her before the next guy. A friend of his from college was in the business, and they'd talked about work once. Though he knew Tom was a great agent, he'd told horror stories about colleagues who cared more about the money and less about the welfare of the people they represented. "So by going to Vegas, someone will hear you sing, you'll get exposure, and you'll get a record deal that way." This was where Fletcher left off a minute ago; he couldn't hide the acrimony in his voice this time, either.

"No, that's not it at all."

He pinned her with his stare, determined to get to the bottom of this before he got up again and left behind that absurd home-and-hearth visual of the two of them, once and for all. "Then what *is* it, Tess?"

Her eyes shone as she held his gaze. She placed her hand over his again, and her robe gaped just a little, but Fletcher was locked onto her face.

"I'm not being conceited when I say that I know I can sing. I've been doing it in clubs all over the country since I was a kid. My dad was a drifter, always moving to some new town or city, singing his songs. It's the only life I've ever known."

Fletcher watched her body language. It didn't take a genius to know that they weren't happy memories for her.

"When he passed away, I stuck to the familiar, and followed the same path. I'd gotten used to sleeping in motels, or the car, going from town to town, but I never liked it. In fact, I hated it."

He listened and began to see things clearly. And his admiration for her grew as she mapped out her game plan.

"I can get by on my voice. But what I really want to do is write songs. Exclusively. I only sing for my supper right now because it helps keep a roof over my head."

"Don't you want to be rich and famous? Singing would do that for you, because you're right, honey—you have an incredible set of pipes. You'd get a contract in a heartbeat."

"Rich, yes—famous . . . no. And the fact that I may be asked to 'hum a few bars' of my music and my voice will only hinder my chances."

One brow rose, and Fletcher wondered if he was really understanding her. "Hinder you how?"

"I auditioned once in New York. The guy was ready to pull a contract from his attaché that minute! But when I told the guy I had no interest in pursuing a singing career, you'd think I'd just kicked him in the gut!"

Fletcher could relate to the poor bastard. Every time he remembered what her voice had done to him last night, he felt his manhood grow heavy and insistent. Even now, as she sat there, animated and energized, her speaking voice was having an effect on him. He had to get up, do something, or he'd be in trouble. He wasn't concentrating on the things she said; instead he was drowning in the way her voice nearly sent him into a frenzy of need, and that was going to be his downfall.

The washer stopped and Fletcher used the opportunity to put some distance between them. He switched the clothes over to the dryer, and the task kept his back to her for a moment, enough for him to get his resurging appetite in check.

A hairbrush lay on the surface of the dryer, and the thought of touching her, even in that simple way, was a temptation he couldn't resist. "So you want to be a songwriter?" he asked, fighting down the flicker of hope he felt. He didn't want it to matter so much, but he wasn't going to start lying to *himself*, too; it mattered a whole hell of a lot.

When he knew he'd be able to trust his own restraint, he sauntered back across the room.

He was grateful when she took the brush from him and carelessly tugged it through the strands, pulling the snarls out until her hair shone, falling long and heavy over her shoulders. He didn't want to harm a hair on that head. And he would have—it was a mess—but if he envisioned her after a bout of lovemaking, the mussed look would be it. She hadn't combed it when she came back downstairs, but she'd taken the time to brush her teeth. She wasn't obsessed with her looks. Fletcher found her gorgeous no matter what she looked like. Man, he was easy!

She handed the brush back to him. His heart squeezed. Women never let men mess with their hair, but Tess trusted him, sat with her back to him, answering the question he'd almost forgotten he'd asked. "Oh, yes. I love to compose music, write lyrics. But I don't want to sing. I want other artists to sing my songs."

God! Fletcher thought. If there was anything that could send a jolt of sensation shooting up his spine, it was the sound of Tess sighing *yes,* while he was so close, breathing in her scent. He was concentrating on what she said, he had to, but he couldn't help just enjoying her company. Something he contemplated doing for a long time to come.

He ran the bristles gently through the dark reddish-brown tresses, and she lazily continued, her body responding to his ministrations. "Justice is *my* last call, Fletcher, the end of the road for me. It's where I want to stay. Forever."

His hands stilled on the silky crown of her head. "Why?" he asked, and realized he was actually holding his breath, waiting for her response.

"I told you. I've been traveling all my life. I want a place to call home. Thanks to my grandfather, Justice is the place. I've only been here a short time, and I already love it."

She spoke with such surety that Fletcher was convinced. But the other—

She must have taken his silence for uncertainty. "Don't you see, Fletcher? If I became a singer, they'd want promotions, tours, publicity, and it would never end if listeners like my voice and style. A year in Vegas to make the contacts I need is worth the reward of never having to uproot myself again, and never having to perform when my heart's not in it. I love singing at Last Call, but it's not my dream to be a star."

The wheels began to turn in his head at a rate faster than he could process them. He was in a position to make her dreams come true. And she could forget about leaving town for a year. He couldn't let her go away. He was foolishly falling in love, and she belonged here—not just in this town, a permanent part of his quiet community, but as a stable, constant fixture in his own life. She had feelings for him, and he'd do everything he could to cultivate them, make them bloom until every time she was away from him, she'd miss him and feel the urgency to return home, to his side.

Fletcher crouched by her chair, turning her face to look down at him. Her expression was drowsy, lethargic, as he set the brush on the table. "I want you to stay, too, darlin'."

"Good. Because I could get addicted to you, Fletcher." She laughed. "I don't even know your first name." Her eyes suddenly focused on him, bright and trusting.

Damn.

Was that the wind being knocked out of him? he wondered. She thought Fletcher was his last name, rather than his middle. "My first name is George," he said, unable to believe he could croak it out when breathing was at a minimum. He watched her face for a spark of recognition, the letters bearing his signature just a glance away. Thankfully, her expression didn't change, and he was able to suck precious oxygen into his starved lungs.

"I'll stick to calling you Fletcher."

"Thanks. My father is George. No one calls me that." He needed to distract her or she'd wonder at the guilt that began to creep into his bones and was going to emanate from his pores any minute.

He did the only thing he could think of. He pulled her head down to his.

He diverted her attention in a most delicious,

sensuous way, and her reaction was more than he'd hoped for: with a moan, she reciprocated his kiss with pure, carnal passion.

She gasped at his ferocious hunger, giving it back in equal measure. Her hand cupped his jaw, her nails scratched at the stubble he hadn't bothered to shave when he got up this morning. He'd left his mark on her earlier with his carelessness. "I'll shave next time," he whispered against her lips.

Tess moaned, tipping her head up, her fingers weaving through his hair as she urged his lips to her throat. "Don't you dare," she warned breathlessly. "I like it so much, Fletcher."

Lost in her excitement, her scent flooding his nostrils, he alternately suckled and nuzzled her soft, heated skin.

His knees dropped to the floor, and he swiveled her in the chair to face him, opening her robe below the belt, spreading her lush thighs, and pulling her to the edge of her seat. Her hands yanked his T-shirt up his chest, encumbered by his arms as his hands dug into her curvy hips.

Her fingers skimmed over his flesh, tangling in the hair she could reach under his shirt, and her touch sent waves of pleasure through him.

He purposely insinuated himself in the vee of her thighs, his hard stomach rubbing against her most intimate place. His head lowered, and he nudged open her robe, his tongue laving the exposed area above her tank top. She moaned, arching in the chair, offering her breast to his rapacious lips, and he took it, cloth and all, into his mouth. He sucked hard at the turgid nipple, and her shriek of pleasure sent a shudder of need through him, to his neglected erection. His hands slid along her bare thighs, and he ached to have his mouth all over her, his cock buried to the hilt inside her.

She ran her fingers through his hair, then tightened and pulled at it—not enough to cause even a stipple of pain, but with a savagery that he willingly obeyed. She wanted his mouth, demanded it greedily, and she lowered her head, sealing her lips to his.

He let her set the pace, but as she devoured his mouth and thrust her tongue past his teeth, tangling and sliding along his, Fletcher didn't think he'd be able to hold back for very long.

Their lips separated and they stared at each other as each drew ragged breaths, both shocked and amazed that they were right back where they started.

But her thighs rode high on his hips, and he could feel her pulsing heat against his stomach through the wet panel of her panties. He was going insane! "God, I want to taste you, Tess," he whispered, his voice rough in the quiet of the room.

"Oh, yes!" she gasped breathlessly, arching her back, just as caught up in the excitement as he was.

A crash of thunder broke the magic of the moment. She jumped like a scared cat, a startled shriek following the rumble of the storm that neither had even noticed was upon them. The one brewing between them had captured their attention. He watched her as she focused on the room, stunned that the lights were the only illumination now.

It was an interruption Fletcher silently cursed, but was grudgingly grateful for. They needed to slow things down. Every time they touched, things went a little further than before. Feeling her heated wetness pressed tantalizingly to his stomach, and staring at the damp spot of her tank top over her still-taut nipple was definitely too far. He wanted so badly to get even closer to her, but his conscience kept nagging at him. He was keeping information from her, things she needed to know and should have been told before they ever got this far. A tumble in the sack wasn't worth the price he'd pay if she found out *after* he bedded her. Not when his heart would suffer.

He tugged her close again, pressing her sweet, swollen breasts to his chest, and just held her to him. "Tess—"

"It's all right, Fletcher. We're going too fast, I know. Not to mention that the rain is coming down, and all over the house, it's coming in."

Thankfully, she'd veered off the subject of sex. "I never did get to the roof, did I?"

She smiled against his cheek, and leaned back to look at him. "Nope. And I'm not sorry. Although, the thought of you all hot and sweaty up there, working in the hot sun, did make me squirm a little."

Fletcher groaned. Damn, but she had a way of making him forget his common sense.

"Unfortunately, since we didn't shore up any

leaks, I have to go put buckets down or I'll have even more water damage than I already do."

"I'll help—"

"No need. I know where to place them all. I think I moved in during the rainy season down here." She grinned. "Besides, your clothes are dry. I don't want to be a tease, Fletcher, and I do like you so much, but . . ." Her voice trailed off.

"Does this thing between us feel as right to you as it does to me?" he asked.

She worried her lip as she pushed her chair back and stood up, looking down at him, her soft palm caressing his cheek. "I rely on my instincts for everything. I've had to, or I'd have gotten hurt a time or two over the years. I know when something is wrong. So unless this southern heat has shorted out my inner radar, I'm right to trust you. Simple as that. And, hopeless romantic that I am, I'm gonna side with the latter. That's why I haven't put the brakes on until now."

Fletcher knew he was a low-down snake to let her believe she could trust him. It didn't escape him that he was on his knees. He deserved it. He should be begging her to forgive him for the lies he'd told. Lies by omission were still lies, and he hated himself for deceiving her.

He was more selfish than he thought. He could make her dreams come true. But pride was a large part of her makeup. If she'd wanted money, she'd have asked Coop, or sold out her dreams and taken a recording contract. No, she wanted to do it on her own terms. He respected her for it, and his heart beat a little faster with pride for her convictions. When he told her that he was the man she'd been doggedly pursuing these past months, she was going to feel betrayed, duped even. It was a chance he had to take now that he was neck-deep. After he made sure she had the option to stay put if she wanted. He didn't want her going to Vegas any more than she did. Maybe she'd forgive him one day.

"Darlin', I think there's a way to get what you want without sacrificing yourself and moving away."

"Really? Fantastic." Tess's eyes lit with interest, but the glow on her face from their fervent coupling flushed her skin, giving her a radiant hue. "Let me go put these buckets down, and you can tell me about it."

She grabbed a stack of pails by the door, backing into the living room, and lining one up. A slow, steady drip began as the winds picked up and howled around the house. She smiled at him indulgently. "It's okay, I'm used to it. I'll just go center these upstairs, throw some clothes on, and I'll be down in a minute." With a swish of that glorious hair, she was gone.

Fletcher pulled his T-shirt down, scrubbed his fingers through his hair, and took a number of deep, cleansing breaths.

Going to the dryer, he fished his clothes from it and put them back on. The room had cooled significantly with the arrival of the summer storm, but the damn dryer had made the rivets on his jeans like a branding iron, burning his skin. He hissed at the contact, and carefully adjusted himself, the lingering effects of his erection making it difficult to zip up his jeans. As long as he was in nothing but those sweats, constantly reminded of how he got that way, his utmost attention wouldn't be on worming his way out of the hole he'd dug for himself. The same hole that he was going to throw Coop in when he got his hands on him. Fletcher wasn't the only one who was guilty of lying by omission.

He grabbed up the phone and dialed The Last Call, knowing Coop would be there. He lived in the apartment above the bar, but when he finally rolled out of bed, he was downstairs working. And Fletcher was going to get the information he needed, but his old friend was going to get a healthy dose of his annoyance, too.

When Coop picked up, Fletcher didn't give him a chance to say a word after the initial "Hello." He had him look up a phone number off the Rolodex in the office, and as soon as he'd jotted it down on one of the letters in front of him, Fletcher rained curses down on his interfering friend. And all the while, Coop chuckled in his ear.

"You're going to hell for this, Cooper Jones," Fletcher vowed. Coop's belly laugh and whoops into the phone brought a reluctant grin to his face. "You swore on a stack of Bibles you wouldn't screw with my love life again."

His friend calmed enough to say, "That was before I knew that the two of you needed each other. She let something slip on the phone when she called me from New York."

"What was that?"

"Never mind. You'll figure it out for yourselves. Sounds to me like you should be thanking me."

"Not yet, buddy. I'm sitting here staring at the same letters I sent to her in New York. I 'bout had a heart attack, staring at my own signature."

"How much does she know?"

"Nothing yet. I don't want to see the look on her face when she finds out that the 'F' in G. F. Graham stands for Fletcher."

"How do you think she'll take it?"

"That's the twenty-thousand-dollar question, my friend. I don't know *how* she'll react to the news."

"I do," came a voice behind him.

Fletcher spun around. Tess stood on the bottom step of the back staircase, her honey-colored eyes wide in shock, but the fury that was gathering strength, as sure as that storm outside, told him all he needed to know. She'd heard everything. "Shit."

Five

Fletcher entered The Last Call forty minutes later, soaking wet, his disposition as black as the turbulent clouds covering the skies of Justice.

Coop looked up as he passed the bar. "Hey, buddy, what the hell happened? You said 'shit,' and the line went dead."

Fletcher cursed under his breath as he stomped down the hall, opening the door to the office with so much force, it hit the wall, his hand stopping it before it smashed him in the face when it bounced back. "It hit the fan, that's what happened!" he shouted down the hall, then slammed the door shut behind him.

He crossed to the desk and slumped down into the chair. Leaning back, he tipped his head up toward the ceiling, then covered his face with his hands. "Damn, what a mess," he whispered.

The door opened and Coop stood in the entry. "She knows, then." It wasn't a question.

Fletcher sighed, bringing the chair upright and dropping his forearms to the surface of the desk. He looked at his friend. "Oh yeah, she knows, all right. Hell, half of Justice probably knows what a bastard I am. That Yank has quite a repertoire of colorful curses." One brow rose, as he remembered just a few of the ones she spit at him when he'd hung up on Coop.

"Did she tell you to drop dead?"

Fletcher's lip curled. "No, she didn't go that far. But she *did* give me directions to a very hot place, though. And I ain't talking Florida, my friend. In fact, she told me that *you* can come with me."

Fletcher gnashed his teeth, recalling that look of betrayal and doubt he saw on her face. He hated it. Her fury quickly followed, but he'd take that any day compared to the lost, bewildered look. Her instincts, the one thing she'd relied on to guide her through life, had failed her, and he actually witnessed the fear dull the sharp, confident brightness in her eyes. He'd shaken the stability of her world, and he might not forgive himself for it. His heart hurt for doing that to her.

"Me? I can go to hell?" Coop's brows lowered. "Why am *I* in trouble?"

Fletcher drew his attention back to his friend. He didn't buy his innocent act for a minute. "Because you're the guiltiest of any of us. You kept us both in the dark, and we're pissed at you. That's something she and I are at least in agreement on."

"And you'll both thank me when you work this out and live happily ever after," Coop replied, nonplussed that two important people in his life wanted to skin him alive.

"So you said on the phone." Fletcher tipped his head. "And yet, if she leaves town, we'll never know, will we?"

Cooper started out the door. "She won't leave." His confidence was solid. But he turned, pointing at his friend. "Do the right thing and she'll never want to leave you."

Fletcher's temples ached with a dull throb as a headache threatened to become a full-blown migraine. He rubbed the pressure points. "And how do you suggest I do that, oh wise one?"

"That's easy." Coop shrugged his shoulders, ignoring the sarcasm. "Make her dreams come true."

The muscle in Fletcher's jaw flexed, his patience wearing dangerously thin as he growled through clenched teeth, "That's what I was *trying* to do when I called you! You remember, Coop . . . it was just before I got caught red-handed in the lies we both told?"

"Yeah, I know. But do it anyway. And your biggest mistake was admitting to an indiscretion without making sure the coast was clear."

"I'll tell that little tidbit of information to the next woman you get involved with," Fletcher said dryly. "But you're wrong, pal. My biggest mistake was not being honest with Tess in the first place. That's why I can be pissed at you, but I can't blame you. This is my own damn fault."

"What can I do to help?"

His gaze rose slowly to Coop, his eyes narrowing. He grinned cynically. "Now, *that* I can put to you in Tess's own words, my friend—*get out.*" He pulled the phone across the desk and picked up the receiver. "I'll handle things myself from here on in."

Coop chuckled, closing the door behind him, yelling through it as he retreated down the hall, "I'll be out front if ya need me!"

"I won't!" Fletcher answered just as loud, flipping through the Rolodex until he found what he was looking for.

Tess paced up and down the kitchen, wearing a path in the already worn floorboards as she tried to hold on to her anger. She had every right to, and yet, what Fletcher had done to make up for his lying, scheming ways had her waffling between seething rage and thrilling elation.

When she'd walked down those stairs and heard Fletcher on the phone, she wasn't really paying attention—not until he mentioned the papers she'd left on the table. Then knots began to twist so tight in her belly that she'd had to breathe through her mouth to take in air. Fletcher was Mayor Graham. She'd been played like a violin! Or a fiddle, as it were, she thought wryly now. Played by Cooper, whom she'd come to trust in the last few months, and Fletcher himself, the man who'd ignored her repeated attempts to contact him and resolve the issue of her inheritance. That part was still unclear.

Of course, it wasn't as if she'd given him the chance to explain. The shame she felt that she was falling in—"No! I'm not in love with that lying bastard!" she shouted, then stopped in the middle of the room as tears welled in her eyes, wondering whom she was trying to convince.

Since she hadn't been dressed when she came down and surprised Fletcher, she went up after he left and showered, trying to cool her anger, but it hadn't worked. She put on shorts and a T-shirt, not really caring how she looked, just needing something to do so she could block out the hurt. She almost whimpered when she brushed her hair after pulling it out of her collar, remembering how it hung, smooth and untangled, down her back when Fletcher had taken such care when he brushed it. No man had ever made her feel so content with such a simple gesture as Fletcher did.

She felt the tingle up her spine again, but valiantly shook off the sensations. Damn that man!

She'd gone back to the kitchen and dialed the number Fletcher had jotted down on one of those blasted letters.

Her heart sank, filling with remorse when she learned whom he was going to contact, *had* contacted, in fact, probably only an hour or so after she'd thrown him out of her house, telling him *just* what he could do with it.

Tess glanced at the clock. It was five P.M. and as of two hours ago, she'd hired herself an agent, and not even forty minutes after she'd made the initial contact with him, Tom Castinguay rang Tess back with a contract for not one but two of her songs. The advance was an amazing amount, and she'd done incredibly well by industry standards for the royalties on both pieces of music. She'd been trying to contact that guy for months! And *he* hadn't gotten back to her, either. Tess snickered, rolling her eyes. *Birds of a feather,* she thought.

But it was *because* of Fletcher that she'd made contact at all. He'd heard every word she'd said to him right here in the kitchen, even as he sweated bullets, fearing discovery of his ruse. *That,* she conceded, and the sweating they both did, trying to keep their hands off each other. She desperately wanted to make a good impression in Justice, and dragging him to her bed would've done the opposite. She suspected *his* restraint lay in the deception he was perpetrating. Still, they'd barely skirted potential disaster, each for their own reasons.

Fletcher must have left her house and gone straight home or to the bar to phone the much-sought-after agent. They were old college buddies, and Fletcher had told Tom to dig her demo tape out of the slush pile. He'd even adamantly pleaded her case, telling Tom that unless he was interested in representing her as a songwriter exclusively, she wouldn't consider making a deal. Her vocal talent wasn't a factor. Tom knew the score before she'd even picked up that phone, and had already set the wheels in motion, calling on an artist to hear the demo.

And Tom was all business, arranging a recording session as soon as he could be assured that Tess was on board. And he told Tess that he was thrilled to represent her, that managing the career of a talented songwriter was more rewarding in many ways than working with the artists who sang the songs. Songwriters were all about the music, and nothing ever got in the way of that, whereas the singers performing the music often became jaded, and the fame became the focus. Dealing with her on her level would suit them both.

Tess's resolve teetered even more as she recalled the conversation again. With a simple phone call, Fletcher had made it so she could pay off her house, live in Justice, and make a heftier income than her job at Last Call provided. An income she'd need if she was going to take on the enormous job of fixing up the Old Vic.

Add to that, he'd made sure she could do that without having to apply for historical status to help defray the costs. No, this house that her great-great grandfather had built would be hers outright, free and clear to tear down walls if she wanted to. She wouldn't, though. Tess knew she wasn't going to change much of the structure of the place, but she loved the idea that she could.

A place to call home, she'd said to him, and he heard. Wow, he'd taken everything she'd said to heart.

He'd gone out of his way to help her, even after she'd told him that he could take her house and shove it. She said it in the heat of anger, but he knew she didn't mean it. She wanted this house, and all it represented to her.

She still couldn't understand why he'd lied. There wasn't a reason for it. Tess could see why he hadn't told her the truth last night when he found out who she was. He was already tangled in the web of lies and deception. She knew Coop was in on it. He was Fletcher's best friend, and he knew damned well that she was trying to contact the mayor about her inheritance.

Of course, she mused, she didn't think she'd ever actually *told* Cooper that she wanted to stay in Justice. Having traveled so much in her twenty-eight years, she played her cards close to the vest, never revealing too much of her plans. The Last Call was the single stop for entertainment within the town limits. If people wanted to know something, they could probably find out at the bar. She didn't want people knowing her business, that she didn't have the money to pay off the house when she hit town and took up residence. Until she'd figured out what she was going to do about that, she'd kept mum.

Maybe if she'd—"No! I am *not* to blame here," she said out loud again, and growled, stomping her foot. Whenever she verbalized her thoughts, it was because she didn't have anyone but herself to argue with. And *dammit,* her conscience was always right, no matter how much she tried to fight it.

"Ah, hell," she grumbled, grabbing her purse, keys, and going to the mud porch to slip on her sandals. It had stopped raining cats and dogs, but the wind still blew enough to spatter her with sprinkles as she made her way over the flagstone path to her car. She groused, hating the taste of humble pie, but for whatever reason those two men had pulled the wool over her eyes, she had to take responsibility for her own part in it. If she was going to become a respected member of this community, *and she would be,* she determined, then she would be accountable. That, and the fact that only a few hours after Fletcher had left her house, she missed him. Totally crazy, but nonetheless true.

As she pulled into The Last Call ten minutes later, Tess knew she was doing the right thing. Of course, she reasoned sadistically, she wasn't going to make it easy on Cooper. He was on her shit list. She and Fletcher had *that* in common.

Putting on a game face, which was a scowl, Tess pulled hard on the door to the bar and marched inside, letting the wind slam it closed behind her. She knew she looked like a force to be reckoned with; the wind and misting rain were shut out, but her march across the parking lot mussed her hair, and she was damp, her appearance miserable. Perfect.

Coop took one glance at her and put his hands up. "Tess—"

"If you know what's good for you, Cooper Jones, you'll only *answer* my questions." Tess let him believe she could actually do bodily harm. She was a tiny woman compared to her boss's hulk, but, she remembered wryly, *hell hath no fury like a woman scorned.*

"Gotcha," Coop replied, obviously familiar with the adage as well.

"You didn't tell me who Fletcher was last night because you didn't know if I wanted to stay in Justice or not?"

"Correct."

Tess took a seat at the bar, and hunched her shoulders. "C'mon, Coop. You're gonna have to do better than that," she implored, needing all the facts before she went to Fletcher.

"Honey, I'm sorry I lied to you. At first, I thought you and Fletch would hit it off, but only if you wanted to stay in Justice. You mentioned it on the phone once when you called from New York."

"I did?" Tess didn't remember saying that to him, but it was possible. It was around the time that she came home from a gig in Boston only to confirm that Jacob had strayed. Not far, though—she'd caught him in her bed with a woman she worked with. She wasn't really surprised, but she *was* pissed. She kicked him out, and since her lease was up in two weeks, she hadn't bothered to renew it.

Then she'd gotten the news that her grand-father had been deceased for two years, but he'd left her an inheritance. It was a crazy time. She probably had slipped and told him that. Coop was so easy to talk to, and his obvious affection for her relative led her to trust him without consciously choosing to.

"But, Tess, you never mentioned it again. I tried to ask you about it, but you always clammed up."

"That's because a bar is to men what the beauty salon is to women. Rumors and gossip were things I didn't need, and couldn't afford. If people knew I didn't have the money to pay the debts on the house, they might have pressured the mayor, Fletcher, to make a decision. I needed time, Coop."

"I know that, honey, now." He sat down on a stool on his side of the bar, "But there are things about Fletcher that you don't know."

"What things?"

"It's not for me to say, Tess. But I kept quiet because if you were to stay, then you and Fletcher would make the perfect couple. He's the only one who liked your kind of music before I converted the bar. I'd bought it about eight months before that. I was only starting to make a profit a few months before I hired you, but I lost it in maintenance and repair."

"Then why did you turn it into a piano bar?"

"Because Fletcher is a silent partner of The Last Call, and as a honky-tonk, we had brawls and the sheriff was here almost every night. We lost more money in broken furniture and glassware than I was taking in."

"Customers get rowdy in any kind of bar, Coop."

He shook his head. "But they haven't here. When Fletch helped me with the finances to convert it, we put in more security, and even my waitresses were trained to spot and cut off those who couldn't handle their liquor. He turned this place around, Tess. Made it a place to enjoy the music, not the drink. Oh, don't get me wrong. It's still got atmosphere, but it's not a stop-off to get hammered."

"You've done a great job with it, Coop."

"Thanks, honey, but I can't take all the credit. And it's more far-reaching than you'd think. The domestic calls into the sheriff's office have dropped dramatically, too. And the doc at the clinic tells me he's seen fewer knuckle scrapes and stitches than before. Fewer alcohol-related injuries. The last drunk driver we had was coming in from a bar in the city. There's less crime to speak of, all because of a facelift on a bar and a change in format." Coop shrugged a shoulder. "We still have country music here—this *is* the South, after all—but without anyone knowing who did it, Fletcher made it clear that inebriation, violence, and unlawful conduct wouldn't be tolerated in Justice."

"He's a good man, isn't he?" Tess asked, knowing the answer already. Her instincts were as sharp as ever. They hadn't failed her.

"He's the best, honey. And *that's* no lie."

She looked up at her boss. "Then why did he tell me that he was a mechanic?" Her brows lowered in confusion.

Coop's brows lowered, too. "He *told* you that?"

"Yeah, he—" Tess stopped mid-sentence as it dawned on her. She closed her eyes, moaned, and banged her head on the bar as she replayed the conversation in her mind. If she hadn't been so aroused by him last night, she might have paid better attention then. "No, he didn't say that," she admitted, sighing, and realizing that she'd let her hormones get the better of her. "*I* did. I assumed it by the way he was dressed last night, all grungy and streaked with grease. You told me he worked for the town, and I told him I'd figured out that he was the town mechanic, taking care of the cruisers and town vehicles. He just didn't correct me. Oh, damn," she groaned.

It didn't help that Coop chuckled and patted her head. "It's okay, honey. We all make mistakes."

The smug look on his face when she lifted hers was a bitter pill for Tess to swallow, but swallow it she would. "I get the point, Coop," she grudgingly granted.

"Good."

Now she was going to have to eat crow too. But if she was going to trust Fletcher with her heart, she had to admit her own part in all of it. She hoped the terrible things she'd said to him could be forgiven.

Throwing caution to the wind, Tess took a deep breath. "Okay, boss. I need your help."

Six

"Dammit!" Fletcher stood in front of the mirror in his bedroom, trying for the fifth time to knot the bow tie of his tuxedo. It wasn't even his fumbling fingers that had him so frustrated. It was the same thing that had been eating at him since he left Tess's house. He wanted to be with her, and he'd blown it.

Before he left The Last Call, he'd tried phoning her, but she didn't pick up. He knew it was a long shot, but he was hoping she'd cooled down enough to hear him out. No such luck.

When he got home, there was a message on his machine. He'd anxiously played it back, but it was just his secretary, Margaret, reminding him of the event at the governor's mansion tonight. It was a formal charity event. He'd all but forgotten about it, having dismissed it as nothing more than politicians hobnobbing, and that wasn't his idea of a good time on a Saturday night.

He still didn't want to go, but if he stayed home, he'd do nothing but think of Tess, would probably do something colossally stupid and go over there. Another mistake he wasn't willing to make. She needed space.

Much as it killed him to back off, and not sit her down to listen to him, he wasn't a violent man unless provoked. And he'd never force a woman to do anything she didn't want to do. But it had only been a few hours, and he already missed her.

A knock drew his thoughts back around. He was glad for the interruption, whoever it was. It pulled him from the reminder of the catastrophe his personal life had become, and he abandoned the task of tying the tie, leaving it to hang around his neck as he went to answer the door.

The knocking became more insistent, and Fletcher yanked hard on the door. "What?" he shouted, but was speechless as Tess stared back at him, a wry grin on her face.

Looking cool as a cucumber in the blasted heat, she stood on his stoop. She crossed her arms under her ample breasts, leaning against the wooden rail, and asked, "Is that how you always answer the door, Mayor?"

Fletcher's jaw flexed; he was so tempted to remind her that it was exactly as she'd greeted him this morning, but he was more interested in taking in her presence.

Her brows rose as she raked her eyes down his body and back up again. The hot summer heat that slammed into him when he opened the door was like a frozen tundra compared to the feel of this woman's appreciative stare. The licks of flame went straight to his groin, and Fletcher shifted his stance before the effect she had on him became obvious.

Her tongue darted out and coated her lips to whistle low. "Whew. You sure do clean up good, Fletch."

That sultry, sensuous voice of hers was like a drug to him. It increased his pulse rate, and upped the furnace temperature his body had become. He had a sneaking suspicion that she was doing it on purpose, too.

Add to that, she was wearing a T-shirt and a pair of cutoffs. Different from what she'd worn last night at the bar, or this morning, when she was wearing nearly nothing, but she was so incredibly beautiful, she'd wear a gunnysack like a gown. And her hair was all messy again, windblown and tangled. Just the way he liked it.

"Come in, Tess." He hardly recognized the hoarse inflection of his own voice.

"Don't you want to know why I'm here?"

"I don't care why. You are—that's all that matters."

Her face softened, and she brushed past him. She waited until he'd shut the door, then, as he turned, pressed herself against him, her hands sliding up his chest and around his neck. "Kiss me, Fletcher."

"Tess, I don't think—"

"Just kiss me," she said huskily. Her fingers tangling in his hair, she drew him to her tempting mouth.

It wasn't as if he really put up much of a fight. It was what he wanted, too. What he ached for. Gawd, but he'd missed her!

His arms went around her slim waist, unable to let her set the pace this time. He held her as close as he could with both of them still fully clothed. With all the love and lust he felt for her, he kissed her deeply, his tongue thrusting into her mouth, showing her what he wanted to do with her. That honeyed sweetness flooded him again, and he growled, remembering how he'd asked to taste her earlier today.

His wet lips slid to her ear; he held her close, whispering huskily, "Say you forgive me, Tess."

"I wouldn't be here if I didn't."

"Good," he breathed, and kissed the shell of her ear, delighting in the soft sigh that escaped her lips. He pulled away and looked down at her. "I'm gonna make love to you now, darlin'."

"Thank God. I thought we'd have to do a lot of talking first."

He chuckled, backing her toward the stairs. "Later. I'll be able to pay better attention if I'm not distracted with need," he said, stepping over her sandals as she slipped them off. His dinner jacket joined the shoes on the floor.

Off came her T-shirt next, her bra teasingly hiding her luscious breasts from view. He couldn't wait to feel her flesh under his hands, his lips and tongue.

He followed her as she backed up the stairs, but stopped her halfway, their eyes level as he stood three steps below. "You're perfect, Tess."

She gasped, surprise and wonder written all over her flushed face. A little giggle escaped her. "Hardly, Fletcher. Just maybe perfect for you."

"Yes," he whispered low as she leaned forward and kissed him, but her lips moved away before he was anywhere near satisfied. There wasn't anyone more perfect for him than Tess.

Her delicate, talented hands pushed the suspenders off his shoulders and traveled to the fastening of his trousers. Good, Lord! He didn't know if he was going to last if they took a long time. He wanted them naked already!

His eyes closed on the incredible sensations, forcing himself to remain still. He had a death grip on the banister, the other hand flat on the wall; Fletcher swallowed hard.

The back of her hand brushed over his fly, tented with the evidence of his hard cock underneath. She turned her wrist and softly gripped him through his trousers. He hissed through clenched teeth, trying so hard to let her play, but it was no use. His hand left the wall, and pulled hers from his engorged, throbbing cock.

Her disappointed expression made him grin painfully. "I'm working with a hair trigger right now, darlin'," he explained.

"Then let me see you, Fletcher."

"You first, sweetheart." His hand reached out, and with a flick of his fingers on the front clasp of her bra, it separated.

"Take it off," he ordered quietly, his eyes transfixed on her.

Tess's breathing became shallow as she slowly

pulled the cups away and her breasts bounced free. She moaned when he licked his lips, her nipples responding to the intimation. As she shrugged her shoulders, the undergarment slid down her arms, and she flung it away, standing proudly for his perusal.

"Now the rest." Fletcher kept a tight leash on his control as she obeyed his rough commands. She was her own woman, but she was just as turned on, letting him take the lead.

She unsnapped the shorts, tugged the zipper down, and wriggled them over her hips.

He absently unfastened the row of buttons down his shirt as he watched with pinpoint focus, but his hands went slack time and again, and he made little progress.

His eyes followed the movement as the shorts dropped to her feet, and she kicked them away. The sight of Tess standing on his staircase in nothing but her panties was the most provocative thing he'd ever seen.

He was hypnotized by her smooth, pale skin as more and more was revealed. The ring that pierced her navel glinted in the light. "This is so sexy, darlin'."

His nail flicked at the tiny golden jewelry, and her belly sucked inward, her breath catching. "Oh, please, touch me," she moaned, her legs too shaky to hold her anymore. She sat down on a step, her arms beckoned him forward, and her lush, pale thighs parted, offering him a place between them.

He leaned down, his hands gripping the step on either side of her head; he hovered over her, lowering just his head, but feeling the heat come off her in waves.

His kisses started at her mouth, lazily lingering, the tip of his tongue tracing her soft, pouty lips. She lifted her face, urging his mouth to satisfy hers, but Fletcher always retreated, teasing her as she'd done to him, leaving her wanting more of his tormenting play.

His breath fanned over her skin as he lowered his head, and she jerked under him, moaning long and low, frustrated as he took his time. His lips curved in a smile as they forged a path, feather-light along her collarbone, until he couldn't taunt her anymore, and his mouth finally, finally lowered and closed over one taut, dark pink nipple.

"Fletcher!" Tess cried out, and her head dropped to the step. Trying to catch her breath, mindlessly aroused, her arms closed around his head, and her back arched like a strung bow.

Gawd, but he loved her responsiveness!

Fletcher drew on her plump breast, his tongue laving over the dark peak before his warm, wet mouth sucked hard. Her erotic moans were like an aphrodisiac. As he moved to the other crest, and treated it to the same loving attention, she twisted and bucked under him, until he was at the end of his own rope, knowing if he kept it up, she'd climax just from sucking her breasts. That wasn't where he wanted to be when she let herself go.

With a last lick at her sumptuous nipple, he said, "I gotta feel you against me, sweetheart." His voice was ragged, rough as sandpaper.

"Hurry," Tess moaned, letting go of him and reclining back on her elbows as he stood up on the step.

As he looked down at her luscious frame, her knees rubbed together, and she opened her eyes; the hunger in them nearly brought him to his knees.

Literally popping the remaining buttons off his dress shirt in a rush to get it off, Fletcher was barely aware of the clasp tearing on his pants, but only because it hindered his efforts to divest them. Dammit! Why did he wear a tuxedo, of all nights? He'd have shucked his jeans in a flash.

When they were finally gone and he was in nothing but his boxers, he noticed that somehow, his black tie still hung around his neck. Fletcher pulled it free, carelessly flinging it aside. He backed down the stairs, but his hands covered her knees as he knelt three steps down.

His eyes journeyed up her body, as did his palms up the outer curve of her thighs. "Lift up," he murmured, scanning her face for any signs of hesitancy. Thank God there were none. Only needy little whimpers as she bit her lip, her cheeks flamed in passion as she lifted her hips for him.

He clamped his fingers around the band of her panties and dragged them down her legs, lifting first one foot, then the other. His gaze didn't waver from hers and both of them held their breath as his hands covered her knees again, and with agonizing slowness, spread them wide.

Her eyes followed his every move as Fletcher gave in to his burning need and looked down. With a sigh, he lowered his head between her legs, murmured "Beautiful" along her sensitive inner thigh, and his hands slid under her buttocks; he breathed in her womanly scent. Cupping her soft cheeks and tipping her hips up, Fletcher held her steady and listened to her shrill gasps as his mouth covered her, tasting her sweet, honeyed center for the first time. He wanted to grin at her reactions, but he was too caught up in his own desires. He went about pleasuring her as he should have done this morning.

His tongue danced up and down her slick, wet lips, and he lapped at her swollen flesh while she bucked under his exploring mouth. He delighted in bringing her to the very edge of her sanity, but retreating every time, pressing kisses on her thighs or along her hip before she could tumble over.

Fletcher imagined driving her like this well into the night, but he wanted to get off the stairs. He needed his big bed to love her properly. And the condoms were in the nightstand.

He brought his hand around from her buttocks, and he slid a long finger into her opening; she sighed, tightening around him. He groaned and his mind reeled, anticipating the feeling of her squeezing around his cock like that.

And oh, did he ache! The throbbing was distracting; his boxers wet again, this time with pre-come, but he needed to feel her climax against his mouth. He wanted to taste the honeyed sweetness of the height of her pleasure.

"Come for me, darlin'. Let me taste you," he whispered roughly into her sensitized skin. His finger pushed in and out, over and over. Driving her on and circling her clitoris, he relentlessly flicked at it, then pressed the rough flat of his finger to the sensitive nubbin of flesh, pressing against it.

She arched up, suspended as her scream pierced the quiet of the house, and Fletcher encouraged her to ride out her climax, keeping to her, and refusing to stop until her fingers tangled in his hair, pulling at it, her body squirming, unable to take the feelings anymore.

Fletcher settled her back down to the step, holding her steady or she might've melted right down the stairs. He took a leisurely trek back up her body, stopping to flick his tongue over her belly, and that tiny ring. A groan of satisfaction rumbled in his chest as she whimpered and cupped his head, not letting go until he was over her, and she was kissing him, their tongues tangling and frenzied. He knew she could taste herself on him, and it drove him wild!

The hair that covered his chest served to rekindle her arousal; she rubbed her swollen, well-kissed breasts back and forth, making cooing sounds, as little shivers wracked her body. Yeah, he thought. They definitely needed that bed.

Not willing to let that luscious mouth go, Fletcher's hands cupped her behind and brought her with him as he got to his feet. Her arms snaked around his neck, and her legs clamped around his waist, her ankles locking behind him. Gawd, but he could feel her wet heat pressed tight to his stomach. The sooner they got upstairs, the better.

She panted as she broke the kiss. "Bed?" she asked, her eyes glowing like pure gold.

"Oh yeah, honey. We definitely need a bed," he growled, taking the steps two at a time.

She laughed, but gasped as he playfully pressed his lips against her shoulder, swirling his tongue over the spot. He couldn't help it; he loved keeping her charged, ready, even as he managed the remainder of the staircase and moved down the hall. She was last night's fantasy, and tonight, it would be real. He wanted to give her the pleasure that he'd imagined she'd given him in his dreams. More than that, he wanted to show her the love that could overcome the issues they still needed to address. Later, he thought. *Much* later.

Tess clung to Fletcher as he made his way up the stairs, tears forming in her eyes. No one had ever taken the time to see to her pleasure first. And when he'd opened that door, standing there in that tuxedo, his black tie undone around his neck, her stomach, tight with nervous butterflies, churned with a whole other feeling: pure lust. He filled it out so well. He was dangerous and sexy in his jeans and T-shirt, but in a tux, he was both those things, and dashing to boot. She didn't know where he was off to, but she was thrilled that her arrival had changed his plans.

She'd made Coop cough up his address and had come over to straighten things out with him. In just a day, he'd come to mean so much to her that she couldn't bring herself to stay away. She didn't like being on the outs with him.

He gently set her down in the middle of his bed;

she was so glad she'd swallowed her pride and followed her heart instead.

He bent to her, but she pushed him up until he'd backed off the bed completely; then she scooted to the edge, her feet on the floor as she looked up at him. Tess couldn't believe she had not an ounce of shyness with him, but the pleasure in his green eyes, dark with desire as he stared down at her, filled her with a sense of empowerment. And his boxers were barely able to cover the state of his arousal only inches from her face.

"Now you," she said, tugging on the material, being careful when she revealed his hard, throbbing erection.

She still stared up at him, but her tongue wet her lips as she took him in her hand, her fist encircling him.

He shuddered, his breath rushing from his lungs, but he made sure she wasn't pressured. "Tess, you don't have to, honey," he murmured, but hissed and closed his eyes when she ignored him, her tongue laving the very tip of his penis.

"Mmm—yes, I do, Fletcher," Tess argued, licking and teasing him the way he had her; with slow, meticulous detail.

His eyes opened and he shuddered to find her staring up at him, watching his reactions. Her hand stroked along the hard shaft; he had to grip the post on the bed when she took him in her mouth, first the head, then her lips slid along the veined shaft, feeling it pulse and throb as more disappeared.

"Gawd, Tess. Harder," he growled, unable to stop the slight rocking of his hips.

She obeyed his throaty command, sucking harder and countering his movements, using her mouth to draw out his pleasure. Her hand came up and cupped his heavy sac, fondling him and driving him to the near breaking point of his restraint.

His fingers tangled in her hair, and she loved it, especially when they tightened—not enough to hurt, but it was just another sign that he was enjoying her treatment of his gorgeous body.

His hard, toned thighs began to shake, and she knew that soon he was going to climax; she anticipated it, sucking him and alternately licking the underside of the shaft.

But before she could send him into sensual bliss, he pulled back, gasping. She let go of him, looking up at his strained face. "Fletcher?"

"Not like this, darlin'," he said, his hand untangling from her hair to cup her face as he tipped up her chin. Leaning down to kiss her pouty lips, he whispered into her mouth, "I want to be inside you, feeling you squeezing me tight when I come."

"Oh, yes," she said quickly, not finding a single thing to object to.

He laughed. "I love a woman who's easy to please," he said, opening the drawer and extracting a condom.

Did he love her? Tess wondered, but there was no way she was going to stop to ask. She ached for him, and relying on her instincts again, went with the magic of the moment. She wouldn't be here if she wasn't already sure he was a good man, an honest man, and one who'd just gotten caught up in something that snowballed out of control.

They'd work it out, she assured herself as she watched him don the condom. He was very well endowed, and Tess could feel the pulsing between her legs from the unbelievable feelings he'd already evoked, and in expectation of their joining.

The mattress dipped as Fletcher settled himself between her thighs. He leaned over her, one hand by her head as his hard arousal grazed along her cleft. He held it as he rubbed her clitoris with the tip, and the feeling was like a jolt of electricity through her body.

She curled a hand around his arm, the other taking a firm grip on his thick hair and pulling his head down for a kiss. The excitement was palpable as their tongues lunged and parried; then she drew her mouth away, staring into his eyes. When he smiled wickedly at her, always intent on drawing out her pleasure, Tess waited until he was right where she wanted him—then she arched her hips, and he sank into her. She moaned, "No more playing, Fletcher. I can't take it."

It garnered a strangled chuckle from him. "Oh, you could take it, and much, much more, darlin'. I know it."

But he didn't attempt to prove it. Instead he pushed in deeper, taking it slow and steady. She wanted to impale herself on him, it felt so damn good, but despite his near-reverent preparation, it was still an incredibly tight fit.

When he was buried to the hilt inside her, he closed his eyes, and except for his deep, even breaths, he remained still, letting her adjust to his size. She was acutely aware of how he filled her so fully, but soon an overwhelming need to feel him move inside her overrode any twinge of discomfort.

She squeezed around him, and the breath whooshed from his lungs, his eyes popping open, staring at her. She cast him a wicked grin of her own. "*Now,* Fletcher," she whispered.

"Yeah . . , now," he agreed and brought her legs around his hips, then interlaced his fingers with hers. "Christ, you're still so tight, Tess."

"I can feel you throbbing inside me, Fletcher." Her eyes closed, not in embarrassment, but at the sensations that washed over her as he growled and pulled almost all the way out of her, then plunged back into her depths.

His voice was rough, tinged with apology. "I'm not gonna last, Tess—I'm sorry." His pace escalated with every deep stroke.

Tess couldn't make her voice work; the friction of the hard and fast movement along her sensitive walls was too heady. She gripped his fingers and tipped her hips up, meeting each thrust and hoping he understood her body language.

Faster and faster they went until one last, deep, spearing thrust and her climax crashed down on her, dragging a scream from her throat. Residual tremors and lip-biting convulsions followed, rippling through her, so strong that they triggered Fletcher's own release, making her whimper as his sex pulsed inside her and his body shuddered over her.

His unsteady groan of satisfaction brought a dreamy smile to her lips before he kissed it away.

Finally succumbing to the exhaustion, he collapsed onto her, pillowing his head on her breast, his body spent and his hunger sated.

Tess's hand came up, fingers idly raking through his dark blond hair; she was tired as well, but utterly content for the first time in her life. Here, with Fletcher, she was right where she belonged.

Seven

"Stay with me, Tess." His appeal fell on deaf ears; she was still asleep.

Fletcher lay on his side, Tess's bottom tucked to him like a spoon while he rested his head in his hand, the other reaching around to play with her belly ring; he was still so fascinated by the adornment. He'd never met a woman who had one, and he loved it.

He'd never taken so much time with a woman, either. Or given so much care to tease and drive her beyond her limits. But with Tess, he delighted in her responses, her genuine pleasure. He just hoped that once they had their talk, she'd stay in Justice. With him.

"Stay with me, Tess," he whispered, not expecting an answer, but needing to say it again and again.

"Do you believe in love at first sight, Fletcher?"

She surprised the hell out of him, but he didn't hesitate. "Not until last night, when I saw you up on that stage."

He felt her sigh, and heard her soft reply. "I don't," she said.

Fletcher's heart began to pound right out of his chest. "Tess, let me explain—"

She twisted until she was flat on her back, pulling the sheet up under her arms; she stared up at him, and he wisely shut up. "But I felt *something*," she amended. "You were drop-dead gorgeous, even all messy and dirty, and I was so flustered when you winked at me. I got the song back on track, but I really didn't hear it anymore. All I could think about was meeting you, and praying you weren't married."

Fletcher chose that moment to interject, "I *was* married once. She hated it here, and eventually, she hated me."

"Why?"

"Because I wanted to settle here, plant roots. I went away to college to get a degree in business so I could come back to Justice with the knowledge to start a business of my own." He absently smoothed his hand over the sheet along her thigh. "What I *didn't* want was to move to the city. She did. I *didn't* want to use that degree to learn how to play and manipulate the market. I didn't want to work on Wall Street, and I didn't want to join the country clubs just to make connections. I didn't want to play at being something I wasn't."

"What else *did* you want, Fletcher?"

His sober eyes connected with hers. "I wanted to love my wife enough so none of that mattered to her. But I didn't. And she couldn't love me enough to give up her need to be the wife of a rich and powerful man."

She brought her hand up to his cheek, her eyes conveying her empathy. "You had different values, different dreams, that's all. Get that look of failure off your face, mister. It doesn't suit you."

He flashed her a fleeting smile, turning his head and kissing the soft pad of her palm. "Tell me your dreams, Tess."

Her hand lowered to the springy hair on his chest. "You know my dreams, Fletcher. In fact, you listened to every word I said this morning. And this afternoon, you made them come true."

"How'd I do that?"

Her eyes brightened to a golden hue as she raised a brow. "Your friend didn't ring you back after you called him, did he?"

"Tom called you?"

"No, I called him."

He swept his hand over his head. "I'm lost."

She chuckled. "You wrote his number on one of the papers."

Fletcher closed his eyes. He'd forgotten. All hell had broken loose right after that.

She went on. "After I threw you out on your ear, and I'd had some time to smash a few things, get dressed, and calm down a little, I saw the letters there, and was just about to crumple them all when I spotted it. I wanted to know who the number belonged to."

"About that, Tess—"

"Do you want to hear this or not?"

Fletcher laughed. "Sorry darlin'. Go ahead."

His anxiety started to wane. Maybe that wasn't wise, but pillow talk with Tess was just about as stimulating as the sex. And the sex was fantastic. He wasn't going to blow it by interrupting now. Not when she didn't look as if she was going to be getting up any time soon.

"He knew who I was when I called, and had already found my demo tape and burned it onto a CD. The quality sucked compared to a professional cut, but it was enough to download and send to an artist for a listen. When he knew I was in agreement, we hung up, and he called back in about an hour with an offer on the table."

"You're kidding. That's great, honey." Fletcher tried to put enthusiasm into his voice, but still, he worried.

"I know it. And because of you, I sold two of my songs to a popular singer. She'll be recording them as soon as the contract is drawn up and signed."

He couldn't stand it. He had to know. He hated feeling weak. "I'm happy for you, Tess. But what will it mean to *us*?"

She smiled. "I wondered how long it would be before you asked that."

"I'm sorry, honey. I don't want to be selfish, but I want you to stay. I know I don't have a right to expect it, but I hope you were honest with me about that."

"Oh, Fletcher. This mess started because I wasn't honest in the first place. I only told Coop once that I planned to move permanently to Justice. I never mentioned it to you in the letters I sent. And you had to consider the citizens first, and that includes your father."

He lifted his head off his hand and played with her hair that he'd taken great, exquisite pleasure in tangling. "You're a citizen of Justice, too, darlin'. If I hadn't been so worried that you'd forfeit the house, and force me to tell my father I'd be damned before I let it be torn down, we could have been helping each other all this time."

She snuggled closer to him. "Oh, I don't know. I think I liked that bit of mystery at first. You were elusive, and even when I was doggedly determined, I couldn't get near you. I was beginning to wonder if there really *was* a Mayor Graham. And Coop says that the minute he heard my voice he knew you'd fall in love with it."

"It's not just your voice I'm in love with, Tess."

She looked at him sharply. "Can we really be in love after only a day, Fletcher?" She tipped her head, doubting the notion, but there was hope sparkling in her eyes.

"I know I can. This isn't like what I felt with Jane. Wanna know how I know?"

She giggled. "Tell me."

"Because when I was getting ready to go out tonight, to the governor's, I wondered if that charity event would be my last one as the mayor of this town."

"I'm sorry you missed your event, but I don't get it."

"I didn't want to go anyway. I just didn't have anything better to do on a Saturday night." He tweaked her nose. "But what I mean is, being mayor, living here in Justice . . . those things didn't mean as much to me as being with you. If you'd forfeited the house and moved to Vegas, I'd have gone with you."

"Really? Sin City? Talk about extremes, huh?"

He chuckled. "I'd have adjusted. But I know I'm in love with you because I wasn't willing to leave my home to follow Jane. But I'd follow you anywhere and I'd be home."

"That's so corny, Fletch."

He knew it sounded like a cliché, but he meant it, and the tears that formed in her eyes told him she knew he was sincere. "Do you love me, Tess?"

She put him out of his misery by nodding her head. "It's crazy, but I do. Head over heels in love with you. And I'm not going anywhere. I told you this morning that Justice is a place to call home." She laughed. "But really, wherever you are is home."

"Are you making fun now, darlin'?" He couldn't fight his grin. He didn't care if she was ribbing him—it felt damn good to hear the words.

Her innocent look needed practice. "Now, Your Honor, would I do that?"

Fletcher chuckled. "I don't care, but say it with conviction."

She took his advice and pushed him back onto the mattress, lying across his chest. Gawd, she was hot!

She lowered her head and gave him a kiss that made all his parts pay attention. She lifted her head, and said quietly, "They say, home is where the heart is. Well, you're here, and you have my heart. So I'm home."

He pushed his advantage, going one step further. "Then marry me."

Tess pushed up off him suddenly, sitting up, back on her heels, and looking down at him. "Are you kidding me? After one day? How is that going to look? What will your constituents say?"

He came up on his elbows, and after popping the question, Fletcher gauged her reaction. Shock, not fear. He could work with that. "They'll say it's a helluva lot better than shackin' up with you. And I *will* be at your house every day after I leave city hall. We've got a lot of work to do if you plan to live there and make a career as a songwriter. I'm going to buy you a piano so you can write at home during the day instead of having to go to The Last Call to compose music and write lyrics."

"Fletcher, I'll be able to buy a piano—"

"But you need a place with good acoustics, and that front room would be ideal. Gawd, I'm gonna love hearing you sing, trying out new songs."

"Fletcher—"

"Just a second, honey, I'm thinking," he said, but he wasn't, really; he was railroading her, giving her too many reasons not to refuse him.

She stalled him right on the tracks, saying quietly, "You really want to marry me?"

He looked at her, with that chestnut-colored hair snarled and tumbling over her naked shoulders, and he wondered how she could be so beautiful and so obtuse at the same time. "Tess, the last impulsive thing I did resulted in divorce. I know those aren't good odds, but my heart and my faith weren't in it."

He picked up her hand and kissed the back of

it. "I'm putting all my faith in you. I love you, and I want everyone to know it."

She raised her eyebrows, considering his offer. "I suppose there are perks that come with being the mayor's wife."

His brow furrowed. "What perks?"

Tess smiled, the irony so poetic. "Well, if I request an audience, he's legally obligated to see me."

Fletcher chuckled, sitting up fully, and pulled her into his arms. "Don't tell my father that. Since this whole thing started, I told him he's got to make an appointment like everyone else, and I haven't been available to him, either. See, honey? It's not just you I was avoiding."

Tess laughed, too. "Well, you can tell George I'm keeping my house. Problem solved," she said, and put her head on his shoulder.

"Not yet."

"What else is there?"

"You haven't actually agreed to marry me."

Tess snuggled down into his lap, and Fletcher had to force his concentration to remain centered. Her answer was too important.

Her soft, naked bottom wriggled and ground against his cock in a bid to get comfortable, but he knew it was just a bit of veiled, torturous payback. Reminding her of his avoidance might not have been such a good idea—another tip he filed away as a lesson learned. But she made it worth his wait as she murmured so low, he had to strain to hear. "Yes, I'll marry you."

He sighed in relief. "Thank God," he exclaimed.

"I thought I was going to have to go down on one knee."

Tess cast him a pouty look. "You didn't want to?"

He kissed her so thoroughly, she had a sleepy, dizzy look about her. "Not when I've got you naked, sitting here, giving me a lap dance."

She giggled and socked him in the arm.

"You like making me suffer, don't you, darlin'?"

Tess wriggled a little more, and tipped her head, considering. "I don't know yet. I think I need more practice." She grinned mischievously, slipping off his lap.

Fletcher hurled himself back down on the bed, and flung his arms wide. "Practice makes perfect, honey. Please, practice away."

Shoving the covers out of her way, she lightly raked her nails up his calf, over his thigh, and finally closed over his now hard, achingly aroused cock. With a gentle squeeze and a teasing flick of her tongue, practice, she did. Perfectly.